I0561221

WIRED SENTINEL

A PARADISE CRIME THRILLER #15

TOBY NEAL

WIRED SENTINEL

Paradise Crime Thrillers Book 15

Toby Neal

Copyright Notice

This is a work of fiction. Names, characters, businesses, places, events, and incidents are either the products of the author's imagination or used in a fictitious manner. Any resemblance to actual persons, living or dead, or actual events is purely coincidental.

© Toby Neal 2026

http://tobyneal.net

ISBNs:

eBook 979-8-9892439-9-0

Print: 978-1-968949-00-6

ALL RIGHTS RESERVED. This book contains material protected under International and Federal Copyright Laws and Treaties. Any unauthorized reprint or use of this material is prohibited. No part of this book may be reproduced or transmitted in any form or by any means, electronic or mechanical, including photocopying, recording, as use for AI development, or by any information storage and retrieval system without express written permission from the author/publisher.

Book Cover Design by: Jun Ares

Formatting by: Neal Enterprises, Inc.

"Family isn't always blood. It's the people in your life who want you in theirs: the ones who accept you for who you are. The ones who would do anything to see you smile and who love you no matter what."

~ Maya Angelou

1

SOPHIE

THE PLUMERIA BLOSSOM'S pinwheel of cream and gold was a drop of moonlight against the polished, dark wood floor of the Bishop Museum. Investigator Sophie Smithson crouched beside it, careful not to interrupt the crime scene tech who was still processing the area.

She bent closer and breathed in the flower's sweet fragrance. The scent hit her like a physical blow, bringing a memory of her fiancé, Jake, grinning as he tucked a plumeria behind her ear, his gray eyes bright. "Every woman in Hawaii should wear one of these, babe."

Sophie's throat tightened. She forced herself to photograph the flower from multiple angles with her phone, maintaining composure even as her chest ached with the familiar weight of grief.

Jake had been gone two and a half years, and the smallest things could still ambush her. It didn't help that her current relationship with the enigmatic cyber vigilante known as Connor was "on the rocks," as the saying went.

"Same as the others." Detective Marcus Kamuela's voice rumbled behind her, pulling her back to the present. The big

Hawaiian man stood with his arms crossed, his expression grim beneath fluorescent lights that turned the early hour into artificial day.

Married to Sophie's good friend, FBI agent Marcella Scott, Marcus was someone she knew well; but even so, he was an intimidating sight when riled as he was now. "Third theft of Hawaiian antiquities in Honolulu, and the third flower left behind. Someone's trying to send a message, and Honolulu PD doesn't have time to dig into this investigation the way the case deserves. Glad the Museum's board decided to hire you and your company."

"Thanks to you. I appreciate the referral." As CEO of Security Solutions, a private security and investigation company, her career had saved Sophie emotionally these past few years, giving her purpose beyond the demands of single motherhood.

Sophie straightened, slipping her phone back into the pocket of her black cargo pants; she always dressed for functionality. The dark tank top and lightweight jacket she wore could handle both Hawaii's humidity and its air-conditioned buildings. Her thick, curly dark hair was kept short to keep it manageable, and the familiar weight of a Glock 19 rested against her side in its shoulder holster—though she seldom had to fire it these days.

"Same variety of plumeria as the other burglaries?" she asked.

"According to the botanist we consulted, yeah. Common white plumeria, nothing special about it except—" Marcus gestured to the empty display case behind them, its glass front cut with surgical precision. "Whoever's doing this has million-dollar taste in Hawaiian artifacts and leaves the flower as a calling card."

Sophie studied the empty case. According to the placard, it had held a *leiomano*—a war club made of koa wood, trimmed in shark's teeth. This one had belonged to the 'Merrie Monarch,' King Kalākaua. It was priceless, irreplaceable, and now gone—despite the museum's state-of-the-art security system.

"Show me the security footage," she said.

Marcus led her through galleries still dim with shadows to the security office, where a nervous guard cued up the recordings. Sophie leaned forward, watching the timestamp tick forward.

"There," the guard said. "Watch the screen."

The monitor showed the gallery in perfect clarity—and then didn't, for just a nanosecond. The image stuttered, pixelated, and reformed.

The display case now stood empty. No motion, no figures, no indication that anyone had been there at all.

"Run it again," Sophie requested. This time, she watched the timestamp, not the video. "Your system didn't glitch. It was fed a ghost recording. See how the shadows are identical before and after? Someone created a loop of empty gallery footage and over-wrote your live feed."

"That's impossible," the guard protested. "Our system is closed-circuit, not connected to any outside networks."

"Then they did it from inside here." Sophie was already moving, following the cable runs along the walls, checking for any aberration. "Your system might be closed, but it still has access points for maintenance. Show me your server room."

Twenty minutes later, she found what she was looking for—a device no bigger than a flash drive tucked behind a server rack, so small it was nearly invisible among the usual tangle of cables and connectors.

"Signal interceptor with local storage," she explained to Marcus as she photographed it in place before carefully removing it with gloved hands. "Military-grade, from the look of it. This isn't some amateur art thief we're dealing with; this was done by professionals."

"I already thought so." Marcus's phone buzzed. He glanced at it and frowned. "Speaking of professional—there's someone here to join us saying he's backup from Security Solutions?"

Sophie shook her head. "I came alone. Who—"

"Sophie, it's Raveaux."

She turned at the familiar French-accented voice, smiling at the sight of Pierre Raveaux standing in the doorway. The ex-Sûreté investigator was immaculate as always, clean-shaven with his silver-touched hair neat. He wore pressed khakis and a crisp white shirt; only she knew its long sleeves covered scars on his arms that were a testament to the day he'd lost his wife and daughter in a car bombing.

"Pierre. I didn't know you were back from France."

"Just a few days ago." Her colleague, a contractor with Security Solutions, stepped into the room, offering Marcus a courteous nod. "Detective Kamuela. I heard through channels that Sophie had been called in on something interesting. Thought I might be of assistance if you don't mind a second consultant?"

"Consult away," Marcus said with a wave of his beefy hand.

"Channels?" Sophie raised an eyebrow.

Pierre's mouth quirked in what passed for a smile with him. "Paula at the office might have mentioned where you were heading this morning. And given my background with art theft cases in Paris . . ."

"The more eyes the better on this one," Marcus said. "Especially since this is the third theft of Hawaiian artifacts and we're no closer to catching these guys than we were after the first."

"Check what I've found so far." Sophie handed Pierre the signal interceptor. He examined it; his years as an investigator showed in quick assessment as he turned the device in his hands.

"Sophisticated," he murmured. "And expensive. Your thief has resources."

"Thieves, plural," Sophie said. "The physical entry would require at least two people, maybe three. One to handle the security system, one to cut the glass of the case, and one to watch for interference or drive a getaway vehicle."

"I heard there were two other thefts besides this one. What were the targets?" Pierre asked.

Marcus pulled out his phone, scrolling through case notes. "Third was this one, a *leiomano* war club belonging to King Kalākaua himself. That was stolen here, as you see, from the Bishop's collection. Second was a royal *kāhili* standard, stolen from Iolani Palace. The first was a feather cape worn only by *ali'i*, owned by a private collector. All were uniquely rare, one-of-a-kind items, significant to Hawaiian culture."

"And the thieves left a plumeria behind at each burglary," Sophie added.

"A plumeria?" Pierre glanced at her, concern in his dark brown eyes. He'd been at her side and helped her through some of the darkest days after Jake's death; he knew plumerias were one of Jake's affectionate gestures toward her. But he said no more, maintaining her privacy with the discretion she'd come to value in their friendship. "This pattern suggests the thieves might be building a collection," Pierre said. "I doubt these items are random grabs for resale. Too difficult a market. Someone's targeting specific items connected to Hawaiian royalty for a reason."

"That tracks," Marcus said.

Sophie's phone vibrated. She glanced at the screen—a text from Bill, the chief of her home security team. *All clear. Kids awake. Armita has breakfast handled.*

The familiar morning chaos was starting without her today: Momi would be demanding to help cook breakfast, while Sean, now an adventurous two-year-old, would be manhandling whatever food her dear nanny Armita tried to put in front of him.

A pang of missing the children was sharp but brief. Sophie would be home soon enough, and the kids were safe with Armita, their dogs, and their beefed-up security team.

That increase had become necessary six months ago when Connor had returned to Thailand, leaving a void that made her uneasy. Not to mention the strain their long-distance relationship was under.

Connor had made his choice—duty to the mysterious Yām Khûmkạn over their life together in Hawaii.

She couldn't really blame him. How could domestic life with her and two small children compare to the challenges and intrigue of running a clandestine ninja stronghold and a powerful organization with fingers in all the world's political and economic pies?

Still, she didn't have to like it. *"Son of a goiter-riddled swine,"* she muttered aloud in Thai.

"Sophie?" Marcus glanced at her, frowning. "You okay?"

"Fine." Sophie refocused on the situation at hand. "We need to figure out the thieves' next target. If they're collecting items connected to *ali'i,* there's a finite number of possibilities."

"I can help with that," a new voice said from the doorway. A young woman in a neat navy blazer stepped forward, her long hair pinned back in a bun. "I'm Dr. Catherine Yoshimura, the museum's senior curator for Pacific cultures. I've been compiling a list of potential targets based on the pattern so far."

Sophie studied the curator: mid-thirties, nervous but trying to hide it, ink stains on her fingers suggesting handwritten notes—someone who cared deeply about the artifacts in her care.

"Show me what you have," Sophie said, after briefly introducing herself and the others.

Dr. Yoshimura led them to a conference room where she'd spread out photographs, catalog entries, and a handwritten analysis. "If they're specifically targeting items that belonged to or were used by the *ali'i,* there are seventeen possibilities in our collection. But if we narrow it to items of the highest cultural significance . . ."

She pointed to three photographs. "The feather standard of Kaumuali'i, last king of Kaua'i. The ivory fishhooks of Chief Ka'eo. And this—" She tapped the final photo almost reverently. "The *kiha pū,* the sacred conch shell trumpet rumored to have announced the arrival of Kamehameha the Great."

"Where are these items kept?" Sophie asked.

"Different areas of the museum. We've increased security on all of them, but . . ." Dr. Yoshimura's voice trailed off.

"But your security didn't stop the first theft," Pierre finished gently.

Sophie studied the photos of the different burglary sites, mentally working through the logistics. The thieves knew exactly what they wanted, where it was located, and how to get it. Each theft had been perfectly executed, suggesting inside knowledge.

"I need full access to your security protocols," she told Dr. Yoshimura. "And a list of everyone who has access to those protocols. Staff, contractors, anyone who might know the system well enough to defeat it."

"That's . . . a lot of people," the curator said.

"Then we'd better get started." Sophie pulled out her phone to text her team. This was going to be a long day, and she'd need backup. "Pierre, can you work with Dr. Yoshimura on the personnel angle? Look for anyone with connections to all three stolen items."

"Of course." Pierre was already pulling out his own notebook, a small leather one with an attached pencil. His investigative interest was clearly engaged.

Sophie turned to Marcus. "I want to walk through each theft site, compare them to the locations of potential targets. There might be a pattern we're missing."

As they prepared to leave the conference room, Sophie's phone rang. The caller ID made her stomach tighten: *Connor Standish*.

Not that that moniker was his real identity—no one knew that. She'd changed his contact from just "Connor" six months ago, adding the Master's last known surname, hoping it would create distance.

It hadn't dulled the pain of seeing his name. *He'd said he loved her, that he'd never leave her or the children . . .*

She let the call go to voicemail. Whatever the leader of the Yām Khûmkạn wanted could wait. She had a job to do, children to get home to, and a life that no longer included a man who'd chosen his work over love.

But as she followed Marcus through the museum's halls and past displays of ancient Hawaiian treasures, the remembered scent of plumeria lingered in her nostrils.

What she'd felt for Connor had never been as strong as her bond with Jake. There was a mercy in that.

2

SOPHIE

Midmorning sun blazed overhead by the time Sophie, Marcus, and Pierre emerged from the museum. The light painted Honolulu in vivid brushstrokes—sparkling off glass towers with emerald mountains rising like ancient guardians behind, and a sky so blue it made Sophie's eyes water.

Sophie paused on the museum's coral block steps, their surface warm beneath her feet even through her shoes. The air carried the mingled scents of plumeria from the museum gardens, diesel exhaust from passing tour buses, and beneath, that underlying salt smell of ocean that permeated everything in Hawaii. A mynah bird hopped along the museum's neatly mowed lawn, its yellow beak and eye patches vivid in the morning light. It pecked at something in the grass—probably remnants from a tourist's crumbs.

Sophie gazed out at the city she'd called home for years now. Tiled and corrugated roofs were clustered in neighborhoods she knew by heart, their streets shaded by wide monkeypod trees where she'd pushed Sean's stroller while Momi skipped ahead to parks where the children played.

Somewhere out there, thieves were planning their next strike, calculating angles and escape routes with the same precision she'd

once used in her former life as an FBI agent. And somewhere else
—she checked her watch—her children were probably halfway
through their snacks, with Armita patiently wiping sticky fingers
and negotiating sharing disputes.

Both realities tugged at her; they were the duality of life as a
working mother. She'd gotten good at walking that tightrope these
past two and a half years; good at compartmentalizing, at being
fully present whether she was analyzing crime scenes or bandaging
scraped knees.

"The flower bothers me," Pierre said, joining her on the steps.
Marcus had gone to retrieve his car from the parking lot, leaving
them momentarily alone with the morning crowds flowing around
them. His shadow fell across hers, and she caught a whiff of his
cologne—something subtle and expensive that he'd worn since
their first meeting. "The plumeria is personal, specific," Pierre
continued, his voice thoughtful. Behind them, a tour group gathered, their guide's voice carrying fragments of Hawaiian history on
the breeze. "A plumeria is symbolic to you . . . It's possible this isn't
just about the artifacts."

"I was wondering about that." Sophie said. Pierre had a way of
cutting straight to the heart of things, seeing past the obvious. It
was what made him such a good investigator, and such a good
colleague and friend in more ways than one.

"Someone wants us to pay attention," he continued, eyes scanning the cityscape as if the answers might be written there. "The
question is—to what? The thefts themselves? The specific artifacts?
Or . . ." He paused, glancing at her. "To you?"

"Too soon to tell," Sophie said. Her phone buzzed against her
hip. She pulled it out, expecting another update from Bill about the
children's morning routine. Instead, she saw a text notification from
Connor's number on the screen. Her jaw tightened, but she opened
the message anyway.

You're going to want my help with this case. I'm sending someone. - C

"Arrogant son of a—" She bit off the curse as a family with

young children passed them on the steps, the parents giving her a disapproving glance. The children, roughly Momi and Sean's ages, were chattering excitedly about the museum's exhibits, their voices high and sweet.

"Connor?" Pierre read her expression with the ease of long practice. His own face had hardened slightly—he knew most of their convoluted history and had opinions about it.

"Connor knows about the case. Of course he does." She gripped the phone tighter with a familiar surge of anger that her on-again, off-again lover could provoke. His organization might be strained, but his surveillance network remained intact, especially when it came to her and her children.

Old habits, old obsessions, constantly updated technology.

"Connor wants to send help." She shoved the phone back in her pocket with more force than necessary. "As if I need his help. As if he has any right to insert himself into my life whenever he—"

"Sophie." Pierre's calm tone cut through her building tirade. A couple of tourists stared curiously, probably wondering about the conflict brewing on the museum steps. Pierre moved slightly, shielding her from view with his body. "Whatever his faults, Connor's resources have been useful in the past."

She wanted to argue, to list every time Connor's "help" had complicated her life, but Pierre was right. Connor's connections through the Yām Khûmkạn had provided crucial intelligence on more than one case. His people had access to information that official channels couldn't touch, moved in circles where badges meant nothing.

"That doesn't mean I have to like it," she growled.

"And neither do I. But we take gift horses when offered." Pierre gave one of his Gallic shrugs, an eloquent gesture that somehow conveyed understanding, resignation, and subtle disapproval.

The Frenchman had never made a secret of his reservations about Connor and the Yām Khûmkạn. He said he'd seen too much of the damage they could do, understood too well the grey areas they operated in. But he was a pragmatist, understanding the some-times-necessary compromise between ideals and reality.

A bus rumbled past, its diesel engine loud enough to pause conversation. Sophie watched it go, noting the advertisement on its side for a luau show—smiling dancers frozen in perpetual welcome, promising tourists an authentic Hawaiian experience.

Everything here in the islands was made up of layers of truth and performance, history and commerce, beauty and practicality.

Marcus's SUV pulled up to the curb, saving Sophie from having to say more on the topic of accepting Connor's help.

The vehicle was spotless despite the demands of his job—Marcus took pride in the details, always had. She got into the front, grateful for air-conditioning that immediately battled the morning humidity. Sophie adjusted her leather seat to her long legs and buckled up as Pierre settled in back.

"Iolani Palace next?" Pierre asked, confirming their plans with typical thoroughness.

"Yes," Marcus confirmed. "You can see where the stolen *kāhili* staff used to be. Its twin still remains."

"Don't you think that's odd?" Sophie asked. "Why would they only take one?"

Marcus shrugged a big shoulder. "Why anything, in this case?"

"I want to see their security setup, compare it to what we found at Bishop."

As Marcus pulled into traffic, Pierre touched Sophie's shoulder. "About Connor's offer—"

"Can we not discuss him anymore?" Sophie interrupted, then softened her tone. "Sorry. I need to focus on the case and not waste attention on Connor's attempts to maintain relevance in my life."

"Marcella told me you two broke up," Marcus observed. "I'm sorry to hear it."

"I'm not," Sophie said, and folded her arms across her chest.

She caught the glance Pierre exchanged with Marcus in the

rearview mirror. They were worried about her, these two men who'd become unexpected supports in her complicated life.

Noted.

Nonetheless, she hadn't asked for it and she was handling things fine on her own. The CEO's desk at Security Solutions and her role as a single mother weren't easy to balance but she had everything under control.

Sort of.

Sophie turned her head deliberately to watch the scenery outside.

Behind them, the Bishop Museum stood solid and dignified, guardian of treasures and secrets alike. Its coral block walls seemed to glow in the morning light, and Sophie found herself thinking about permanence and change, about things that endured and others that crumbled.

The museum had stood for over a century, protecting Hawaii's heritage through kingdom and territory and statehood, through wars and economic booms and devastating storms. It would outlast them all—the thieves, the investigators, probably even the memory of this strange case.

But for now, it was her responsibility to protect the treasures it held. Her skills, her determination, her refusal to let the past dictate the future—these were her tools.

The men filled the silence with discussion of a recent soccer match—football, as Pierre insisted on calling it. Sophie half-listened to their debate about offensive strategies and referee calls until her phone buzzed again. This time it was a photo from Armita —Momi and Sean at the kitchen table, faces smeared with what looked like mango, grinning at the camera. The simple domesticity of it made her chest tighten with fierce love.

She would solve this case on her own terms, with her own team. Connor could keep his help—and his distance. That's what he'd chosen when he'd walked away, when he'd decided that power mattered more than the tentative future they'd been building. He didn't get to waltz back in now, playing puppet master from that jungle throne where he'd taken up residence.

Even so, Sophie found herself rubbing the spot on her inner arm where Connor had implanted a tracking chip years ago. The scar was barely visible now, just a tiny line that could have been anything. That chip had saved her life once—though not Jake's. It had been too late for Jake by the time Connor found them in that overflowing lava tube . . .

The technology was probably obsolete now, but she'd never had the chip removed.

Some reminders were worth keeping, if only to remember the cost of them.

Marcus navigated through downtown traffic with the ease of long practice, weaving between delivery trucks and tourist rental cars. The city flowed around them—businesspeople heading to late morning meetings, tourists clutching maps and phones, locals moving with the unhurried purpose of people who understood that in Hawaii, everything happened on island time.

"The pattern still bothers me," Sophie said suddenly, needing to voice the thoughts spinning in her head. "Three thefts, three different types of institutions, but all were important Hawaiian cultural artifacts."

"Private collector?" Marcus suggested, signaling to change lanes. "We've seen it before. Rich person decides they want to own a piece of history."

"Maybe," Sophie said. "But the technical sophistication, the plumerias, the level of planning . . . seems like something more than just acquisition."

"You think there's an endgame we're not seeing," Pierre said.

"Yes. Maybe someone's sending a message," Sophie said slowly. "I just don't know what it is yet."

3

SOPHIE

IOLANI PALACE ROSE from its manicured grounds in downtown Honolulu like a Victorian dream trapped in tropical amber. Sophie had scanned a historical search on her tech pad on the drive, quickly absorbing as much background information as she could.

Built in 1882 by King David Kalākaua, Iolani was the only royal palace on American soil, however wrongfully claimed that soil had been.

Once they had parked, Marcus produced their authorization at the security checkpoint—a modern addition. Sophie paused at the palace's entrance, taking in the American Florentine architecture that had cost the Hawaiian Kingdom $340,000 in currency of that era, nearly bankrupting the nascent nation in its bid to prove itself equal to any European monarchy.

Gentle trade winds carried scent from the plumeria trees King Kalākaua himself had planted, their white and yellow blossoms cascading over a wrought iron fence—the same type of blossom they'd found at this morning's crime scene. Sophie noted the Iolani Barracks to her left, a smaller but similarly designed building where the Royal Guard had once been housed, which now served as the visitor center.

The grounds were still empty, the first tour groups not scheduled until eleven a.m. "We have to finish before they arrive,"
Marcus said. "Since this is just a follow-up visit."

They climbed the broad steps where Queen Liliʻuokalani had
been arrested in 1895, passing between four Corinthian columns
that supported the wide lanai. Sophie touched one of the etched
glass doors imported from San Francisco, thinking of all the history
the fragile panels had witnessed.

Inside, the Grand Hall stretched before them, its gleaming koa
wood staircase ascending gracefully to a second floor. The walls
displayed portraits of Hawaiian royalty in European dress; the kingdom's response to the colonizers' language of power had been to
match it.

Crystal chandeliers hung from coffered ceilings, their light
dancing across walls that had witnessed both glittering state
dinners and the illegal overthrow of a sovereign nation.

"The throne room is this way," Marcus said, leading them
through a reception hall where a plaque denoted the name Blue
Room, describing King Kalākaua receiving dignitaries here from
around the world. Sophie noticed an alarm system discreetly inte-
grated into the crown molding—one of many modern updates
necessary to protect what remained of Hawaii's royal treasures—
not that it had worked.

Truth was, nothing in the world was safe from a determined
and tech-equipped thief.

The throne room itself took Sophie's breath away with its luxurious, traditional appearance. Twin elaborate golden chairs sat on a
raised dais beneath a scarlet canopy, empty now but still radiating
dignity and *mana*. One had been King Kalākaua's, the other his
queen Kapiʻolani's. Behind them hung the royal coat of arms with
its motto: *"Ua Mau ke Ea o ka ʻĀina i ka Pono"*—The life of the land is
perpetuated in righteousness.

"There." Marcus pointed to an empty pedestal beside the
throne platform. "That's where the stolen *kāhili* was displayed."

Sophie studied the empty pedestal where the feather standard had once stood. *Kāhili* were symbols of royal authority, made of thousands of feathers from native birds, some of which were now extinct. This particular one had belonged to Kamehameha I himself, its red *'i'iwi* and yellow *'ō'ō* feathers worth far more than gold.

"Same MO as the other burglary." Marcus gestured to the security camera mounted in the corner. "That was disabled. The burglars knew exactly where every camera was, every motion sensor."

Sophie crouched beside the pedestal, examining the base. The *kāhili* had been mounted using the same system installed in the 1960s during the palace's restoration. "No tool marks. They knew which screws to remove, in what order. This was likely an inside job, or at least directed by someone with inside knowledge."

Raveaux emerged from examining the entrance points, having checked the staff entrance near the basement kitchen where King Kalākaua had once hosted poker games. "The windows show no signs of forced entry. They came through the main doors, which means—"

"They had access and knew the alarm codes," Marcus finished.

Sophie's phone buzzed. Another message from Connor appeared on the screen: *My operative will arrive tomorrow. He's my best.*

Sophie deleted the message without responding. She had more pressing concerns than Connor's unsolicited interference.

"Dr. Yoshimura mentioned an inter-museum loan program when we were talking," Pierre said. "Artifacts move between institutions for special exhibitions. The palace loans items to Bishop Museum, the Hawaiian Mission Houses, even mainland institutions. Sometimes private collectors participate. Perhaps we should look at—"

A loud creak, as if from a footfall, came from the floor above

and interrupted him. The sound had come from the second floor—
the private quarters where the royal family had actually lived.

"No one is supposed to be in here." Marcus pulled his weapon
and Sophie matched his movement. They whirled to face the doorway. "Building's supposed to be empty. Let's check it out," Marcus
said. They moved as a pair toward the grand staircase, footsteps
muffled by the crimson carpet runner as they ascended, weapons
ready. Pierre, unarmed, brought up the rear.

Sophie's heart rate stayed steady despite her alertness as she
reached out to touch the koa wood banister. It was smooth under
her hand, polished by thousands of visitors and, before that, by the
hands of Hawaii's last monarchs.

The creaking sound came again—definitely from the King's
Suite above, the corner bedroom. Marcus took point, Sophie
covering his six, Pierre bringing up the rear.

The door to the suite stood ajar. Through the gap, Sophie could
see the room's Victorian furnishings: an ornate carved bed where
Kalākaua had slept, the desk where he'd written correspondence to
other monarchs, asserting Hawaii's place among nations, and
composed the lyrics to "*Hawai'i Pono'ī*," now the state anthem.

Marcus counted down on his fingers—three, two, one—and
swept inside with Sophie on the other side of his advance. "HPD!
Nobody move!"

But the room was empty except for an open window, its lace
curtains billowing in the light trade winds. A gilded candlestick lay
on its side on the polished floor beside Kalākaua's writing desk.
Next to it was a plumeria blossom, so fresh that dewdrops still
clung to its petals.

"Dammit." Marcus holstered his weapon as he bent to examine
the blossom. "They were just here."

Sophie moved to the window, careful not to touch anything.
Below stretched the palace's manicured grounds—the same view
the king would have seen every morning. The Coronation Pavilion,
built for Kalākaua and Kapi'olani's formal coronation in 1883,

stood empty on the lawn and cast geometric shadows across the grass.

No sign of anyone on the grounds.

Had the intruder chosen this room specifically? Why not the Queen's Suite across the hall where Lili'uokalani had been imprisoned under house arrest after the overthrow, not the library where she'd composed *"Aloha 'Oe,"* but Kalākaua's personal space? Could the choice of location be a piece of the puzzle?

Sophie frowned. "What is this thief playing at?"

"I don't know," Raveaux said, reaching her side.

Marcus got on his radio, calling for backup to sweep the area—all eleven acres of the estate.

"They must have known we'd be coming," Sophie said, unease causing her spine to prickle. "Someone could be watching us."

"But why take this kind of risk and . . . not steal anything?" Raveaux gestured around the King's Suite with elegant hands, his movements encompassing the Victorian furnishings, the heavy koa wood furniture, a crystal chandelier that had witnessed the last days of Hawaiian independence. Sunlight streamed through tall windows, illuminating dust motes that danced like spirits of the past. "They didn't even take those." He gestured to the mantelpiece.

Sophie studied the silver candlesticks resting on the raised shelf —nineteenth-century pieces that could fetch considerable sums on the black market. They were undisturbed, their surfaces still bearing the careful polish of the palace preservation staff. Above them hung a portrait of King David Kalākaua, the "Merrie Monarch," his eyes seeming to follow her movements with an expression both regal and melancholic.

"The whole thing is bizarre," Marcus said, watching as Sophie photographed the plumeria. The flower lay against the deep burgundy of the carpet like a fallen star. The morning light revealed subtle variations in its coloring—not pure white as she'd first thought, but touched with the faintest lemon yellow, like sun on sand.

Sophie pulled on latex gloves with practiced efficiency, the familiar snap of rubber against skin grounding her in the present even as the room's history pressed in from all sides. She carefully lifted the flower noting how it had been placed with deliberate precision at the exact center of the room, equidistant from all four walls. Someone had cared about the presentation.

"Evidence bag?" she asked, and Marcus handed her one from his kit. The plastic crinkled as she sealed the plumeria inside, another piece of the puzzle.

Standing in the room where Hawaii's last king had once paced the floors, dreaming of preserving his nation's independence against the rising tide of American imperialism, Sophie felt the weight of years pressing down. King Kalākaua had died in San Francisco's Palace Hotel in 1891, far from these shores he'd fought to protect. His sister, Queen Lili'uokalani, had been imprisoned in an upstairs bedroom of this very palace after the overthrow, composing mournful songs that would outlive her kingdom.

And now someone was using these rooms as a stage for their own drama, leaving blossoms like breadcrumbs in a dangerous fairy tale.

A feather brush of anxiety traced down Sophie's spine—not for herself, but for what the flowers might mean.

Three crime scenes, three flowers, each deliberately chosen. In her experience, such specificity meant personal connection. Personal threat.

"Something tells me I need to increase security at home," she said, already reaching for her phone. The device in her hand felt heavier than usual, loaded with responsibility and all the calls she needed to make. "In case these plumerias are a message for me." Sophie forced herself to think like an investigator rather than a mother whose instincts were screaming warnings. "The specificity matters. These aren't just any flowers—they have meaning for me."

"They could as easily be a message for any one of us," Marcus said, though his tone suggested he didn't quite believe it. "But I can ask to have patrol units do extra sweeps of your neighborhood. HPD takes care of its own."

Sophie smiled at her friend, grateful for the offer even as she knew its limitations. "Thanks, but I doubt that will help." Her tone carried the firm certainty of someone who'd learned the hard way that conventional security measures meant little against serious enemies. "I have a very secure home. We won't need anything but possibly some additional personnel, which Security Solutions can provide. I must minimize disruptions for the children."

The children. Always, her thoughts circled back to them. Momi, now five, with her father Alika's stubborn chin and her mother's quick mind, still asking why Uncle Connor had vanished from their lives like smoke. The questions came at unexpected moments— during bath time, over breakfast, in the quiet minutes before sleep. "Where did Uncle Connor go, Mama? Did we do something bad?"

And Sean, two and a half years old and brimming toddler energy, had finally stopped calling for "Unco!" every time the gate alert chimes rang.

He'd never known his father Jake, would have no memories of the man who'd died before his birth. But he'd had Connor for those early months, had learned to walk holding those skillful hands, had been sung to sleep by a man who ordered death with equal gentleness.

Her children didn't need more upheaval; they'd already lost enough.

"At least accept the help Connor's offering," Pierre suggested, his voice gentle but insistent. He knew her well enough to recognize the signs of her internal debate—pride warring with pragmatism, independence fighting with protectiveness. "Additional trained security couldn't hurt."

Sophie moved to the window, looking out at the palace grounds where history had been made and unmade. Below, a docent was leading a tour group, her voice carrying faintly through the glass as she explained how the palace had been the first building in

Honolulu to have electricity, even before the White House. Progress and tradition, innovation and preservation—these were forever in tension in Hawaii.

"I'll use him," Sophie decided, the words tasting like compromise in her mouth. "Connor's operative, I mean. As long as I know that this person answers to me, not to the Master of the Yām Khûmkạn."

They spent another forty minutes processing the scene, documenting every detail of the King's Suite with meticulous care.

Pierre examined the windows with their original wavy glass, checking for signs of entry. Marcus dusted for prints on every surface that might have been touched, though they all knew it was likely futile. Whoever they were dealing with was too professional to leave such obvious traces.

Sophie used her specialized equipment to scan for electronic signatures, finding the same sophisticated loops in the security footage that had marked the other scenes. A digital ghost had been here too, dancing through walls as easily as the nineteenth-century ali'i had once danced with political alliances.

By the time they finished, the late morning sun had transformed the palace grounds into a tourist mecca. Sophie watched from the window as buses disgorged their passengers—families with children posing by the Kamehameha Statue, its bronze surface gleaming in the sun; couples taking selfies on the palace's distinctive stairs, the same steps where Marines had once stood guard over a deposed queen; elderly visitors moving slowly through the gardens, stopping to smell the plumeria trees whose flowers fell like blessings on the grass.

All of them were oblivious to the darker currents flowing beneath the surface of paradise. Sophie envied their ignorance.

"We should check the third location," Marcus said, securing his evidence kit with efficient movements. "I'd like to get your opinion on the private collector's home, see if there's any pattern to the physical locations."

"Geographic pattern," Sophie said, though her mind was already racing ahead to other patterns: digital footprints, personality signatures, possible psychological profiles of someone who left plumeria at crime scenes. "And I'm curious to see if the perpetrators follow our movements there, as well."

She couldn't suppress the chill that touched the back of her neck, a cold kiss.

Someone was watching them.

4

SOPHIE

THE THIRD THEFT had been from a private collector's home in Kahala, one of Honolulu's most exclusive neighborhoods. Sophie knew the area well—she'd investigated cases there before, always struck by how much wealth could exist just miles from where local families struggled to afford even basic housing.

The drive took them along the coast, around and past Diamond Head's distinctive profile. Sophie found herself checking the rearview mirror more than usual, looking for surveillance on their tail. From the back seat, Pierre was doing the same. They caught each other's eyes in the mirror.

Pierre's mouth twitched in his almost smile, and he leaned in to address her when Marcus took a phone call on his Bluetooth. "I missed a lot while I was away in Europe. Tell me about Connor's departure. If you don't mind my asking."

Sophie kept her eyes on the passing scenery—surfers catching morning waves, joggers on the roadside path, people working in tropical yards, mynahs fluttering out of the way of their tires. Normal life continued alongside and around them.

"Connor got restless," she said finally. "We fought about his desire to leave for weeks, before things came to a head when there was an attempted coup of his position as Master of the Yām Khûmkạn. He left for Thailand then, citing 'urgent matters' that he couldn't or wouldn't explain. I told him he had to choose—his duty to the Yām Khûmkạn, or his life with us."

"So he chose duty."

Sophie nodded. "He said it was temporary, just until he could stabilize things there. But temporary became a month, then two, then six." Sophie's chuckle was bitter. "I'm an expert at losing men. At least this time no one died."

"It does seem you've had more than your share of loss. As have I." Pierre was quiet for a moment. Pierre had lost his wife and daughter in a horrific way. He knew about grief, about the spaces people left behind, about living with scars. "Even so, not all deaths are of the body."

Sophie met his gaze; her eyes stung as she glanced away. "I'm sorry. Here I am complaining when you—"

"It isn't a competition, Sophie. Your loss is real, even if Connor still walks the earth."

Marcus swore as he ended his call. "We've got a problem. The Kahala collector just called 911—someone tried to break into his house again. He scared them off, but they left something behind."

Sophie's stomach tightened reflexively. "Let me guess—a plumeria?"

"You got it. He's freaking out, wants us there, ASAP."

THE COLLECTOR'S house was a sprawling modern mansion, all clean angles and shining glass, set on a rise with ocean views. They pulled into a large turnaround planned around a copper statuary fountain that created melodic water sounds.

A silver-haired mixed-race man in his sixties, radiating nervous energy, met them at the immense glass double doors leading into his home. "Thank God you're here. After what happened to my collection already, I've been paranoid. Good thing, too, or they might have taken another piece."

"Show us where they tried to enter," Sophie said.

"Let's go inside."

The burglary victim, who introduced himself as Gary Tavares, led them through light-filled rooms filled with museum-quality art and Hawaiian artifacts. Sophie noticed Pierre gauging the items with professional interest and making quick notes in his leather notebook.

Tavares took them to a climate-controlled gallery where his most precious items were displayed. The would-be thieves had attempted to access through a skylight and had triggered a silent alarm.

"I put in cameras everywhere after last time," Tavares said proudly. "Caught the whole thing on video."

Security footage, revealed on Tavares's laptop, showed two figures in black, faces obscured by masks. They moved with professional efficiency, opening the skylight and descending on ropes— until the alarm triggered. They then pulled back up and vanished; one had taken time to drop a plumeria through the skylight's opening before fleeing.

"Can you enhance this section?" Sophie pointed to a moment when one figure turned toward the camera.

Tavares zoomed in, but the image remained frustratingly unclear. Still, something about the person's build, the way they moved . . .

"That's military training," Pierre said with certainty. "The way these men use cover, their tactical movements—I saw plenty of it working with Interpol."

"I agree," Sophie said. Their precision and discipline pointed to military or paramilitary background.

"But that could describe thousands of people in Hawaii, with our large military presence," Marcus observed.

"What were they after?" Sophie asked Tavares. "Your best

guess."

He led them to a specific display case closest to the attempted point of entry. "I imagine they were after this—the *lei niho palaoa* of Queen Lili'uokalani. The last queen of Hawaii's own necklace. It's worth . . . well, beyond price. It's irreplaceable."

Sophie studied the piece. Tiny braids of black human hair were themselves braided to form a thick cord, from which hung a hook-shaped pendant carved from a sperm whale tooth. The hair rope seemed to absorb light while the tooth's ivory gleamed in contrast, barbaric and beautiful. The *lei* was magnetic to look upon, radiating the *mana* of its provenance.

"How did you come to own this?" Sophie asked.

Tavares threw his barrel chest out with pride. "I am related to one of the Queen's retainers. She gave it to him in thanks for his service during the overthrow, not wanting it to fall into foreign hands. I've promised it to the Bishop Museum in my will so it can be enjoyed by all *Kanaka Maoli*."

"That's good to hear," Sophie said. "It appears to be an exceptional piece."

"As were all the items that the thieves have taken. They seem to be trying to build a collection," Pierre said. "Something that speaks of Hawaiian royalty, perhaps?"

Sophie's phone rang; it was her security chief, Bill. She stepped away to answer, and her body went rigid at Bill's urgent tone.

"We've had a breach attempt, Sophie. Perimeter sensors triggered about ten minutes ago. We deployed quickly and scared them off."

"How many?"

"Two. Got them on camera, but they were all in black wearing masks. And they left something odd behind."

"Let me guess," Sophie said. "They left a flower."

"How did you know? It was a plumeria. Right by the wall they attempted to climb. Want us to bag it for evidence?"

"Don't touch it. I'm on my way." She ended the call and turned to Marcus and Pierre. "They tried for my house. Two in black. Left a flower behind."

Marcus was already moving toward the door. "I'll call for backup to meet us there."

But Sophie held up a hand. "No marked units, lights or sirens. I don't want to frighten the children. Pierre, can you stay here and finish processing the scene and the details with Mr. Tavares?"

The Frenchman nodded. "Of course. I'll cover everything and get in touch with you later."

Sophie headed for the door, anxiety humming along her nerves and the bile of fear sour in her mouth. *The children had to be safe.*

THE DRIVE to Sophie's Kailua home after the alarm had come in stretched like an eternity, though Marcus wove through Honolulu's midday traffic with the practiced aggression of someone who'd spent years navigating the city's arteries.

Sophie pressed her forehead against the cool glass of the window, watching familiar landmarks blur past—the H-1 merge where traffic always bottlenecked, the Pali Highway exit that led to the mountains, the stretch where downtown's glass towers gave way to older neighborhoods with their monkeypod trees and bougainvillea-draped walls.

The SUV's air-conditioning hummed steadily, fighting against heat that shimmered off the asphalt. The leather seats warmed despite the climate control. A faint scent rose from them, a mix of the faint smell of Marcus's cold coffee from earlier, and the lingering perfume of plumeria that seemed everywhere, even when no flowers were present.

Her children were safe. Sophie repeated it like a mantra, matching the rhythm to her deliberately steady breathing.

Armita would have taken them to the safe room the moment the alarm triggered. The vault beneath the house could withstand anything short of a direct military assault. Bill and his team were the best private security money could buy—all former military, all personally vetted, all understanding that their job was to protect not just clients but family.

The house itself had become a fortress over the years, especially after Connor had lived with them. His improvements to the AI monitoring system had taken her original designs and elevated them to something that approached prescience. Cameras that could read microexpressions, sensors that detected chemical signatures, algorithms that learned and adapted to patterns of behavior. The system had made Security Solutions a world leader in defensive home protection technology, their waiting list stretching two years out for residential installations.

"The response time was impressive," Marcus said, breaking into her thoughts as he swerved around a tourist rental car going twenty miles under the speed limit. "Your team knows their stuff."

"Yes," Sophie said. "When you have children, thirty seconds can be a lifetime."

"Don't I know it." Marcus and Marcella were parents too.

The breach scenario summoned unwanted memories—another time, another threat, her mother's elegant face twisted with determination as she'd tried to take the children for her own twisted purposes. Pim Wat, master spy and assassin, was a grandmother who'd never held her grandchildren with love, only calculation.

The CIA black site where she now resided was designed for people like her—those whose skills made normal incarceration inadequate and whose networks ran too deep for conventional justice.

Sophie checked her phone reflexively, scrolling through secure contacts. No alerts from her CIA liaison. No warnings from the State Department connections she maintained. Her mother remained contained, at least physically. But Pim Wat had taught her daughter well—physical walls were just one kind of prison. Influence could seep through the smallest cracks.

"You're thinking about your mother," Marcus observed.

"Always, when someone threatens my home." Sophie tucked the phone away. "But this doesn't seem like her style. Too elaborate, too indirect. Mother would just—" She stopped, unwilling to voice the brutal efficiency Pim Wat was known to employ.

They passed through Kailua town proper, its surf shops and shave ice stands catering to the beach crowd. The salt breeze carried through the SUV's ventilation system now, bringing with it the promise of the ocean just beyond the residential streets. This was the Hawaii tourists dreamed of—laid-back vibes, local fruit stands on corners, kids riding bikes with surfboards tucked under their arms.

"I keep coming back to the question of why," Sophie said, watching a family walking, all three licking rainbow-colored shave ice. Such normal life, such easy joy. "I don't have artifacts at home. My art collection is decorative, nothing that would interest a thief targeting Hawaiian cultural items. So why . . ." A thought crystallized as she spoke it. "What if the artifact thefts were just to get my attention? What if I'm the real target?"

Marcus glanced at her sharply, his knuckles tightening on the steering wheel. "You think someone's using million-dollar heists as a calling card? That's an expensive way to send a message."

Sophie touched the scar on her cheekbone, a ridge of tissue that caught the light filtering through the windshield.

"And how would they know you'd get involved with the thefts?" Marcus navigated around a delivery truck, his movements automatic even as his mind worked the problem. "I was the one who recommended Security Solutions to the Bishop Museum. Unless . . ."

"Unless they knew our connection. Knew you'd call me." Sophie's mind raced. "The artifacts themselves might be secondary. Valuable, yes, but not easily monetized. Most are too recognizable for the black market, too culturally significant to move without attracting attention."

"Likely they're symbolic of something we haven't figured out yet." Marcus flexed his hands, the leather covering the wheel creaking slightly. "I hate puzzles like this. Give me a straightforward homicide any day." He glanced at her with rueful brown eyes that held depths of concern. "Wish I could be more help."

They turned into her neighborhood, the change immediate and palpable. Here, mature *kukui* and monkeypod trees created canopies over the street, their shadows dappling the asphalt in constantly shifting patterns. The houses sat further back from the road, hidden behind walls and tropical landscaping that provided privacy and beauty in equal measure. This was old Kailua, where *kama'aina* families had lived for generations, where the sound of the ocean was a backbeat beneath the birdsong.

Sophie's house stood behind its distinctive wall—black lava rock quarried from the Big Island a century ago, now softened with patches of grey-green lichen that looked like ancient script in the afternoon light. The wall stood eight feet high, topped with modern additions that were invisible but effective—pressure and movement sensors, infrared beams, electrified wire disguised as decorative metalwork.

Bill met them at the gate, his sturdy frame radiating controlled tension. The middle-aged former Army Ranger had led her security team for over two years, earning Sophie's trust through countless quiet nights and several not so quiet days. He input the code at the featureless security plinth—biometric scanners reading his palm print, retinal pattern, and gait recognition simultaneously before the metal gate swung open on silent hinges.

Marcus pulled through, tires crunching on the driveway. The house revealed itself in stages—warm ochre walls that glowed like honey in the afternoon sun, reddish terra-cotta roof tiles imported from Italy decades ago, and deep cobalt ceramic ones lining the deep veranda. It was a house built for both beauty and defense, its sight lines clear, its approaches limited.

The dogs met them on the front steps—Ginger bouncing with

yellow lab enthusiasm, Anubis maintaining Doberman dignity until Sophie's hand touched his head. Then both dogs transferred their attention to Marcus, who'd made the mistake of keeping treats in his pockets on previous visits.

"Down, beasts," Sophie commanded with fond exasperation, shooing them away from her friend. "Marcus isn't here to play."

"The children are inside with Armita," Bill reported, falling into step beside her. His blue eyes carried the crinkled concern of a father himself, though his own kids were college aged. He pushed a hand through hair that had gone grizzled during his time with her team, the Hawaiian sun and job stress taking their toll. The black polo and khaki shorts of Security Solutions' uniform looked almost military on him. "They're playing in the secure room. We made it seem like a game—told them we were practicing camping underground."

Sophie nodded, relief loosening something in her chest. "Good thinking. They love that space, heaven knows why." She shook her head at the irony. "I can barely stand being down there for five minutes."

The secure room was a relic from the Cold War, a bomb shelter built by the home's original paranoid owner and updated with modern amenities. Reached only by a cramped elevator that triggered every claustrophobic tendency, it was simultaneously her greatest comfort and deepest dread. The space was stocked for a six-month siege—food, water, medical supplies, entertainment systems, air filtration that could handle everything from volcanic ash to biological weapons.

But for Sophie, small dark spaces would always carry echoes of her first marriage, and of locks that only opened from the outside.

"Breach attempt was at the southwest corner," Bill continued, his voice shifting to mission-brief mode. "Professional approach—they'd done their homework. Picked the section with the most tree cover from the neighbors, furthest from the street. Used some kind of electromagnetic device to try to fool the sensors."

"But?" Sophie prompted.

"But they didn't know about the underground grid Connor installed last year. Pressure sensors extending fifteen feet beyond the wall perimeter. The moment they stepped into the zone, we had them. Clement was first responder—reached the area in under twenty seconds. They were already retreating by then."

"How many?"

"At least two, based on the footage. All in black, faces covered, moving like they'd trained together." Bill's expression darkened. "These weren't standard B&E artists, boss. These were operators."

They rounded the corner of the house, following a path lined with white ginger that filled the air with perfume. The attempted breach point showed no obvious signs of disturbance.

But there, dropped with care on a flat lava rock just inside the fence line, lay another plumeria. The afternoon sun caught its creamy petals, making them seem to glow against the dark stone.

5

SOPHIE

"WELL, THAT'S NOT GOOD," Marcus said. He pulled on latex gloves with practiced efficiency, then crouched to photograph the flower from multiple angles. "Same type, same placement style. Our thief has a signature."

"How are they moving around the island so efficiently?" Sophie studied the scene, her analytical mind clicking through possibilities. "The museum, the palace, now here—that's a lot of ground to cover."

"Multiple teams?" Marcus suggested, carefully bagging the plumeria. "Or really good knowledge of traffic patterns and back routes."

"Double the security rotation," Sophie told Bill, already revising defensive plans in her head. "I want someone inside the house at all times, not just patrolling. And review all the footage from the last week—let's see if we had surveillance we missed."

"Already in motion, boss. Brought in Rodriguez from the B-team, plus I've got Ferragut coming in tonight. She's good with kids, in case we need someone who can be inside without making them nervous."

Sophie nodded, grateful for his forethought.

"Whoever's doing this knows too much," Sophie said, the words tasting bitter.

"Agreed. You keep a low profile for someone running a major security firm," Marcus observed, sealing the evidence bag.

"But there are always leaks. Employees talk, contractors gossip, clients make connections." Sophie was already building lists in her mind, categorizing potential sources of information. "I'll have Paula pull everything—employment records for the last five years, contractor agreements, client lists that overlap with the museums. Financial records for anyone who might have a grudge."

"Send me the names as you get them," Marcus said, straightening from where he'd collected the plumeria. "I'll run them through our databases, see what pops. And Sophie?" His voice gentled. "I'm opening a formal stalking and harassment case. This goes beyond property crime now."

The official designation carried weight—resources would be allocated, federal databases accessed, inter-agency cooperation activated. It also meant paperwork, interviews, her family's life under official scrutiny. But Sophie had learned long ago that privacy was a luxury she couldn't afford when it came to protecting her children.

"Thank you," she said simply. "And tell Marcella I'll call as soon as things stabilize. If this crosses state lines or involves cultural patrimony, we might need FBI resources too."

"Already texted her. She's standing by." Marcus squeezed her shoulder, the gesture conveying support. "Lock down tight tonight. I'll have units do extra patrols, but your people are better equipped than anything HPD can offer."

Sophie walked him back to his vehicle, the dogs trailing hopefully until they realized no treats were forthcoming. As Marcus drove away, she stood for a moment in her driveway, feeling the weight of the afternoon sun on her shoulders.

Her phone buzzed. Another text from Connor, as if he could

sense her thoughts from whatever monastery or boardroom currently held his physical presence.

My operative arrives tomorrow morning. He reports only to you for this mission. Trust him, Sophie. Please.

The "please" stopped her from deleting.

Connor commanded, manipulated, occasionally requested. He rarely pleaded. *Received,* she responded, then added after a pause: *He stays outside the house. The children don't need to have their hearts broken by another "uncle."* She couldn't resist the jab.

Understood. Connor refused to take the bait.

Sophie deleted the conversation and headed inside, needing to see her children, to hold them and reassure herself that they were safe.

But first, she paused at her front door, hand on the carved teak panels that had weathered half a century of storms.

Someone had brought a war to her home. They'd made it personal.

Her mother had taught her many things, most of them terrible. But one lesson served her now: when someone brings a fight to your door, you don't just defend.

You make them regret it.

SOPHIE ENTERED THE HOUSE, walking down the simply furnished terra-cotta tiled hall to the family room. Armita had moved the children there after the security alarm was called off. Once she reached the comfortable room with its short-napped carpet and sturdy furniture, she paused in the doorway, her heart filling with tender emotion as she gazed at her children.

Sean and Momi were building block towers with their nanny. Armita, a petite Thai woman dressed all in black with her hair in a no-nonsense braid, looked up to meet Sophie's eyes with a reassuring smile.

Not for the first time, Sophie thanked the deities that Armita had come into her life. Her mother's former handmaiden could not have been more devoted and capable, and her care of Sean and Momi made Sophie's working life possible.

In addition, she was an actual ninja who had trained with the Yām Khûmkạn.

Momi looked up from her blocks, her face lighting with a smile that reminded Sophie of her daughter's father, Alika, a handsome Hawaiian man Sophie had fallen in love with after escaping her sadistic husband. Alika's features had influenced Momi's tawny skin, large brown eyes, and the cascade of ringlets trailing down her back. "Mama! Look, I made a castle."

"It's beautiful, Little Bean," Sophie said, kneeling to admire the elaborate construction.

Sean toddled over, arms outstretched. She scooped his sturdy body close, breathing in his baby shampoo scent and then blowing a raspberry on his neck. The little boy's giggle shook his whole body.

"Mama pretty," he said, patting her cheek with a chubby hand.

Sean had a pale version of Sophie's golden skin and curly brown hair, resembling her more than his father—but his personality and demeanor were all Jake's.

"Thank you, sweetheart," Sophie said. "Now show me what you were making. Maybe I can help."

Sean didn't reply but wriggled out of her arms to lead her to a pile of blocks that had so far assumed no recognizable shape. She began to stack them, with Sean adding new pieces between her choices.

"Now that you're here, I'll go get dinner started," Armita said. "We can catch up about the day's events after the children are in bed."

"Thank you, Armita. Good plan," Sophie said. "Momi, why don't you tell me about your castle."

"It's actually a museum inside a castle," Momi said. "A lot of treasures are inside." She pointed to tiny items from her dollhouse she had stashed in the block rooms.

"Nice job," Sophie said. "I like that idea."

But even here, in a fortress of a house, Sophie couldn't shake the feeling that their safety was an illusion.

An enemy was out there stealing pieces of Hawaiian history and leaving flowers like breadcrumbs, forcing Sophie toward some kind of revelation or confrontation that had begun to feel inevitable. Whatever it was couldn't be good.

She forced her attention back to the simple joy of the moment at hand, as Sean sat his padded bottom firmly in her lap and inserted a thumb in his mouth, watching her stack the blocks. She leaned her scarred cheek on his sweet curls.

For now, this was enough.

Her children were safe, her team was solid, and she had allies like Pierre and Marcus to help solve this mystery. Whatever game someone was playing or message they were trying to send, she and her team would figure it out.

Hopefully they could do that before the next plumeria appeared.

6

SOPHIE

SOPHIE AND ARMITA met in the kitchen after the children were in bed. After she finished loading the dishwasher and wiping the counters, Sophie made them a pot of fragrant Thai tea and settled at the small breakfast nook.

She watched Armita prepare a simple meal for when the children woke, mixing the ingredients for a tasty, protein rich hot cereal with practiced grace. "How did the evacuation down to the safe room go yesterday?" Sophie asked. They spoke in Thai—a comfort for them, heritage in this island paradise. "Let's keep this short, though. I want you to get some rest."

"And I want you to do the same." Armita sliced a papaya with quick, efficient gestures. "It was a busy day." Her dark eyes met Sophie's with steady calm. "The children did very well. We reached the safe room in under five minutes with no problems."

"Even Sean? He didn't do great last time we drilled." Sophie's youngest had struggled with the practice evacuations, not understanding why they sometimes had to interrupt play to go down to the restrictive underground bunker.

"He cried a little when we arrived, but Momi sang him a song.

The one you taught her." Armita's voice warmed. "She does love being a big sister."

Sophie felt a tightness in her chest—not guilt, but fierce protectiveness and joy. Her children were adapting, surviving, just as she'd had to do while growing up in Thailand. She'd been tugged between her American ambassador father with his long absences, and a mother who suffered chronic depression while living a secret life.

"Sophie," Armita said gently. "The children are strong. Like their mother. But strength doesn't mean we have to carry everything alone."

Armita had been Sophie's nanny before she became her children's. Sophie had brought Armita into her home not just for her training with children, background as a ninja, and cooking skills, but for the deeper level of commitment and love they shared. Armita understood without judgment, offered support without pity. She was another survivor of the evil that was Sophie's mother. She too had rebuilt her life far from where it started; there was much only Armita really understood about what Sophie had lived through in the past.

"Thank you," Sophie said. "For taking care of them. And me too."

Armita smiled, the expression transforming her narrow, serious face. "Family takes care of each other." She poured them each a mug from the pot Sophie had started. "Speaking of, here's your tea. Strong as you like it."

Sophie gave the woman a brief hug and took the fragrant beverage, heading to the private office Pierre jokingly called her "Batcave."

The room was a converted bedroom, windows covered with blackout curtains, walls lined with servers and monitors, floor covered in sound-absorbing matting. This inner sanctum was where Sophie the mother became Sophie the tech expert, using skills she'd always had a natural talent with.

Sophie settled into her chair, bringing her systems online. Six monitors flickered to life, displaying feeds from various sources as she activated her three computers: Jinjai, Amara, and Ying.

The house's security cameras showed peaceful scenes—Sean sprawled in his crib, Momi curled in bed with her favorite stuffed elephant.

But it was the monitor holding the case file that drew her attention. She activated the file, pulling up digital evidence from the museum thefts, surveillance footage from nearby businesses, and traffic cameras from routes between the targeted locations. She'd spent years building her network of access—some legal, some in grey areas.

"Show me what I'm missing," she murmured, fingers flying across the keyboard.

She pulled up the footage from the Bishop Museum theft first, running it through enhancement filters she'd developed herself. There—a shadow that didn't quite match the lighting. A reflection in a display case that showed movement where there should have been none.

The work was good. Better than good. They'd edited the security footage in real-time, creating a perfect loop that showed empty galleries while they did the job.

But perfection itself was a signature, and Sophie had learned long ago that everyone had tells.

She isolated the timestamp discrepancies, overlaying them with code analysis from the signal interceptor. A pattern emerged— subtle, almost musical in its rhythm.

Her breath caught as recognition dawned.

"No," she whispered, but her fingers were already moving, pulling up archived data from her past life.

The Yām Khûmkạn's technical division had been legendary in certain circles. Their encryption methods, their signal manipulation techniques, their ability to make technology bend to their will —it had been one of Connor's most valuable assets. Sophie had been given access during their time together, had learned from masters of the craft.

She pulled up comparison algorithms, letting her program analyze the signatures. The match came back at 94.7%—too high to be coincidence, too low to be the original source.

Someone had learned from the Yām Khûmkạn's methods. Someone with access to their techniques but not quite their level of mastery. A student rather than a teacher.

Sophie frowned, thinking through possibilities. Connor's organization had begun fracturing after his departure when he came to live with her. Some had waited for him and been rewarded when he returned. Others had scattered to the winds. But some might be, even now, working against him by trying to get to her.

The theft pattern wasn't random. She'd known that from the start. But now she saw another layer. The stolen artifacts weren't just valuable or culturally significant. Each one had a connection to warrior traditions, royalty, and protection: the values of the Yām Khûmkạn. Someone was building a collection with a purpose.

Sophie pulled up the museum's network architecture, her programs sliding through firewalls like water through silk. There—a backdoor, elegantly hidden but not invisible to someone who knew what to look for. The coding style was familiar. "Son of a pox-ridden yak," she murmured in Thai. "Who are you, and what do you have to do with the Yām Khûmkạn?"

Sophie began a deeper dive into the museum's systems, documenting every trace of intrusion. If she was right—if someone from Connor's former organization was involved—then the thefts were, indeed, targeting her somehow.

The Yām Khûmkạn never did anything without layers of purpose. If the burglars were a faction, there was an endgame she hadn't seen yet—but it was time to talk to Connor about it.

She glanced at the security feed showing her children sleeping peacefully. Whatever was coming, whoever was behind this, they'd made a mistake. They'd threatened her family.

The computer chimed softly—another anomaly detected, this one in the Bishop Museum's HVAC system. Sophie leaned forward, eyes narrowing. Someone had been mapping the museum's infrastructure for weeks, learning its rhythms, its vulnerabilities.

"Got you," she whispered, documenting the digital fingerprint.

She saved her work to encrypted drives, then began the careful process of covering her own tracks. Old habits and hard-learned lessons: always clean up after yourself. Never leave a trail that could lead anyone back to you.

As she worked, part of her mind was already at the museum, imagining the conversation with Pierre and Marcus and the museum staff. They needed to know what she'd found.

But first, she had one more search to run.

She pulled up shipping manifests, customs records, flight plans. If someone was moving stolen artifacts, they'd need transportation. And if they were connected to the Yām Khûmkạn, they'd use specific routes, certain trusted channels.

There. A private jet, registered to a shell company, had made trips between Honolulu and Bangkok six times in the last month. Sophie memorized the tail number, then erased her search history. She'd give the information to Marcus, let him run it through official channels. Her role was information, not action, at least at this time.

She secured her systems, triple-checking the encryption before powering down. As she stood, her phone buzzed.

It was Connor, persistent as always—and as usual, his timing was perfect.

She was ready to deal with him; it was past time he answered for a few things.

Sophie punched the answer button on her phone with her thumb. "Are you finally calling to tell me what's really going on?"

7

CONNOR

SOPHIE'S NAME lit the screen as she answered his call. Her slightly husky voice with its crisp British accent took him by surprise, braced as he'd been for another aborted call. "Are you finally calling to tell me what's really going on?" she demanded.

"Sophie." Instead of answering, he leaned back in his padded ergonomic chair and deliberately slowed and softened his tone. "I was beginning to think you were ignoring me."

"Too busy putting children to bed and hunting expert thieves to deal with you and your schemes." Her voice carried the blend of frustration and anxiety that had become familiar. "Connor, we need to talk about the museum thefts."

He closed his eyes briefly.

He needed to see her. Craved it, even. Plus he wanted to gauge her responses by watching them. "Can we switch to video?"

Sophie didn't answer—but a moment later, his phone screen bloomed to life, filled with her frowning face.

Something inside him unknotted, relaxed. Just looking at her soothed him, even when she was backlit by unflattering blue monitor glow that highlighted how her eyes were circled with tiredness. The scar from a near-fatal case stood out on her cheek more when she was fatigued. The scar pulled her eye down on one side, a faint ridged line paler than the rest of her golden-brown skin.

Nothing could dim her beauty, but she was more precious to him for these frailties and flaws.

Sophie seemed to be studying him too. She glanced away at last, blinking those luminous eyes and giving a little shake of her head. "Damn you," she said.

"I've missed you," he said. "So much."

"You have a funny way of showing it, as the Americans say." There was no mistaking the bitterness in her tone.

"There's a lot going on over here. I had no choice but to return. I can't explain everything, but the consequences could be catastrophic—for whole countries."

"You do realize how grandiose that sounds," Sophie said icily. "And whatever you've been trying to do isn't working. Someone's coming after us here—and they have ties to the Yām Khûmkạn."

Of course she'd already found the connection. Sophie's brilliance with technology matched his own skills. "You found the digital signature."

"Yām Khûmkạn protocols, but watered down. As if a student learned from an apprentice." She glanced down and he heard the soft click of keys in the background. "Another thing you might know about. There's a jet held by a shell company making runs between Honolulu and Bangkok. Tail number November-Four-Seven-Nine-Kilo-Papa."

"Yes." Connor's jaw tightened; he knew that plane. "That used to be one of ours."

"Used to be?" Sophie's tone sharpened. "Connor, what haven't you told me?"

Connor stood and moved away from his desk. He paced the large stone chamber whose chill walls were softened by luxurious tapestries. His bare feet sank into silken rugs. Through the narrow arrow-slit type windows, dawn was breaking. He stepped outside onto a stone balcony and paced. "When I came back to Thailand, not everyone accepted my return to leadership. Some felt I'd . . . compromised the organization by leaving. By choosing you and the children."

"And these people are now on my island, threatening my family's safety?" The controlled anger in her voice made him wince.

"I've been tracking them. I have people in Honolulu, watching. They won't get any further with this play."

"These perps are stealing from museums using your organization's techniques, and they tried to breach my home. Your splinter faction is operating in my territory." She took a breath and blew it out forcibly, calming herself. "How many are involved?"

"As I've regained control over here, those that left the compound—maybe twenty, but well-trained and higher in leadership—have been recruiting, training others who have no connection to us." He paused. "I don't know exactly. But that could be why the programming was—different."

Sophie was quiet for a moment. She was pacing now too, the low light of her office caressing her profile like a silver finger. "The artifacts they're taking aren't random. There are themes." She described the items that had been stolen. "Is this group making a statement? What are they doing with these symbols of royalty? Does it have something to do with the original mission of the Yām Khûmkạn, as Thailand's guardians of the royal family?"

"It could," Connor said. He thought back to an earlier conversation with Feirn, his majordomo and confidante, where they'd brainstormed motives. "I believe the burglaries are a ploy to draw me in. The question is if they're using you to do that, or they have some other plan."

"Does it matter? Either way, they're a threat." Another pause, longer this time. She turned to face him in the camera; her eyes were wide, hypnotic. He wished he could see her in person and read the color of her energy field. "Connor, I need complete transparency. No shadows, no half-truths. The children's safety depends on it."

Sophie's words landed like blades between Connor's ribs, each one precisely placed. He had known this moment would come—had rehearsed versions of it during sleepless nights when the weight of his position pressed down like the humid Thai air before a monsoon. Even so, nothing could prepare for the reality of disappointing Sophie.

"The faction is led by someone called Sunan," Connor said. The name felt strange to say aloud, like disturbing a grave—they'd avoided using it in discussions here. Through the tower's stone-lined windows, fruit bats began their evening hunt, dark shapes against a purple sky. "He was one of the Master's most devoted students, a true believer in the old ways. Blood for blood, strength through fear, loyalty proved through pain."

The stone floor beneath Connor's bare feet still held the day's heat, radiating upward with the memory of violence. Connor had walked these same stones the night he'd taken the Master's life. The ancient floor had been slick with blood, and his own body battered by a fight to the death.

"When I eliminated the Master, Sunan tried to raise resistance but was rebuffed. He left and that wasn't long after your mother had disappeared. She was the Master's lover, as you know." He could still see them together in his mind's eye, Pim Wat's elegant beauty complementing the Master's coiled power. They'd moved through the ninjas in the stronghold like paired jaguars, leaving unease in their wake. "We assumed he'd gone to ground permanently, possibly even been eliminated by Pim Wat during her flight. She was never one to leave loose ends."

"But this man has been building a following instead." Sophie's voice carried across the miles and in the tiny screen, her level brows drew together in a frown. "Waiting for his moment."

"We think so. No one has actually seen him." Through the windows, the jungle around the fortress began its evening chorus—gibbons calling their territories, insects beginning their night songs, the distant scream of a hunting bird. Familiar sounds now seemed full of foreboding.

"The timing can't be coincidence," Sophie said. "Why surface now? What's changed?"

Connor moved to the window, pressing his palm against stone worn smooth by centuries. The dampness of evening was beginning to creep in, carrying the green smell of jungle rot and growth, life and death intertwined. Below, mist rose from the canopy, ghostlike in the failing light.

She deserved honesty, even if it burned. "Next month marks an anniversary since my ascendance in the Yām Khûmkạn." The words felt heavy. "In our laws—old laws that even I cannot change —that's when leadership can be formally challenged. Before that, any move against me would have been rebellion, would have united the organization against him."

"So he's preparing his challenge by stealing artifacts in Honolulu?" The skepticism in Sophie's voice was sharp enough to cut. "That doesn't track. The Yām Khûmkạn doesn't care about Hawaiian cultural pieces."

"No, but they care about strength." He gripped the window's edge until the stone bit into his palm. "Every theft on your island that goes unpunished by the Yām Khûmkạn is a public declaration that I've grown weak. That my connection to you, to the children, to the outside world has compromised my ability to lead. He's building a case that I've lost my way."

The truth of it lodged in his throat; Sophie and the children *had* changed him. Made him dream of being something more human than the leader of a shadow organization. But in Sunan's world, such dreams were blasphemy; they showed vulnerability.

"Politics." Sophie's laugh carried no humor. "Even criminal organizations can't escape bureaucracy and power plays."

He heard the creak of her chair as she sat back down. Sophie's eyes dropped to her keyboard. Rapid keyboard clicking followed. "I've recorded everything I found tonight," she said. "Digital fingerprints from the museum intrusions, network signatures, correlation patterns between the thefts. I'll pass it all to Marcus in the morning, let him run it through official channels . . ." She added, "Though we both know they won't find anything actionable—your people are too good for that. I'm also going to reach out to Agent MacDonald, my contact with the CIA. They might have intelligence on Sunan's movements."

"Sophie—" Connor ran his hand into his hair, gripping hard enough to ground himself. The ache in his scalp was nothing compared to the constriction in his chest. "I wish you'd wait. This is an internal matter. Let me handle it through our channels."

"Connor." Just his name, but weighted with the years of their relationship in all its many phases. Her voice softened, though steel remained beneath. "My children are practicing drills getting to a safe room because someone tried to breach my home. I don't have the luxury of waiting for your cult to resolve its issues."

"It's not a cult," he said automatically, but her words hit hard. Sean and Momi, whom he'd taught to swim in the gentle waters of Lanikai Beach, called him Uncle Connor and loved stories of his travels and roughhouse play. These beloved children shouldn't have to know about secure rooms and evacuation protocols.

"I'm not going to sit here like bait in a trap," Sophie continued, her fingers never pausing on the keyboard. "Armita has the evacuation plan refined to five minutes. All my systems are updated with the latest countermeasures. Bill's team is on high alert. And now I know what we're really facing, which is more than I did an hour ago."

Sophie's protective instincts were fierce as any lioness. She'd survived her mother, her ex-husband, and numerous threats that came with her work.

But the Yām Khûmkạn was different—older, deeper, more embedded and dedicated. Its reach was global and hidden.

"I can send more people beyond the operative already en

route," he offered. "Additional security teams, satellite surveillance—"

"No." The word was flat, final. "Your people can maintain their distance watch, but this is my territory to defend. I'll handle it my way, with my rules."

He recognized that tone, had been on the receiving end of it enough to know argument was futile.

"Then at least let me share what intelligence we have," he said. "Sunan's preferred methods, his known associates, patterns of behavior that might help you predict his moves."

"Send the intel through the encrypted channel. I'll review it tomorrow." She paused, and he heard her take a breath. When she spoke again, her voice carried the weight of a mother's deepest fear. "Connor, I need you to be completely honest. Are the children in danger?"

Outside, he saw that something large moved through the canopy—a leopard perhaps, or one of the smaller jungle cats that hunted at twilight. Predators and prey in their eternal dance. Which was he, this time?

"I don't believe Sunan would injure the children directly." Connor forced himself to analyze coldly, as the Master would have. "It would violate every code we have about involving innocents. Such an action could turn the organization against him, even those who support his challenge. But . . ."

"But desperate people do desperate things." Sophie's voice was steady, controlled, but he knew her well enough to hear the fear beneath. "And fanatics don't always follow their own rules."

"No," he said quietly. "They don't."

"Then, as I said, I'll handle it." No dramatics, no accusations— just Sophie facing reality with her usual unflinching resolve. "I need to go. It's late here, and tomorrow will be complicated."

"Sophie, wait." He pressed his forehead against the cool stone of the window frame, struggling to find a way to convey his love, his regret, his determination to protect her despite the distance and barriers. Words failed him, as they always did in moments that truly mattered. "Please. Just ... be careful."

"You too, Connor." Her voice gentled for just a moment. "Whatever Sunan is planning, it won't stop with a few museum thefts and cryptic messages. He's building to something bigger. He probably wants your head. Literally."

The line went dead with a soft click and she vanished from the screen, leaving Connor holding a silent phone while the jungle breathed below him.

She was right, of course. The Yām Khûmkạn had ancient ways of handling succession—trial by combat and obstacle. Sunan wouldn't be content with simply defeating Connor; he'd want to make an example of him, wash away what he saw as weakness with Connor's blood.

Connor would have to eliminate him first.

He set the phone down carefully, though his hands wanted to hurl it against the stone walls. Violence shimmered just beneath his civilized veneer—the Master's true legacy was hardwired into him now.

Outside, a night wind picked up, setting the prayer flags on nearby turrets snapping. The breeze swept in over the ancient stones of the stronghold, lifting the silk tapestries that covered doorways, carrying the scent of approaching rain. The air grew thick with moisture and electricity—monsoon season coming early, or perhaps just a brief storm.

He could feel the disturbance in his bones. Storm season was approaching Thailand in truth, but also metaphorically approaching Oahu, approaching everyone that he'd tried to protect by leaving them far behind.

Connor hit the intercom on his desk, the modern device incongruous against the hand-carved teak. Feirn answered immediately —the man never seemed to sleep, a useful trait.

"Master?"

"Gather the inner circle. Main conference room, twenty

minutes." Connor was already moving, pulling on a shirt, sliding his feet into the soft leather shoes he wore indoors. "I have intelligence to share about Sunan's activities. I want updates from all our Honolulu assets, and I want strategic options prepared."

"Aye, sir. I'll have them assembled." A pause, then carefully: "Lethal or non-lethal options, Master?"

Connor stopped in the doorway, one hand on the ancient wood that defined the stone portal. Through the window, he could see the first drops of rain beginning to fall. One of them landed on his skin, warm as blood.

With Sophie and the children in danger, he felt a darkness rising inside. Some part of him had always known this moment would come—when he'd have to choose between the man he wanted to be and the monster he'd been shaped into.

"Lethal," he said quietly, the word falling into the humid air like a stone into still water. "This must end with Sunan's death. Prepare options that ensure it."

He disconnected and moved through the stronghold's corridors, feeling the weight of centuries in these stones. Monks had prayed here once, before the Yām Khûmkạn had claimed it. Perhaps their spirits lingered, witnesses to how sacred spaces could be corrupted.

The rain was falling harder now, drumming against the roof tiles, running down in sheets that distorted the jungle beyond. Somewhere out there, Sunan was moving his pieces into position, confident in his righteousness, certain that Connor's feelings for a woman and two children were proof of weakness.

Connor paused at a window overlooking the central courtyard, watching rain pound the stone courtyard where he'd trained for years. His gaze fell on the row of pikes where heads of the disobedient were displayed. They were empty now, but this was where he'd learned that love was liability, that connection was vulnerability, that strength came through isolation and self-mastery.

Sophie might pay the price for his hubris in believing he could have both worlds—the shadow kingdom he ruled, and the light she represented.

The storm was coming in truth now, lightning flickering through the clouds, thunder rolling across the jungle like war drums.

Connor turned from the window and walked toward his council chamber. The man who loved Sophie and her children would always exist, locked away in his heart.

But now, the Yām Khûmkạn would remember why they'd feared him enough to follow him after he'd killed their Master.

8

SOPHIE

Sophie drove out the gate of her house the next morning, the automatic barrier closing behind her with a soft mechanical whir and a *clunk* that felt more final than usual somehow; it had been difficult to leave today.

The familiar curve of Kailua Road stretched before her, lined with shower trees whose pink blossoms carpeted the asphalt in a display that the tires of her pearl white Lexus SUV rolled over like so much confetti.

Morning sun slanted through ironwood trees as she navigated the gentle curves toward the Pali Highway, their needlelike leaves creating shifting patterns of light and shadow across her windshield. To her left, the Koʻolau Mountains rose in their ancient majesty, their fluted cliffs dark with last night's rain. Waterfalls threaded down the green faces like silver ribbons that would vanish by afternoon.

Her eyes were gritty despite the extra hour of sleep Armita had gifted her by keeping the children occupied. After last night's revelations, even that mercy hadn't been enough.

"Even so. Armita is a treasure," she muttered.

Guilt pricked at her for all the woman had taken on. Not just nanny and household manager, but cook, bodyguard and crisis counselor. Sophie instructed her phone to send that sentiment as a text message, adding thanks in Thai that felt inadequate for the depth of her gratitude.

She yawned as she merged onto the Pali Highway, reaching for a thermal mug of extra strong English Breakfast tea. The familiar nip of flavor and caffeine began to clear the fog from her mind as she drove the upward-curving route toward the tunnels through the mountains. The temperature dropped as she gained elevation, mist clinging to the craggy green mountainsides like torn silk. Through gaps in the junglelike foliage, she caught glimpses of Kāneʻohe Bay spread out below, its usually turquoise waters turned to steel by an overcast sky.

The Pali Lookout flashed by on her right, tourists already gathering despite the early hour and questionable weather. She'd stood there herself, enjoying trade winds that could literally push you backward, contemplating the ancient battle where King Kamehameha had driven enemy warriors over these very cliffs.

Descending now through the tunnels toward Honolulu, she placed her first call. The transition from mountain mist to urban concrete was always jarring as lush, residential Kailua gave way to the more densely packed neighborhoods of town. "Paula. Can you prepare the meeting room for a video conference and send invites? I need Pierre Raveaux. Marcus Kamuela from HPD, and Marcella Scott from the FBI. Full security briefing protocols for confidentiality."

"Sure, Sophie." Paula's perpetually upbeat tone was like audio sunshine. "Sounds like you've got a hot case brewing. Should I alert the coffee machine to work overtime?"

"That's putting it mildly," Sophie said, appreciating her assistant's attempt at levity. She passed Punahou School, its manicured grounds a stark contrast to the grittier neighborhoods that would follow. "This one's going international. I might need to have you loop in my CIA contact—still tracking down the best way to reach him. I'll let you know. See you soon." She ended the call as she navigated the merge onto the H-1 freeway.

Traffic was building as she joined a river of commuters flowing into downtown. The freeway carved through older neighborhoods where modest homes crouched beneath the shadows of new high-rises. Honolulu's growing pains were visible in the contrast of older wooden buildings versus concrete and glass. Assembly cranes dotted the skyline like mechanical birds, testament to the island's hunger for growth despite limited space.

"Now to call Agent McDonald at the CIA. Ugh," Sophie muttered, bracing herself for the interaction. She'd never liked the beefy, blustery Cold War operative who seemed frozen in a spy novel from the eighties. McDonald consistently tried to bully her into operations that served CIA interests more than hers, and he had an unfortunate habit of using gender diminutives like "little lady" despite repeated corrections. Dealing with him required focus and an iron spine.

Sophie hit a button on the steering wheel and called Agent McDonald. Geared up to ask him about the status of her mother in prison and to leverage that information with passing on Sunan's threat, she was deflated by an automated recording telling her to leave a message at a series of digits that sounded like coordinates to a missile silo.

"Agent McDonald. I hope this is still your personal number; it's the only contact number I have for you." She kept her tone brisk, professional. "I'm calling to check on the status of a certain prisoner. You know which one. I also have intelligence regarding her former associates that would be of interest to the agency. Please call me back at your earliest convenience."

Sophie ended the call, frowning as she navigated the familiar turns toward her office building. Hopefully McDonald would ring her back, or someone else from his department would. Otherwise she'd face the Kafkaesque nightmare of trying to reach him through the CIA general switchboard, where "need to know" was a weapon wielded against civilians.

"Didn't want to talk to that nasty old yak fart anyway," she muttered in Thai, the profanity rolling off her tongue with satisfying emphasis. Her mother was the one who'd taught her that cursing in Thai was more expressive than English—one of the few useful lessons she'd kept from that woman.

Her mind drifted over the late-night conversation with Connor as she passed the gleaming towers of Kaka'ako, a neighborhood that had transformed from industrial wasteland to luxury condos in barely a decade.

She mulled over what he'd said, what he'd carefully omitted. The weight of unspoken truths lay between them, but what felt new—almost foreign—was the emotional distance she'd maintained when she heard his voice and saw his face on her screen. Those sea blue eyes that had once undone her had seemed shadowed and dull. The sensual mouth that had whispered promises in the dark seemed like it belonged to a stranger.

Feelings that had reawakened when he'd come to her during last year's crisis had subsided like a fever passing, leaving her weak but clearheaded.

She was done with that complicated man and his divided loyalties. For the first time since he'd left for Thailand six months ago, she was relieved he was gone.

"We're over," she said aloud, testing the words as she took the Vineyard exit toward downtown. They rang true, settling into her with surprising peace. No dramatic pain, no surge of longing or regret. Just . . . *acceptance.* "He's made his choice. So have I. I'm single now." She smiled. "Single. And feeling good."

The downtown skyline rose before her with its glass and steel monuments to commerce. Aloha Tower stood sentinel over the harbor where cruise ships disgorged tourists seeking paradise, unaware of the shadows that moved beneath the surface of island life. She passed the Prince Kūhiō Federal Building where the FBI used to have their offices, its architecture a stark contrast to graceful palm trees that tried to soften its harsh lines.

Sophie had time for one more call as she descended into the parking garage beneath her building, fluorescent lights replacing the morning sun. This one was personal and would be a touchstone of normalcy—or so she hoped.

Ambassador Frank Smithson answered the phone in the deep, warm voice that never failed to lift her spirits—as if Morgan Freeman spoke to her with paternal affection. "To what do I owe the pleasure of a call from my best girl?"

"Just catching up, *Pa*." She used the Thai honorific that had become her pet name for him. Her father had been through hell last year—a cancer diagnosis, difficult treatment, and an assassination attempt by her mother Pim Wat that had nearly succeeded. The last thing she wanted was to stress him with news of the Yām Khûmkạn entering her life again. "How is retirement treating you? Still finding it boring?"

"Ha! I'm busier than ever," Frank said with evident satisfaction. "You know me, I can't sit still. I'm consulting for the State Department on Pacific Rim relations, and I've been lobbying Washington for more funding for Native Hawaiian programs. Did you know they're trying to cut the budget for language preservation? Over my dead body." He paused. "Poor choice of words, given last year's events. But I'm back on-island at last. When can I see you and my grandchildren?"

Sophie pulled into her reserved parking space and cut the engine. "How about dinner next week? Tuesday maybe? The kids would love to see their Grandpa Frank." Hopefully by then, things would have settled regarding Sunan's threat. If not, she might need to activate protection for Frank too.

"Perfect. I'll bring that chocolate *haupia* pie from Ted's Bakery they love. And Sophie?" His voice gentled. "You sound tired. Everything alright?"

"Just work stuff, *Pa*. You know how it is." She kept her tone light as she gathered her work things from the seat beside her. "I'll fill you in next week."

She ended the call and sat for a moment in the artificial twilight of the parking garage, the engine ticking as it cooled. Through the open concrete pillars around the upper level, she could hear the morning sounds of downtown Honolulu—traffic, construction, the distant squabble of mynah birds arguing over territory.

They were the normal sounds of a downtown Hawaii day, at odds with the medieval succession drama in which she was a bit player.

"One crisis at a time, Sophie," she told herself, checking her appearance in the mirror. Her professional armor was in place: subtle makeup, fat pearl earrings, a slim fitting navy silk blouse that made her feel both feminine and formidable. "Don't borrow trouble from tomorrow."

She locked the Lexus and headed for the elevator, low heels clicking against the concrete with a determined rhythm. The elevator doors closed on her reflection—composed, professional, ready for anything in pearls and pin-striped slacks.

The external elevator rose toward her office, carrying her from the depths toward the top of the building. Outside, the first drops of a misty rain began to fall on Honolulu, creating a rainbow and washing the city clean for another day's sins.

If Sunan thought she'd be an easy target, a weak point to exploit against Connor, he was about to learn why her reputation in security circles was legendary. Sophie had survived being raised by Pim Wat. She'd survived a sadistic ex-husband, and having her heart broken repeatedly. She'd survive this threat too, and come out the victor.

Time to brief her team and figure out how to protect her family from an international threat. Time to be Sophie Smithson, security expert and strategist—not Sophie the mother, a woman who loved unwisely and too well.

9

PIERRE

PIERRE RAVEAUX ADJUSTED his laptop screen to avoid the glare streaming through the window of his ground floor apartment in Waikiki. The late morning sun painted golden rectangles across his polished floor. Visible in the distance was Diamond Head, the famous crater rising like a sleeping giant against the cerulean sky. The beach where he swam each morning was a short walk away, close enough that he could smell the ocean on the trade winds. His place was on a quiet side street near the yacht harbor, far enough from the tourist chaos that he could hear mynah birds arguing outside, and when the wind was right, the clang of boat rigging.

He liked to think that his minimalist living space—clean lines, white walls, modern furniture—reflected the orderly nature of his mind. The truth was more complex. After Gita's death, he'd stripped away everything that might trigger memory. When he'd moved to Honolulu for a fresh start he'd left behind her textiles, plump pillows, little icons, and paintings that had once covered their walls in a riot of color. He'd kept only one, wrapped in acid-free paper in his bedroom closet: an impression of their child, four-year-old Lucie, building a sandcastle with her characteristic focused intensity.

Even five years after their funeral, he couldn't look at it.

Currently, the only concession to chaos in his life was Lisette, his young gray tabby cat. She had draped herself across his keyboard with feline entitlement, and emitted a loud purr while curling a paw and twitching her tail, clearly expecting petting.

"*Non, ma petite*," he murmured, gently relocating her to his lap where she settled with a reproachful huff. "We have work to do."

He poured his Perrier, always with two lime wedges and a generous measure of ice. The ritual was as important as the beverage itself. He was years sober now, though the thirst never truly left. It lived in his chest where his grief did, manageable but ever-present.

He wiped condensation from his fingers on the linen napkin he kept folded beside his workspace. Small civilities, Gita used to say, made the difference in quality of life.

He'd been notified by Paula about an imminent team meeting; it was perfect timing as he'd been readying to check in with Sophie about a plan for the investigation today. The case intrigued him—not just the puzzle of it, but the way it seemed to be pulling Sophie into dangerous emotional territory.

The video conference window opened, revealing Sophie in the Security Solutions conference room. Her style was sophisticated today and highlighted how uniquely beautiful she was.

"*Bonjour*, Pierre," she said.

"*Bonjour*, Sophie. May I say, that blouse is very good on you?" Pierre cocked his head. The silk caught the light, its deep blue tone setting off her golden skin. "You should wear it more often."

"I will, now that Sean isn't spitting up on everything." She smiled, touching the V-neck of the fabric. "*Merci*."

Marcus Kamuela joined next, his massive shoulders making the video frame look cramped; the HPD detective filled any space like a force of nature. "Hey," he said, his casual greeting at odds with tension visible in his mouth and jaw.

FBI Special Agent Marcella Scott appeared last. Even in a black suit, wearing no makeup and with her hair scraped back in a bun, the agent was a stunning woman: all cheekbones, flashing eyes, sensuous lips. "Good morning, all." She and Marcus exchanged a nod, the only indication the pair were married, before she turned to Sophie. "Nice to see you, Sophie. It's been a while."

These people had history—shared cases and long friendships that formed a complex web where the professional and personal were inseparable. Pierre sipped his Perrier, the bubbles sharp against his palate, content to wait and see how his role intersected with theirs.

"Glad each of you could make time for this meeting." Sophie's voice was steady despite tension around her eyes. She pulled up a file and shared it to their screens. "I'll dive right in with my news. The antiquities burglaries at the Palace and the museum aren't just high-end theft. They're connected to the Yām Khûmkạn."

Pierre's eyebrows rose as Lisette kneaded his thigh through his linen trousers. Marcus shifted uncomfortably, his bulk making his office chair creak, as he frowned.

Marcella leaned forward with focused attention. "The Thai organization?" Marcella's voice was sharp. "Are you sure?"

"Unfortunately, yes." Sophie clicked through some images of code that were meaningless to Pierre. "The level of expertise and a digital signature . . ." she paused, seeming to choose her words, ". . . also, confirmation from a reliable source. All point to a splinter faction of the group being involved."

Reliable source. Pierre's chest tightened. That meant she had to have talked to her former lover Connor Standish about the case.

He took another sip of Perrier, catching the lime slice in his teeth and letting its sourness ground him.

He was Sophie's colleague and her friend. The fact that he dreamed sometimes of her laugh, of the way she moved—that was his burden to carry.

Sophie went on, emotion excised from her tone. "It's likely the burglaries are connected to a succession dispute within the organization. Someone is trying to prove their worthiness to lead by acquiring artifacts of power."

"Power?" Marcus's skepticism was evident even through the digital connection. "We talking symbolic or literal?"

"Both," Sophie said. "The stolen items aren't random selections. It seems their strategy has been to pull me in, using the plumerias as a message. It's possible the pieces may have significance to the organization's mythology."

Marcella straightened. "If this is confirmed Yām Khûmkạn activity, then this case now falls under federal jurisdiction. Specifically, the Terrorism Organization Incursion protocols."

"Wait." Marcus's voice rose. "Marcella, this is my case. I've been working—"

"Had been working," his wife corrected gently. "Marcus, you know how this goes. The moment international terrorism organizations are confirmed as operating on U.S. soil, the FBI takes lead. This is no longer a burglary investigation. It's a national security matter."

"Message received," Marcus said. "I'll send my work product to the FBI office when you send confirmation. See you all later." He disconnected abruptly, his window going dark as abruptly as a slammed door.

The silence that followed was awkward. "I'll need access to all your files, too," Marcella addressed Sophie. "And your source. We'll need to verify—"

"My source's identity remains confidential," Sophie said; of course she wanted to keep Connor's name out of any FBI investigation. The enigmatic leader of the Yām Khûmkạn had tangled with all the federal agencies in the past. "But I can provide corroborating intel through secure channels."

Lisette chose that moment to stand, stretch luxuriously, and resettle in Pierre's lap, her tail flicking across the screen and drawing the women's gazes. The feline interruption provided a distraction.

"I see you've got some feminine company," Sophie said, her smile genuine for the first time. "Hullo, Lisette."

The cat disappeared as she lay back down. Pierre stroked her silken fur, grateful for the excuse to look away from his screen. "Perhaps," he suggested, "if these criminals are seeking specific artifacts, we can predict their next targets, *non*? What else might they make a play for? Perhaps set up a trap for them?"

He was offering Sophie an escape route from the direction of Marcella's questioning, and from the flash of gratitude in her eyes, she knew it. "I'm working on that. There are several possibilities, both in private collections and public institutions. I'll work with the curator of the Bishop who has been helping us and have a list of possible targets ready by tomorrow."

"Good." Marcella was typing, probably drafting the paperwork to process the case. The rapid click of her keys carried through the connection like hail hitting a window. "I'll need a full briefing with our Special Agent in Charge once I'm officially assigned. I'll have my office reach out to schedule it."

Federal involvement meant more resources but also more scrutiny. More questions about Sophie's role in the case. That was bound to be uncomfortable, given Connor's history of operating in the shadows between legal and otherwise.

"One more thing," Sophie said. "We need to consider protective details. Not just for the artifacts, but for people who might be leveraged." The words carried weight beyond their surface meaning.

"You thinking the thief might escalate to kidnapping?" Marcella asked.

"The Yām Khûmkạn doesn't hesitate to use any means necessary to reach its goals. If someone is desperate enough to challenge the current leadership, they won't stop at theft," Sophie said.

Current leadership. The lime in Pierre's Perrier had gone bitter and the ice had melted to nothing as he finished the drink and filed that comment away. Another careful phrase that danced around Connor's name like a waltz around a land mine.

"I'll include threat assessments, then," Marcella said. "I'm aware of the attempted breach at your house, Sophie. You must be thinking of your father, too, now that he's retired and no longer has a Secret Service detail." She made eye contact with each of them. "Pierre, I'm not sure we'll have a role for you once I have official jurisdiction, but we'll reconvene another time at least. Thank you both."

The FBI agent's window went dark, leaving Pierre and Sophie alone in the digital space.

"Well," Pierre said after a moment, setting his empty glass on the coaster—always a coaster, small civilities—"that was illuminating."

"Was it?" Sophie shook her head, and he could see her stress now that the official meeting was over. "I worry we'll be squeezed out of the investigation entirely. Just when I've confirmed the faction is targeting me because it's after Connor." She sighed. "I can say his name now, but I'm going to do my best to keep it out of Marcella's files. She's my friend, but she's ambitious. She might see this as a career-making case and bringing in someone like Connor would be . . ." she didn't finish. "Anyway, she's never liked him."

"Meanwhile, Marcus sees it as his wife stealing his investigation." Pierre absently scratched behind Lisette's ears, finding comfort in the simple pleasure of making another creature happy. "I hope their dynamic won't complicate things."

"I've dealt with complicated before." Her smile was rueful. "The FBI has resources we'll need. Marcella is competent. I trust her."

"But?" He could hear a reservation she hadn't voiced.

"But trust has limits when national security is involved." She looked directly at him, and he felt the weight of her gaze. "Pierre, I may need . . . help. If things go wrong."

"You have it," he said simply. "Always."

"Thank you, *mon ami*." Something had shifted in her expression —surprise, perhaps, or recognition. Of what, he couldn't guess— because he didn't want to wish for more.

After she ended the call, Pierre sat back, staring at the monitor. The apartment felt larger in the silence, empty in ways that had nothing to do with minimalist décor. Outside, someone was grilling on a hibachi, the smell of teriyaki mixing with charcoal—the perfume of urban Hawaii.

He'd done his best to suppress and deflect his feelings for Sophie, but hope had become a persistent weed, springing up through cracks in his resolve now that Connor's desertion was clear. Sophie's attachment to the man seemed to be fraying. The way she'd said his name—like touching a bruise to test if it still hurt.

"Plus ça change," he murmured to his cat, *"plus c'est la même chose."* The more things change, the more they stay the same.

He stood, carrying Lisette to her favorite perch by the window, and then returned to reach into the refrigerator for another Perrier. The bottle was cold against his palm, sweating in the humid air, as he freshened his glass and came to stand beside Lisette's carpeted sun spot.

The bright light outside reminded him of his wife. Gita had painted with her whole body, dancing in front of her canvases as if creating art was a celebration. She would have liked Sophie.

"Watch over Sophie, *ma chérie*," he whispered to the empty air, the words a prayer. "She has children who need her."

Pierre sat back down and opened a new browser window. He began online research into the background of the Yām Khûmkạn, and another file pulling together provenance on the artifacts.

Anything he could do to prepare for what was coming their way —and to fill the void of his loneliness.

10

SOPHIE

THE FEDERAL BUILDING'S lobby hit Sophie with its aggressive chill, the air-conditioning set to support computers rather than humans. She shifted a paper bag of sandwiches to her left hand, warm oil from her Italian sub already starting to seep through the white paper.

The security guard's nostrils flared at the scent of garlic, aged provolone, and the particular blend of oregano and red pepper flakes that made Marcella's parents' sandwiches legendary.

"Smells like someone's having a good lunch," the guard said, waving her through after checking her ID.

Sophie's heels created a rhythm on the hard tile floor, each click echoing until she got on the elevator. The doors closed; odors of cleaning solution and someone's cologne (probably the suited businessman who exited on the third floor) surrounded her.

The FBI offices on the seventh floor carried their own distinct atmosphere: gray walls and nothing but flags and seals decorating them. Marcella had once joked that the whole floor felt like justice and bureaucracy had a baby. The space was very familiar from her five years working there, though she'd spent most of her time in the basement where the tech heart of the agency resided.

She signed in and then was buzzed back to Marcella's small office. Once shared, Marcella's partner had returned to the Continent, leaving her solo on her cases. Three empty paper coffee cups decorated Marcella's desk, and her chignon, perfect this morning, was unraveling around her face and neck as she looked up with a smile for Sophie.

Outside, the sun beat down on downtown Honolulu, making heat mirages shimmer off the surrounding buildings' windows. But here in Marcella's arctic office, Sophie was grateful for the blazer she'd grabbed at the last minute.

"Thanks for coming to the Bureau," Marcella said, standing up behind her desk. "I wanted to get started strategizing with you the minute I got the go-ahead on the case from SAC Waxman. And . . ." Marcella's large brown eyes lit with an almost religious fervor as her gaze landed on the bag in Sophie's hand. "Tell me that's my mother's hot sub sandwich special and I'll name our next child after you."

"If Marcus ever sleeps with you again. He seemed upset this morning. That you took over the case and dropped him from it." Sophie walked over to set the bag on the small conference table by the window, careful to avoid files spread across its surface.

Marcella flapped a hand dismissively and locked her file drawer away with a definitive metal thunk and practiced efficiency. "He'll get over it. There's always a new one down at HPD and plenty to go around."

"Meanwhile, extra peppers, oil on the side, lettuce shredded not chopped. Your mama sends her love." Sophie took two sandwiches out of the bag, along with a stack of napkins. "She was delighted when I told her I was bringing you lunch. Then she lectured me for ten minutes about how we're both too skinny."

"She thinks everyone's too skinny. Feeding people is her love language. That and guilt."

Sophie unwrapped her own sandwich, the paper crackling, releasing a fresh scent wave of vinegar and herbs as Marcella joined her at the table after fetching a couple of bottled waters from a box in the corner of the room.

"So." Marcella bit into her hot sub with predatory satisfaction, a drop of oil escaping to glisten on her chin before she caught it with a napkin. "Let's talk about Connor."

Sophie's hands stilled as she picked up her sandwich. "What about him?"

"Come on, Soph." Marcella spoke in her investigator tone, friendly but inexorable. "The man compartmentalized his life like a digital vigilante, which he was. Multiple identities, hidden assets, connections to international terror groups . . . and you took him back. After he faked his death and broke your heart." She tore a huge bite off her sandwich as if it were a piece of the man himself.

"I did." Sophie took a deliberate bite, using the chewing time to formulate her response. The sandwich tasted like comfort and nostalgia—she'd been eating the Scatalinas' subs for years since they opened their cute little Waikiki restaurant. "He made it up to me for that, and he's always been good to me."

"Good in bed, you mean." Marcella winked.

Sophie rolled her eyes, smiling. "That too."

"What's he been up to? Late nights, unexplained absences, mysterious phone calls?"

"He's moved out. We're not together now. It's been six months." Sophie kept her tone level, focusing on the texture of the bread, the way the oil had soaked just far enough into the crust without making it soggy. "I haven't kept you updated because . . . it's been hard to talk about. At first I thought his departure was temporary. That he'd be back. But things kept coming up. He's working overseas. International business." She met Marcella's penetrating gaze. "Don't forget, he's the founder of Security Solutions, even though he signed the company over to me."

"That was just to avoid our investigations," Marcella rapped out, her eyes flashing.

"But we resolved those investigations. And as you know he has clearance from the CIA to be in this country."

"I know. But—" The office phone rang; Marcella got up and went to her desk. She hit the speaker button, her eyes never leaving Sophie's face. "This is Agent Scott."

"Agent Scott, there's a team from DEA here. They say you scheduled a two o'clock?"

"Tell them fifteen to twenty minutes." Marcella hung up without waiting for confirmation. "Sophie, I'm not trying to put you on the spot. But if we're going to raid that plane and its hangar that you tracked down, I need to know what we might find. And if your boyfriend is involved."

So Marcella had already scanned the files Sophie had sent over and found the only real lead they had, the private plane Sophie had discovered that the group might be using to travel back and forth to Thailand.

She set down her sandwich, her appetite evaporating. "I hope you will find the missing artifacts there in some kind of storage, but to be honest, I doubt it."

"What makes you say that?"

"Seems too easy." Sophie shrugged. "But a search of the plane and its hangar might tell you more about the thieves. If they're moving the artifacts on that plane, etcetera. We should do it."

"There's no 'we' here. I'm getting a warrant and gathering a team to search, but you won't be coming with us. Sorry." Marcella grabbed an electronic tablet, sat back down, and resumed eating. "You and Pierre are 'consultants' for us now, okay? You know the drill. We'll do our thing, and we'll ask you for information when we need it."

"I expected as much." Sophie had started her career as an investigator with the FBI; she was familiar with their protocols. "You don't need to remind me that I'm a civilian now."

"And you didn't answer the second part of my question. About your boyfriend being involved." Marcella narrowed her eyes.

"Connor's not my boyfriend, as I just finished telling you. And he's not involved." Sophie kept her voice steady and her gaze trained on Marcella's.

"But is he still involved with the Yām Khûmkạn?"

Sophie pushed aside the sandwich, abandoning any attempt to eat it.

If she didn't answer the question directly, it would erode Marcella's trust in her, and Marcella would find out who the organization's leader was, eventually, anyway. "Yes. But he is not involved with the thefts."

Marcella made a note on her tablet, the stylus clicking against the screen. "Is he your source? The one who told you the Yām Khûmkạn is involved in these thefts?"

"It's a splinter group. Not the main one that he's in charge of. And I cannot confirm or deny anything about my source."

"Oh, please." Marcella rolled her eyes.

Sophie's phone buzzed in her purse. She ignored it. Marcella's eyebrow arched.

The sound came again, insistent.

"You should get that," Marcella said, but her tone suggested they weren't done with this conversation.

Sophie took out her phone, seeing Armita's number. Her stomach tightened; her nanny never called unless something was wrong.

She stood and turned her back as she answered. "Armita?"

"Sophie, I'm sorry to bother you." In the background, Sean was crying—not the angry wails of a tantrum but frightened, hiccupping sobs that made her chest ache. "Sean had a bad nightmare at nap time. He woke up screaming for you, and nothing I do helps. He keeps saying 'Mama' and pointing at the window like something terrible is there."

Sophie's body had already made the decision before her mind caught up, her muscles responding to primal maternal programming that overrode everything else.

She pivoted to reach for her handbag. "Take him to my bedroom—sometimes the big bed helps. Close all the curtains and dim the lights. Sing him the rainbow song. I'll be home as soon as I can get there."

"I'm glad you're on your way. This is not normal for him."

"I know. You did right to call." Sophie slid her phone into her bag.

Marcella wore an expression that mixed understanding with a touch of regret. "Emergency at home? It's been a bit since I've had one of those calls. Jonah is in school now, and the baby's daycare is Marcus's sister or his mom. They handle her so well I feel like an appendage."

"We're both lucky. Armita's amazing, but Sean's having a rough time," Sophie said. "He's been unsettled lately."

"Kids pick up on stress." Marcella bundled up Sophie's barely touched food with efficient motions, the paper crackling, and handed the sub to her. "Even when we think we're hiding it."

The observation hit too close. Sophie shoved the wrapped sandwich into her bag. "I've got to go."

"Sophie, we're going to need to finish this conversation." Marcella cocked her head. "Even if it gets uncomfortable."

"There's nothing more to say. All I've got is in that file I sent you." Sophie had created a subfile with the tip about Sunan for the FBI, without Connor's name attached, of course. "Can you keep me posted on the plane situation?"

"Will do." Marcella stood and gave her a quick hug. "Thanks for the food. Now go take care of your baby."

SOPHIE HAD TEXTED Bill that she was incoming; the gate to her house opened automatically, ushering her into her personal oasis after a hectic, hurried drive home.

Sophie was glad that Momi was at her preschool because she

could hear Sean before she opened the front door: exhausted sobs seemed to vibrate through the walls of the house. She kicked off her shoes at the door, her bare feet silent as she hurried to follow the sounds of distress.

Armita was in the master bedroom as instructed, walking Sean around the bed that took up most of the room. His face was blotchy and red, snot mixing with tears, his fists clutching Armita's shirt. But the moment he saw Sophie, his whole body arched up as he reached for her.

"Mama!" The relief in that single word nearly broke her.

"I've got you." Sophie took Sean's warm, damp weight, and he immediately burrowed his hot face into the crook of her neck, as if trying to crawl inside her skin. His hair smelled of shampoo and sweet baby sweat. "Thank you, Armita. Why don't you take a break? Get some lunch. Have a rest."

Armita nodded, exhaustion clear in every line of her petite body. "I'll be in the kitchen if you need me."

Alone with her son, Sophie sank into the rocking chair she'd nursed him in as an infant. The familiar creak of wood, the way the afternoon light filtered through the filmy inner curtains Armita had drawn—it all combined to create a cocoon of safety. Sean's sobs settled to hiccups, his body relaxing incrementally as she rocked.

"Bad dream, baby?" she murmured into his hair.

He pulled back to look at her, his light brown eyes with their ring of gray—Jake's eyes, though she tried not to think about that—were serious and still frightened. "Bad man," he said, pointing to the window.

Sophie's blood chilled, but she kept her voice calm. "There's nobody there, sweetheart. It was just a dream. Mama's here now."

He studied her face, then settled against her again, thumb finding his mouth. Within minutes, his breathing had evened into sleep.

A man at the window. Just toddler nightmares, surely. The pediatrician had warned her about night terrors, about how vivid they could seem to small children.

But as she rocked her sleeping son, Sophie found herself studying the filmy closed curtains.

The faction knew where she lived. Knew about her children. Probably had a schematic of her house.

Could he have seen someone? Or one of her security detail, doing a perimeter check?

Her phone vibrated with a text. The world was trying to demand her attention, pulling her back to the shadow games Connor had sucked her into. But Sean's weight anchored her to this moment, to a priority that outweighed all others. She closed her eyes, savoring the warm spot where Sean's hot face rested on her shoulder.

She let his breathing regulate hers.

An afternoon shower blew in; raindrops pattered against the window, washing the world clean. In this chair, in this room, they were safe. For now, she was just a mother holding her child, guarding a baby from nightmares dreamed and real.

But just in case there was something she needed to know, she peeked at her phone. A text from Connor: *"My operative is arriving this evening."*

"Spawn of a flatulent toad," Sophie cursed, but softly—so as not to wake the baby.

11

PIERRE

PIERRE RAVEAUX CHECKED his reflection in his car's rearview mirror before getting out in front of Sophie's Mediterranean style house that evening. Dusk pressed against him like a damp cloth, carrying the scent of plumeria and distant rain.

His linen shirt was wrinkled, and he probably should have shaved—but Sophie's summons to dinner with the family (and to hear about Dr. Yoshimura's list of target antiquities) hadn't left him much time for grooming, once he'd torn himself away from his Yām Khûmkạn research deep dive.

He grabbed a bottle of wine from the passenger seat—a modest Côtes du Rhône, along with a bottle of Perrier for his own consumption.

"Pierre, perfect timing!" Sophie's voice brought him around. "Momi's been asking every five minutes when 'Uncle Perro' would arrive." She stood in the tiled entry, wearing running shorts and a Security Solutions tank top that highlighted the lean muscles of someone who treated fitness as a job requirement rather than hobby. Her short curls were pinned back, exposing her exquisite profile. The porch light caught the sheen of perspiration on her collarbones—she'd just finished a workout.

"Uncle Perro?" Pierre asked as he approached. The evening light brought out warm tones in her tawny skin. "Momi's still calling me that?"

"Better than some nicknames, believe it or not. Last week she called our insurance adjuster 'the boring paper man' to his face." Sophie accepted the wine with a quick smile. "*Merci*. Come in—and fair warning. Sean got up from his nap late and is—extra."

"Extra what?" Pierre cocked a brow.

Sophie shook her head. "It's been a day with him. You'll see."

Once inside, the house smelled like Thai basil, lemongrass, and bubbling rice. Overhead fans fought a losing battle against heat from the kitchen, where something sizzled in a wok. Through the doorway, Pierre spotted Armita attempting to contain a shirtless Sean who was careening around, covered in what might have been peanut sauce. His gleeful shrieks echoed off the tile floors. Momi sat at the table, humming tunelessly as she arranged plastic dinosaurs on her plate in what looked like a complex battle formation.

"Uncle Perro!" Momi abandoned her prehistoric army to hurl herself at him, small arms wrapping around his legs with surprising strength. "Where have you been?"

"I've missed you as well, Little Bean." Pierre's heart swelled painfully as he picked the little girl up, her weight familiar and precious. He gave her a kiss on each cheek in the European style, smelling the faint residue of fruit juice on her skin. He'd spent considerable time with the family prior to Connor's return to Sophie's side; after that, he'd been a fifth wheel and had taken work overseas whenever he could.

Momi, at least, was glad to see him again.

"You haven't come to see us in forever," Momi's large brown eyes were serious. "I thought you left. Like Uncle Connor."

Pierre glanced quickly at Sophie, catching her slight wince. "I would not do that, *ma chérie*," he said, making eye contact with the child. "But I do have to take trips now and again. I was in France, working." He put Momi down gently and took the chair beside hers, the woven seat creaking. "And now, I am glad to be back."

Dinner unfolded in controlled chaos. Sean was wrestled into his highchair, where he proceeded to conduct a percussion symphony with his spoon. Armita and Sophie brought an array of Thai dishes to the table. The complimentary aromas of coconut, soy sauce, and lemongrass made Pierre's stomach growl.

"I'm looking forward to discussing our findings after dinner," Sophie said, sipping the wine he'd brought. "Dr. Yoshimura's come up with the list of possible targets she promised. She's particularly worried about the security of the museum's pieces."

"As she should be." Pierre caught an escaping wad of noodles from Sean's plate before it could join the growing collection on the floor. He wiped his hands on a napkin. "The feather capes alone are priceless. Literally—they can't be valued in conventional terms."

"Because they're made from extinct bird feathers?" Momi piped up, handling her chopsticks dexterously for a five-year-old.

Pierre blinked. "How did you—"

"I like birds and I know how to find out things about them with Mama's phone," Momi said with the nonchalance of a child raised in the digital age. She speared a chunk of chicken with precision. "The 'ō'ō birds are all gone. That's sad."

After dinner—which ended with Sean requiring a head-to-toe washing down and Momi negotiating for dessert like a tiny lawyer, Armita herded the children toward bath time. The sounds of protest and splashing water drifted down the hallway.

"Goodnight, Uncle Perro!" Momi called. "Next time tell me what you and Mama are talking about!"

Sophie rolled her eyes, but her face held love and pride, too.

"She's too smart," Pierre said. "Is that girl only five?"

"I know. It's hard to stay one step ahead of her. Always has been," Sophie said. Her demeanor shifted like a switch being flipped; the indulgent mother vanished, replaced by the professional. "Let's go to my office. We need to review Yoshimura's list."

Her workspace was a study in contrasts, with technology and family life finding an uneasy coexistence. Multiple monitors cast blue light across her desk, showing feeds from around the property in crisp detail. Children's drawings—stick figures under rainbow skies—shared wall space with logistics flowcharts and a topographical map of Oahu marked with red pins. A BowFlex workout set, pull-up bar, and Peloton occupied one wall area. A gun safe with a biometric lock was positioned for easy access.

"Tea?" Sophie offered, heading to a sleek setup on a small wet bar. "Let's do something herbal since it's evening."

"Please." Pierre settled onto a section of the low gray leather built-in couch in one corner, the material cool against his skin. Through the window, security illumination created pools across the lawn. "You mentioned the curator's list of possible targets—and I'd like to share what I've learned about the Yām Khûmkạn's historical background. It's given me some ideas about why the faction might be interested in Hawaiian antiquities."

"Good. That's been a knowledge gap." Sophie filled a clear glass kettle from the tiny sink and placed it on its electrical base. She returned to sit kitty-corner to him on the sectional. Opening a file on the coffee table, she spread out photos like tarot cards. "I'll share my part first. Here's what Dr. Yoshimura has put extra security on." She tapped a finger on images that seemed to glow with their own power. "These pieces were chiefs' possessions. Feather capes, carved serving bowls, weapons. They're not just artifacts. To the Hawaiians, they embody spiritual power—*mana*—made physical."

The clear teakettle began to bubble, condensation fogging the glass. Its electronic chime seemed too modern for the spell cast by the relics' images.

Pierre studied the photos as she rose to tend to the tea: a feather cape that seemed to shimmer even in the photograph, a *lei niho palaoa* whose carved whale tooth hook was barbarically beautiful.

Sophie brought over a tray bearing two delicate glass cups and a small, enameled teapot, along with a jar of honey glowing liquid amber in the low light. She settled close enough to Pierre that he caught a whisper of vanilla and jasmine perfume mixing with the clean scent of her skin. The leather sectional creaked as she tucked one leg beneath her, catlike, and cradled her cup as if her hands were cold.

"Tell me more about the Yām Khûmkạn," she said, her voice carrying an edge of urgency. "I need to know all I can about the organization Connor's the leader of."

Pierre opened his leather satchel to remove his tablet. The screen bloomed to life, revealing a curated digital folder. "What I found explains why Hawaiian royal artifacts would appeal to the splinter group you described."

Sophie shifted closer for a better view. Her proximity was distracting as Pierre opened the file of his digital evidence: historical texts, organizational charts that looked like twisted family trees, photos of ancient Thai manuscripts.

"It took me hours to find anything substantial," he said. "But eventually I discovered a cache of documents on the Thai government website, buried in their historical archives. The Yām Khûmkạn began in the 14th century as an elite guard for the Thai royal family—think of them as a cross between Secret Service and a ninja CIA. Their recruitment process, protocols, and training methods are all highly guarded secrets."

"This much Connor told me." Sophie said. "The remote jungle compound where he lives is ancient. It's their main training facility."

"Yes. But here's what he might not have shared." Pierre used his fingertips to zoom in on a genealogical chart that resembled a spider's web. "They never stopped being loyal to the Thai royal line. For generations, they were the shadow protectors of the throne, specializing in assassination, espionage, and eliminating threats before they materialized. Over time, they transformed into something resembling a cult."

Sophie frowned. "I threw that word at Connor more than once because it seemed like one to me. Cult how, exactly?"

"They believe in a sacred power—*sakti*—that flows through royal bloodlines and their possessions like an invisible current." Pierre pulled up a document dense with references. "The organization is always led by a Master, someone who's supposedly achieved enlightenment through combat and ritual. Members train from childhood in martial arts, philosophy, and what we might call mysticism."

"You're describing warrior monks," Sophie's curls had escaped their pins, framing her face. "To think I knew Connor before he got mixed up with them. He ascended fast within their ranks."

"Yes. His position with them is highly unusual. And, not only are they something of a cult . . . they're also an organized crime syndicate." Pierre's fingers flew across the tablet, pulling up information he'd harvested from encrypted forums. "Data I found on the dark web shows that, though Thailand as a whole has moved away from poppy cultivation, the Yām Khûmkạn maintains hidden fields. Much of their financial power comes from heroin production and distribution networks that span the Pacific."

He pulled up another document—a grainy scan of a report from a French intelligence officer in 1960s Indochina. The paper looked water-damaged, the ink faded but still legible. "Here's what's most relevant to our current investigation. According to multiple sources, the organization teaches that power can be transferred between objects and people. Royal artifacts don't just represent authority—they contain it, store it like batteries. And there are rumors . . ." He hesitated.

Sophie raised her eyes to his. "Tell me."

"There are rumors of ritual cannibalism. Consuming the flesh of defeated enemies to capture their strength."

Sophie's expression remained carefully neutral, but she stood abruptly, still cradling her teacup with both hands. She paced, her bare feet silent on the dense carpet, her lithe form graceful.

He cleared his throat; it must be devastating to know that her lover was this shady organization's current Master. "I know it sounds insane, but multiple sources mention cannibalism. Always in the context of defeating a powerful opponent. The ritual supposedly transfers the vanquished enemy's power to the victor."

"Connor certainly never mentioned it." Sophie set her teacup on the tray with deliberate precision. "I'm having a hard time imagining him participating in something like that."

"Maybe the faction Connor represents has modernized, moved away from old practices. Could be why this more radical group is breaking away—they want a return to past traditions." Pierre attended to his tablet, spreading out more records with practiced gestures. "Here's something more. Look at the pattern. Every major Thai antiquities dealer has ties to certain families. Families that trace back to known Yām Khûmkạn lineages and connections. It's a kind of hidden network, a shadow economy."

Sophie returned to sit beside him. He could feel tension and warmth radiating from her. "They keep their antiquities close. In-house, if you will."

"Yes. It seems to be part of how they preserve their beliefs, and their obsession with royalty and sacred power." Pierre pulled Sophie's manila folder closer, tapping the photos of Hawaiian artifacts. "Now think about what Hawaiian *ali'i* pieces represent. *Mana* made physical. Power you can hold, wear, possess. This belief aligns with that of the Yām Khûmkạn."

"The feather capes," Sophie breathed. "Worn by kings. Made from birds that no longer exist."

"And *lei niho palaoa*—the hook pendants worn only by royalty. Also, war weapons that killed rivals and supposedly absorbed their *mana*. To the Yām Khûmkạn, these items wouldn't just be artifacts. They'd be considered spiritual batteries, charged with royal authority."

Sophie swore softly in Thai. He wished he understood what she was saying, but her tone conveyed enough.

Pierre continued. "If this is an old guard faction trying to over-throw Connor and seize control, they'll want every piece of trans-ferable power they can acquire. The Bishop Museum's collection would be like a spiritual arsenal to them."

Sophie leaned in, peering at the tablet; her bare arm brushed his sleeve. "Pierre, this research is incredible. How did you find all this?"

"I can't take all the credit; I had help. A colleague in Paris who specializes in Southeast Asian secret societies. He's been tracking Yām Khûmkạn references for years." He gestured at the spread of digital documents. "They've been hiding in plain sight, using global trade and their shadow network to move power—both literal and figurative—for generations."

Sophie leaned back against the couch. Pierre did too.

"This is not a group you want to have as an enemy," Sophie murmured.

"No. But you didn't choose any of this," Pierre said.

"I did choose Connor, though. And he brought the Yām Khûmkạn to my doorstep."

Pierre cleared his throat. "I've also put together a dossier of sorts on all the artifacts that were stolen. And additional ones that might be at risk."

He opened a new digital file. "I worked with Dr. Yoshimura today to gather provenance records, authentication documents, and even statements from cultural practitioners about each piece."

"That's great. Not sure what we will need that for, but I have a feeling it could be useful. *Merci,* Pierre. You were busy today."

The house had gone quiet around them except for the elec-tronic hum of Sophie's tech equipment and the distant rumble of the dishwasher running. Despite the darkness of what they'd discussed involving the case, the moment felt oddly peaceful as they sat in companionable silence.

Sophie spoke, her voice barely above a whisper. "I'd forgotten what it was like to have someone to really talk to."

Pierre's chest tightened. "Different perspectives can be valuable," he said lightly.

"More than valuable." She turned to face him fully, and something in her expression made his heart rate spike. "Pierre, knowing I can count on you . . ."

The moment stretched between them, fragile as a spiderweb, until a monitor across the room erupted in a series of electronic chimes.

Sophie was on her feet instantly.

She crossed to the screens. "Someone's at the gate." She pulled up the camera feed. "Bill's on it. He's . . . talking to someone. This must be Connor's operative arriving."

Pierre moved beside her to see the screen.

A sleek black car had pulled up to the gate kiosk. The driver was visible through the windshield—a simply-dressed Asian man with his hands visible on the steering wheel, his posture relaxed but alert.

"I recognize him," Sophie said sharply. She fumbled her phone from her pocket, her fingers finding the speed dial without looking. "Bill, let him in. It's Feirn, Connor's second in command."

"I recognize him too." Professional caution came through her phone's speaker in Bill's voice. "We're checking the vehicle first to make sure it's clear."

On the monitors, Sophie's security team materialized around the black car. They surrounded the vehicle with practiced efficiency, running bomb detection wands along its chassis, popping the trunk to verify its contents. A moment later the gate retracted and the car glided through like a shark entering a lagoon.

Sophie turned to Pierre. "Thank you for all this research. I need you to pass it on to Marcella and the FBI team immediately. But right now I have to deal with Feirn's arrival. Connor said he was sending someone to help, but I didn't expect it to be his closest lieutenant."

"It shows how much he values you," Pierre said carefully.

Sophie snorted and fired off what sounded like a particularly creative curse in Thai as she headed for the door, leaving it ajar for him to follow.

As Pierre began forwarding his research to the FBI team, he couldn't shake the feeling that something had shifted between them. The tiny spark of hope in his chest burned a little brighter.

12

SOPHIE

"TWENTY MINUTES TO WAILEA." The pilot's voice crackled through their headsets as the FBI helicopter banked over the Kaiwi Channel. Sophie pressed her face close to the window as the late afternoon sun painted Molokai's sea cliffs in shades of green, black, and rust. The turquoise waters below churned white where the currents collided. She could almost taste the sea in the recycled cabin air.

Her stomach did a flip—not from the turbulence, but from familiar pre-mission tension coiling in her gut. She and Feirn, her new bodyguard, had been summoned by the FBI to accompany Special Agent Marcella Scott to the scene of the latest antiquity theft. This time the mysterious burglars had hit a private collector on Maui.

"So much for Dr. Yoshimura's likely list of targets," Sophie muttered.

Belted in across from her was Feirn, and beside him, Marcella. Feirn sat ramrod straight in his black Security Solutions tactical outfit. Connor's choice to send Feirn still surprised Sophie. The Thai man was young, only in his twenties. Though strong and well-trained, there were more experienced and deadly ninjas Connor could have sent.

Her former lover had few he let into his inner circle, and Feirn was one of them. It must be as Pierre had said: Connor had sent the young man to Sophie because he trusted Feirn to protect her.

Meanwhile, *Pierre.*

She'd thought about kissing him last night. Almost had, in fact.

The way he fit in with her family was so comfortable; his interest in her children was genuine. Something about the intimacy of working together and the way his scent meshed with hers had been magnetic. Last night's slightly rumpled expensive linen and unfamiliar beard shadow had made him almost . . . irresistible.

She wasn't sure if she was relieved or disappointed the gate alarm had stolen the moment.

Marcella adjusted her FBI windbreaker and leaned forward, her brown eyes catching Sophie's. "The collector's name is Harrison Whitmore. He's old money from San Francisco and has been acquiring Hawaiian artifacts for forty years." Her voice was a little tinny in the comms; Sophie wondered how much Feirn was picking up. The young Thai had been diligently studying English since becoming Connor's right-hand man, but he wasn't fluent. "Whitmore's alarm system is state-of-the-art—or supposed to be."

"What kind of system?" Sophie asked, running through possibilities in her mind.

"Dynatech 9000 series. Motion sensor video, pressure plates, infrared grid. The works." Marcella said. "Didn't matter. They bypassed everything. In and out like ghosts."

"Was there a—plumeria left at the scene?"

"Not sure. Wasn't in the report."

Sophie gave a brief nod. "Interesting."

Feirn caught Sophie's eye and gave a slight inclination of his head, his expression unreadable behind sunglasses. She took it to mean that he was following what Marcella had said.

"The *mahiole*, the feather headdress—belonged to a lesser *ali'i* from Maui, circa 1780s," Marcella went on. "Red and yellow feathers, extremely rare. Museum-quality. Whitmore bought it at auction fifteen years ago. Weirdest thing is, he never displayed it. Kept his Hawaiiana collection very private. How did the thieves know about it?"

"Good question," Sophie said. "If we knew that, we might be close to catching them."

As the helicopter descended, Maui's massive silhouette filled the windows with Haleakala's volcanic slopes, golden in the fading light, the resort corridors of Kihei and Wailea spread along the shoreline like a blanket of bright pearls. Manicured golf courses and pristine beaches with luxurious homes tucked behind gates and tropical landscaping came into view as they neared their destination.

"There," Marcella looked up from a display on her tablet and pointed. "The white house with the blue tile roof is the Whitmore estate."

The mansion sprawled across what had to be two acres of beachfront property. As they approached, Sophie counted three structures—main house, guest house, and what looked like a private museum building, all connected by covered walkways. Coconut palms swayed in the trade winds, and an infinity pool seemed to pour directly onto the beach and into the Pacific.

Their aircraft lowered toward a landing pad near the main house. Maui PD cruisers were already on scene, their strobing lights painting red and blue streaks across the white coral parking area and walkways. The helicopter touched down, and the rotors' downdraft sent plumeria blossoms pinwheeling across the manicured lawn. Their scent hit Sophie as soon as she stepped out: flowers mixed with cut grass and a whiff of helicopter fuel.

As the three of them approached the house, a man who must be Harrison Whitmore met them on the lanai. He was an overly tanned, thin septuagenarian wearing a bright and cheerful Tommy Bahama shirt that clashed with an enraged scowl. His hands shook slightly as he gestured.

"Forty years of collecting," he bellowed. "Forty years, and they took the one piece I treasured most. That *mahiole* has real *mana*. It protected the *ali'i* in battle, and now these . . . these criminals have it."

"Mr. Whitmore, I'm Special Agent Marcella Scott. These are my investigative colleagues." Marcella spoke in a crisp, professional tone. "I need to see your security footage, the breach points, everything. The more we understand what happened and see any trace left behind, the faster we can track them."

"Let's get to it, then." Whitmore nodded curtly and led them through sliding glass doors into a living room the size of a football field that could have graced the pages of *Architectural Digest*. Koa wood furniture, museum-quality Hawaiian quilts on the walls. A view that stretched from offshore atoll Molokini to larger offshore island Kaho'olawe made Sophie's feet drag as she slowed to take it in.

"This way," Whitmore said, leading them down a hallway lined with Hawaiian artifacts—poi pounders, a feather cape in a climate-controlled case, ancient fishhooks made from human bone.

"Seems like you have everything here for a complete set of feather clothing," Marcella observed.

"I did," Whitmore said. "But without the *mahiole*, it's incomplete. That headdress belonged to my wife's ancestor. She was part Hawaiian, traced her lineage back to the *ali'i* of Lahaina. She died last year, and I promised . . ." his voice cracked . . . "I will donate all of this to the Bishop Museum in my estate."

"I'm sure that will honor her memory," Marcella said.

They reached a heavy door marked "Security Center." Inside, multiple screens showed feeds from around the property. One screen was frozen on a timestamp of 3:47 AM.

"There," Whitmore pointed. "That's when they entered."

Sophie leaned closer, studying the grainy footage as Marcella activated it. Two figures in black, moving with the fluid precision she recognized, approached the house from the beach and climbed the high wall surrounding the property.

Feirn gave a sharp intake of breath beside her. When she glanced at him, his face had gone pale beneath his tan. He spoke in Thai: "*Not our people. But trained by us. I can tell by the way they move.*"

Confirmation of the splinter group. "I'll translate for you later," Sophie told Marcella, with a glance at Whitmore.

Marcella nodded, understanding the confidentiality issue. "Can you enhance this section?" she asked, pointing to a moment where one of the figures turned slightly. "Maybe we can get more detail there."

As he zoomed in, Marcella's phone buzzed. She stepped away to answer, her brows drawing together.

"That was SAC Waxman," she said when she returned. "There's been another theft, this one on the Big Island. Another feather piece—a *lei hulu* from the Kamehameha dynasty." She paused, swallowed. "And this time, there's a casualty. The relic's owner tried to stop the thieves." She met Mr. Whitmore's widened gaze. "I'm glad you slept through the burglary last night."

The older man shook his head. "I recognize their cultural, monetary and historical value, but none of these things are worth dying for."

"Now we know the thieves will kill for them," Marcella said.

The room fell silent except for the hum of electronics and the distant sound of waves on the beach. Sophie felt the weight of what they were dealing with settling on her shoulders.

"We need to get ahead of them somehow," Marcella said to Sophie. "At this point finding where they're taking and storing the items might be our best bet, rather than trying to guess what they'll hit next. Show me the rest of the video."

As the action resumed, Feirn touched her arm lightly. His eyes were dark with concern as he whispered: "The Master needs to know. The group are escalating the stakes."

Sophie nodded. Connor would have to be told, but she didn't

want to be the one to do that. As if reading her mind, Feirn said, "I will call and update him."

"Yes," Sophie said, relieved.

He stepped outside, removing the satellite phone he'd arrived with from a belt holster.

The sun dipped below the horizon, and the skylight overhead automatically adjusted, bathing the room in artificial light that couldn't capture the magic of the Hawaiian sunset they had missed.

Done reviewing the recordings, Marcella saved the video to a drive and ejected it. "Let's go check the display case they breached," she told Whitmore. "I want to know how these guys got through a Dynatech 9000 security system."

Whitmore led them through the house to a set of French doors opening onto a lanai that faced the private museum building. The trade winds had picked up, rustling through the coconut palms with a sibilant whisper.

"They came through here," he said, pointing to the doors. "But look—no damage. Nothing forced."

Sophie knelt beside the lock mechanism, pulling out a penlight. The smooth brass keyless lock showed no scratches, no tool marks. She ran her fingers along the doorframe, feeling for any irregularities.

"Feirn," she called softly. He materialized beside her, crouching with fluid grace. She pointed to the lock, then spoke in Thai: *"What do you see? What would your comrades do to breach this?"*

Feirn's tilted dark eyes narrowed as he examined the mechanism. Then he stood abruptly, scanning the lanai floor. He moved to a potted bird of paradise plant near the door and carefully tilted it. Beneath was a small electronic device, no bigger than a matchbox.

"Signal interceptor," he said. *"Very expensive. Military-grade."*

"They cloned your door's key fob signal," Sophie told Whitmore as Marcella photographed the device *in situ*, then bagged it.

After they examined and photographed the locked case which

had been penetrated with a glass cutter, Marcella gestured. "We should get going. Waxman wants us on the Big Island case."

As they exited the mansion, Sophie moved to the edge of the lanai, studying tropical landscaping that bordered the walkway. Something caught her eye—a plumeria tree heavy with pink and white blossoms. At shoulder height, several flowers had been deliberately broken off, their stems twisted: they'd been tossed on the walkway.

Maybe this was the plumeria marker that had so far been missing from this theft.

"Feirn," she called.

The bodyguard's face went still when he saw the torn off plumeria. *"An old custom. Asking forgiveness from the spirits before taking something sacred. This is someone who was trained in the deepest traditions."*

"What are you talking about?" Marcella asked, joining them.

Sophie translated once she saw that Whitmore was out of earshot. "The Yām Khûmkạn believe certain objects carry spiritual weight. According to Feirn, before taking them, they perform ceremonies to avoid spiritual retribution. Breaking off and offering a plumeria—frangipani—is one way. These flowers represent offerings to the gods."

Feirn spoke rapidly, filling Sophie in more about the Yām Khûmkạn's traditions. Sophie summarized for Marcella. "They believe they know how to handle objects with *mana* without bringing a curse on themselves. This is deep cultural knowledge."

"So we're dealing with true believers," Marcella said. "Fanatics."

"It seems so," Sophie said.

She bent down and carefully collected one of the broken plumeria blossoms, sealing it in an evidence bag Marcella handed her. The flower's perfume was sweet and slightly citrusy up close.

"Mr. Whitmore," Marcella called. "I need a list of everyone who knew about your collection. Staff, guests, anyone who's been to the house in the last six months."

"Most of my serious pieces aren't public knowledge," Whitmore said, as they joined him. "I only show them to other collectors, scholars . . ."

"That's why it's important," Marcella said. "We're tracking similar lists from the other thefts. When we find someone who overlaps, we will find our inside source."

"Of course. I'll get it to your office as soon as possible."

The sunset was fading into indigo as they headed for the chopper. Sophie wished she had longer to spend on Maui—maybe even time to see her friend Lei—but they were on to their next crime scene.

This one, the site of a murder as well as the theft of a priceless *lei hulu*.

13

SOPHIE

THE HELICOPTER DESCENDED through darkness toward the Kohala Coast off the Big Island of Hawaii, fighting crosswinds that made Sophie's stomach lurch.

Below, the island's northwestern shore curved like a broken backbone, its scattered lights fragile definition against a vast black Pacific. The aircraft bucked suddenly—here, trade winds funneled between the towering volcanoes of Mauna Kea and Mauna Loa with vicious force, creating air pockets that dropped them ten feet without warning.

"Five minutes," the pilot announced, his voice tight with concentration.

Meanwhile, Marcella was in a heated exchange with local law enforcement; Sophie read her lips as she spoke through her headphones on a private channel. "Yes, I understand Detective Multon wants jurisdiction . . . No, this case is part of an ongoing federal investigation . . ." Her knuckles were white where she gripped her phone. "I'll explain it to him when we land."

Sophie caught Feirn's eye. He'd been silent since calling Connor, but his stillness had the quality of a cobra coiled before striking. In the cabin's dim lighting, his eyes gleamed with intelligence. The young ninja's hand rested casually on his thigh, inches from where a knife was concealed—and that was only one of the many weapons he carried.

A landing pad materialized below them; it was a parking lot, ringed by police vehicles whose flashing lights turned the world into a disorienting disco.

They touched down hard with the pilot fighting the wind until the last second. Sophie glimpsed the estate beyond: a sprawling single-story plantation house hugging a bluff above the sea, its silvery metal roof reflecting the red and blue lights.

They exited the aircraft into air so different from Maui's humidity it made Sophie's sinuses tighten. The Kohala Coast sat in Mauna Kea's rain shadow, creating a microclimate that smelled of dust and drought-tolerant *kiawe* trees. Warm wind carried traces of the incongruous sweetness of a nearby bank of plumeria trees.

A thick-necked plainclothes officer stalked toward them, his tight polo shirt sporting sweat rings under the arms despite the evening hour. "Special Agent Scott? I'm Detective Fred Multon, Kona PD." His pidgin-accented English carried anger. "I need fo' know why the FBI thinks this murder on my island is federal jurisdiction."

Marcella squared her shoulders, her FBI windbreaker snapping in the breeze. She pitched her voice to carry over the gusts. "Detective, this murder is connected to a series of thefts across multiple islands that may have international connections with a terrorist organization. That makes it federal. I'm not here to steal your case, but to support you. Work with me, or I call your chief and take it over. Your choice."

A muscle jumped in Multon's jaw. Behind him, three other Kona uniformed officers formed a loose semicircle, their crossed arms and spread legs telegraphing 'backup.'

Finally, Multon ducked his head in a gesture that indicated he had made up his mind. "The victim is Samuel Akamu," Multon finally said. "Aged sixty-three. Retired from Silicon Valley. Dude moved here ten years ago to 'reconnect with his roots.'". Sarcasm dripped from his tone. "Started buying up Hawaiian artifacts like he was shopping for groceries."

"Sign in and I'll take you up to the house." Marcella signed the crime scene log and fell in beside him; the backup boys remained at the crime-scene-taped perimeter as Sophie and Feirn signed as well, and then trotted to catch up.

"The Medical Examiner has been and gone. The body's already at the morgue," Multon said as they approached the front of the house.

"Now you tell me," Marcella said, scowling. "I wanted to see the victim *in situ*."

"The crime happened last night. Akamu's wife found him. We'd been working the scene all day before we heard the Feds were interfering," Multon snapped.

"You mean helping," Marcella said. "How was he killed?"

"Throat slashed. Looks like he surprised the thieves as they were looting the collection in his study." Multon glanced back to Sophie and Feirn. "These your people?"

"Consultants," Marcella said. "Specialists in the field." She didn't introduce them. Sophie was relieved. Explaining their roles to a cop like this wasn't going to go well.

Crime scene tape that had come loose and whipped in the wind seemed to usher them through massive koa doors. Inside, the house was all soaring ceilings and polished concrete. Every surface gleamed with the kind of perfection that required a big staff. Contemporary Hawaiian art hung on whitewashed walls; each piece lit by hidden LED probably cost more than most people's cars.

Sophie noticed a child's tricycle parked in an alcove. Showplace this might be, it was also a family's home.

"This way." Multon led them down a hallway that smelled faintly of lemon polish. The coppery tang of blood soon overshadowed that as they approached an interior door that gaped open like a mouth.

Sophie paused in the doorway as Marcella and the detective went inside, approaching a dark red pool that took up the center of the room. The smeared shape of a body marred it, showing Akamu's death position. A plumeria flower was smeared and stuck in the coagulated fluid.

"The victim must have completely bled out," Marcella said. "That's a lot of volume."

"Yup," Multon said. "M.E. said the cut went to the bone. Knife must have been hella sharp; there are a lot of ligaments and tendons to get through in a slash like that."

Sophie pointed to the plumeria, its creamy color stark against the purple-black of congealed blood. "Where was this flower originally?"

"On the body."

Feirn's sharp intake of breath was almost inaudible. He touched Sophie's arm and hissed in Thai. *The flower placement is wrong. Should be offering to spirits, not decoration for the dead.*

"What's your boy saying?" Multon had noticed the exchange, his eyes narrowing with suspicion.

Sophie chose her words carefully. "There were plumeria left behind at the other theft scenes." She gestured to the empty display cases around the room where interior lights illuminated black velvet backgrounds impressed with the items they'd held. "It's significant that it was touching the body."

"An apology?" Marcella said, crouching beside the blood pool and photographing it with her phone.

"Sending some kind of message," Sophie said. She skirted the area, studying the violated display cases. The precision of the glass cutting was surgical, perfect, as it had been elsewhere.

Feirn moved to the windows, examining locks with gloved fingers that barely seemed to touch the glass. He caught Sophie's eye and shook his head—no breach there.

"Detective, tell us about the security system," Sophie said.

"No video. Just a burglar alarm on the outside of the house. The wife said it was turned on once they went to bed. It was disabled from inside near the front door," Multon said. "Security company says someone used Akamu's personal code."

"Akamu let them in?" Marcella's head snapped up.

"Or they made him give up the code," Multon said. "But there were no signs of torture or other injury on the body, just the cause of death, which was obvious. The medical examiner is still working on the victim, but we guessed the time of death to be pretty close to when the alarm was deactivated." Multon indicated a small box with pushbuttons near the entry; a time flashed above the display. "This is a junction box connected to the main one. We think they came in through the front, turned off the alarm there, then came here."

Marcella approached the alarm box and frowned as she noted the time. "This is too near when the other place was hit to have been the same doers," Marcella told Sophie. "They must have two teams working."

"That explains how they were able to hit so many places on Oahu in the same time frame," Sophie agreed. She took her tablet out of her backpack to make a note in her case file and take some photos, then studied the room's geography.

Akamu's teak desk faced the door, positioned so he could survey his treasures while working. The leather chair behind it was askew, as if he'd risen quickly. She could picture it—the collector working late, maybe admiring his acquisitions, when death walked through his door.

"He might have seen his killer's face," she said. "Maybe that's why they killed him."

"The thieves in the other burglaries kept their faces covered," Marcella said. "Probably because they knew they'd be videoed."

"As I said, Akamu's security wasn't that fancy," Multon said. "No video."

"And they seem to know a lot about the security at every place they've been. So they might have known that," Sophie said.

"Tell me about the *lei hulu*," Marcella said. "That's the item that triggered a connection to our other thefts."

"As you can see from the cases, they cleaned out his collection. But that was his prize piece." Multon pulled out his phone, swiping to a photo that made Sophie's breath catch when she viewed it. The feather *lei* glowed like captured sunlight; thousands of golden 'ō'ō feathers woven into a collar that would have graced a king's shoulders.

"Kamehameha dynasty piece," Multon said. "Akamu bought it from a dealer in Kyoto three years back. Caused big *pilikia*—Native Hawaiian groups wanted it returned for proper museum display."

"Instead it ended up locked in this room," Sophie murmured. She thought of the artifact's journey—from *ali'i* warriors to Japanese dealers to a tech millionaire's private hoard—then stolen by fanatics.

"Detective," Marcella said, "I need every record connected to Akamu's collection. Receipts, authentication documents, correspondence—"

"Already bagged," Multon cut her off, pride evident. "We know how to work a scene."

"We're also looking for a common thread between this and the other burglaries. Someone in common who could be leaking information to the thieves. So we need to know, as much as possible, everyone who was familiar with the contents of the collection."

"For that, you'll have to talk to the wife," Multon said. "She was too hysterical to interview earlier."

"Does 'the wife' have a name?" Marcella's voice was clipped; she was offended at Multon's attitude. "And I spotted a trike on the way in. Do they have children?"

"Two grown kids off-island, one young grandkid who visits. Wife's name is Sandra Akamu. I'll punt you her contact info." Multon took a minute with his phone to forward something to

Marcella. "She told us he had a computerized catalog of his items on his laptop. Their provenance and whatnot." He gestured to the desk where the computer lay closed. "It's password-protected and the wife didn't have access to it."

"I'd like to have a look at that," Sophie said. "The password won't be a problem."

"Whatever. It's your case now," Multon said. "We dusted it for prints. None on it but the victim's."

Sophie approached the desk and took the computer, slipping it into her backpack.

A young crime scene tech appeared in the doorway, her face flushed with excitement. "Detective? Found something out back."

They followed her into the yard where drought-adapted native plants grew in decomposed granite. The tech's Maglite carved a cone of white through the darkness, illuminating disturbed earth near a garden shed. The wind had died to occasional gusts, but Sophie could hear the ocean crashing against lava rock in the distance.

"Footprints," the tech announced. "Two sets."

Sophie squatted beside the prints. The tread pattern made her pulse accelerate; these looked like they were made by similar tactical boots to those worn at Whitmore's scene. They had a distinctive heel depth, that of someone trained to move on the balls of their feet. "They surveilled from outside," she said. "Probably learned when he'd be alone."

"But why kill him?" Marcella's frustration bled through. "The other thefts were surgical. No violence."

"Maybe because Akamu knew every major collector in the Pacific," Multon said. "And likely, the world, with his tech background. He was part Hawaiian, too. I'm guessing that's different from your other collectors."

"True," Marcella said. "Maybe he let them in, but they killed him because he could have identified the link between all of the burglaries. We're still looking for who that is. Sophie, when you have time, I need Akamu's contact lists cross-referenced with our other victims' contact lists. Let's look for anyone with ties to Southeast Asia and Thailand."

"Is this guy from Thailand?" Multon's gaze swiveled to Feirn. "What's the angle?"

"We have intelligence suggesting the thieves may have connections to that region," Marcella said, her tone closing off further questions.

"I need to get to my office, or at least somewhere quiet and secure, to break into this laptop and do the work you're asking for," Sophie said. "Feirn will stay with me."

Marcella nodded, then addressed Multon. "Detective, I'd like to make a visit to the morgue and see the body. Then I'd like to speak to Mrs. Akamu about her husband. Can Ms. Smithson here use your department's computer lab to do her work?"

"It's getting late," Multon said. "The lab and the morgue will already be closed."

"Give me your captain's number. I'll call them myself and get things opened up," Marcella said. "Time is of the essence with this case."

The two continued to wrangle as they headed toward the helicopter. Shortly after, Marcella, Sophie and Feirn were aloft, leaving Multon staring after them resentfully, his arms crossed on his barrel chest.

"We'll get more done without him," Marcella said at last.

Sophie nodded, but her eyes were growing heavy. She would have to grab a catnap on the floor of the lab. She texted Armita that she might not be home tonight.

The helicopter banked south toward Kona and the closest police station, fighting crosswinds that made the fuselage groan and the aircraft bounce. Below them, the Big Island slumbered; its ancient valleys and hidden caves potentially harbored a cult assembling a spiritual arsenal.

14

SOPHIE

THE KONA POLICE DEPARTMENT'S computer lab was a windowless box of a room in the building's basement that smelled of burnt coffee and ozone from the machines. Sophie settled at a workstation in the corner, Akamu's laptop open before her. Feirn positioned himself by the door, his back to the wall, eyes tracking the occasional officer who passed in the hallway beyond.

"*Coffee?*" Sophie asked him in Thai, gesturing to a pot that looked like it had been brewing since morning.

Feirn's nose wrinkled as he answered in the same language. "*I'd rather drink water buffalo urine.*"

Sophie smiled grimly and turned her attention to the laptop. The login screen taunted her with its password field. She pulled out her portable drive containing her toolkit—a collection of scripts and programs that had served her well over the years.

First, she tried the obvious: variations of Akamu's name, birth date, anniversary. Nothing. Then she booted into recovery mode, accessing the command line. Her fingers flew across the keyboard, muscle memory from hundreds of similar intrusions.

Within ten minutes, she'd reset the admin password and logged in. The desktop wallpaper showed Akamu with what must be his family—a smiling woman, two grown children and a grand-daughter on a beach with Diamond Head visible in the background.

"Here we are," she murmured, then began copying the hard drive to her external storage. While that ran, she opened Akamu's email.

The inbox contained thousands of messages. Sophie sorted by sender, looking for patterns. Tech newsletters, collector forums, auction house notifications—the digital detritus of a wealthy collector's life.

Then a name made her pause.

Dr. Catherine Yoshimura.

Sophie's pulse quickened. She filtered for emails from the Bishop Museum curator. Dozens appeared, stretching back three years.

"Feirn," she called softly. "Come look at this."

The young warrior materialized beside her. He read over her shoulder as she opened the most recent exchange from two weeks ago:

Sam,

I understand your concerns about the lei hulu's provenance, but I assure you, the documentation from the Kyoto dealer is legitimate. As we discussed, items of this cultural significance deserve proper care. I'm always available if you need authentication or storage advice.

Best,

Catherine

Sophie scrolled to Akamu's response:

Catherine,

I appreciate your ongoing support. You know how much these pieces mean to me—not just as objects, but as connections to our heritage. BTW, I've been meaning to ask: do you know a good security consultant? After those thefts on Oahu, I'm getting paranoid.

Sam

Yoshimura's reply sent a ripple down Sophie's spine:

Sam,

I share your concerns. The Bishop Museum has upgraded our security recently. I can't recommend anyone specific, but I'd suggest someone with experience in art protection. The thieves seem quite sophisticated.

Stay safe,

Catherine

"She's asking leading questions," Feirn observed. "Probing his security without seeming to."

"Seems like," Sophie said, pointing to Akamu's reply: *I definitely need to do something. We only have a basic burglar alarm.*

Sophie opening another email thread from six months earlier. This one discussed authentication for a Fijian war club Akamu was considering:

Sam,

The club is magnificent! Definitely 18th century, possibly connected to Ratu Cakobau's warriors. If you acquire it, I'd love to document it for our database. As you know, I maintain records of all significant Pacific artifacts in private collections—for research purposes, of course.

Catherine

"For research purposes," Sophie murmured. "Hmm." She opened a new search, looking for mentions of the database.

What she found made her lean back in the uncomfortable chair.

Email after email showed Yoshimura systematically cataloging private collections across the Pacific. She was building relationships with every major collector, positioning herself as the helpful expert, a cultural guardian and coordinator who understood their passion.

"She must have a complete inventory built by now," Sophie said. "Every piece, every security system, every collector's schedule and habits."

"So educated and well-positioned." Feirn's expression darkened as he scowled. "The perfect inside source."

Sophie dug deeper, cross-referencing names. Harold Whitmore

appeared frequently, as did the other victims. But it was a thread from three months ago that made her pause:

Dear Collectors,

As discussed at our last gathering, I'm creating a comprehensive digital archive of ali'i-related artifacts. This is purely for academic purposes—to ensure these treasures are documented for future generations. Please send updated photos and provenance documents at your convenience.

Dr. Catherine Yoshimura

Head Curator, Pacific Collections

Bishop Museum

The recipient list read like a who's who of their case: Whitmore, Akamu, the collectors from Oahu, and a dozen others who might be future targets.

"She's been building this for years," Sophie said. "Gaining collectors' trust, collecting data."

"But is she communicating with the splinter group from the Yām Khûmkạn?" Feirn asked. "Or just being used?"

Sophie opened a new search, looking for connections to Southeast Asia: a conference attended in Bangkok five years ago. A visiting professorship at Chulalongkorn University. Published papers on the spiritual significance of warrior artifacts across cultures. "This is not enough," Sophie muttered.

Then she found it—a single email from an address that made Feirn jerk sharply beside her: ancientways_preservation@protonmail.com.

Dr. Yoshimura,

Your presentation on the metaphysical properties of ceremonial weapons was enlightening. We share your belief that these items are more than mere artifacts. They carry the mana of their makers, the power of their purpose. Perhaps we could discuss preservation strategies?

A fellow Seeker of the Ancient Ways

Yoshimura's response was cautious but interested:

Dear Seeker,

I'm always happy to discuss preservation of cultural heritage. However, I must emphasize that my position at the Bishop Museum requires strict ethical standards. Any strategies I share must be legal and appropriate.

Dr. Yoshimura

"She's covering herself," Sophie said. "Plausible deniability."

She pulled up the museum's staff directory, studying Yoshimura's bio and trying to remember their brief meeting. An attractive mixed-race woman in her forties, Yoshimura had the polished demeanor of someone comfortable in both academic and social circles. Her curriculum vitae mentioned a PhD from Harvard, numerous publications, and a black belt in karate.

"Martial arts background," Feirn noted. "That's not common for curators."

"Another reason she might be attracted to the Ancient Ways group." Sophie's phone buzzed with a message from Marcella: *At morgue. ME confirms throat cut with precision. Almost surgical. No other wounds on body or signs of struggle/defensive wounds. How's the laptop contact search going?*

Sophie typed back quickly: *Looks like we found our leak. Yoshimura from Bishop Museum has been cataloging private collections for years. All victims were in contact with her.*

The response was immediate: *WHOA. Can you find any connection to our rogue group?*

Working on it.

Sophie returned to the emails, now searching for travel patterns. Yoshimura had been occupied during each theft—conferences, research trips, family visits. Always a rock-solid alibi.

"Too perfect," she muttered. "She's establishing distance while feeding them information."

A new email thread caught her attention, dated just three days ago:

Colleagues,

Due to the recent tragic events, I feel compelled to offer the Bishop

Museum's resources to help secure your collections. We can provide temporary storage in our climate-controlled vaults until this crime wave passes. Several collectors have already taken advantage of this offer.

Please contact me directly if interested.

Dr. Yoshimura

"Brilliant," Sophie said. "Create the threat, then offer salvation. I bet the items in the museum's 'protection' are the next targets."

Feirn stroked his concealed knife. "Or she's gathering them in one place for Sunan."

Sophie began documenting everything, taking screenshots, and copying files. The computer lab's ancient printer wheezed to life, spitting out page after page of evidence for the case file.

"Look at this," she said, pulling up a spreadsheet hidden in a subfolder labeled "Tax Documents." It was Akamu's personal inventory, complete with purchase prices, authentication details, and—crucially—security notes.

One entry made her stomach clench:

Lei Hulu (Kamehameha dynasty) Acquired Kyoto 2019 - $2.8M - Displayed in study. Alarm combination: grandmother's birthday

"He gave her everything," Sophie said. "Trusted her completely."

"And she betrayed that trust," Feirn's voice carried an edge; in Thai culture, betrayal was among the worst sins.

Sophie continued digging through the files, building a comprehensive picture of Yoshimura's network. The curator had been methodical, patient, building relationships over years before the Ancient Ways group recruited her.

A sound in the hallway made Feirn tense and turn toward the door. Footsteps, multiple sets, moving with purpose, were coming their way.

"Sophie," Feirn hissed. "Company."

The door burst open. Detective Multon entered, flanked by two uniformed officers. His pugnacious jaw was clenched.

"Ms. Smithson, move away from the computer."

"What's going on?" Sophie kept her voice level, even as Feirn shifted into a defensive position beside her.

"Got a call from the Bishop Museum. The curator there, Dr. Yoshimura, reported a cyber intrusion. Someone is hacking into private correspondence connected to an ongoing federal investigation." Multon's hand rested on his service weapon. "Funny thing, the IP address traced right back to this room."

Sophie's mind raced; Yoshimura had been monitoring her own emails, had seen Sophie's breach.

"Detective, I'm working with Agent Scott, as you know. Everything I'm doing is part of the investigation and being admitted into evidence . . ."

"Agent Scott's at the morgue. And until I hear different from her, you're coming with me." He gestured to the uniforms. "Secure that computer. Everything gets bagged as evidence."

"Call Marcella," Sophie told Feirn in rapid Thai. *"Tell her Yoshimura knows we're onto her."*

"English only," Multon barked. "And your boy there keeps his hands where I can see them. Matter of fact, I haven't seen ID from either of you."

Feirn streaked out the door before he could be detained.

As the officers moved in, Sophie glimpsed her phone screen lighting up with messages she couldn't check as Multon pocketed her phone. The officers bagged the laptop and took her external drive even as Sophie protested about federal jurisdiction.

"Fine, I'm cooperating," Sophie said, letting apparent defeat color her voice. "But you're making a mistake, Detective."

As they cuffed her, "procedure," Multon insisted—Sophie thought ahead.

Yoshimura had made a critical error. She'd revealed herself, shown she was monitoring the investigation in real time. The curator thought she was protected, untouchable in her position; instead, she'd confirmed she was the key to everything.

"Where are we going?" Sophie asked as the officers led her toward the exit.

"Holding cell until we sort this out," Multon said. "Your equipment stays here as evidence."

"Son of an ignorant swineherd," Sophie swore.

"English only!" Multon barked, and Sophie rolled her eyes. Hopefully Feirn had made it out of the building and got Marcella on his satellite phone, or she was in for an uncomfortable night.

As they walked her down the stark hallway toward booking, she wondered how long Yoshimura had been playing this game. How had the Ancient Ways group gained leverage with her? Could she be a victim too?

But by calling in the breach, she'd exposed herself.

That mistake could cost Yoshimura everything—and as her wrists chafed in the cuffs, Sophie hoped it did.

15

SOPHIE

THE HOLDING cell's fluorescent light hummed, monotonous, as Sophie finished her morning sun salutation.

The concrete floor was cold against her bare feet, the bed had been hard and the smell, rank—but she'd endured worse in her past. Being the only occupant of the cell had been optimal; she'd spent some time meditating, detaching from her worries about children, relationships, and the case. This discipline had freed her enough to relax and get a surprisingly good night's sleep on the lumpy cot with its scratchy synthetic blanket.

Now, her morning yoga routine was there to keep her mind sharp and body limber. She was ready for the day.

As if on cue, the heavy door with its wire-embedded window clanged open. Detective Multon stood there, his jaw working like he was chewing glass. Behind him, Marcella's thunderous expression showed her Italian temper, while Feirn looked fresh and ready to demonstrate some of his more aggressive training.

Sophie smiled at the trio. "Good morning."

"Ms. Smithson," Multon grunted. "You're free to go."

"Thank you, Detective." Sophie slipped her shoes back on.

"I . . . apologize for the misunderstanding." Each word seemed physically painful for Multon to produce. "Agent Scott has clarified your role in the investigation."

"Misunderstanding?" Marcella snapped. "You arrested a federal consultant conducting authorized research. After I specifically told you she was working with us."

"She wasn't arrested. Just detained. And Dr. Yoshimura's complaint seemed credible—"

"Dr. Yoshimura is now a person of interest." Marcella cut him off. "We've been through all this. Step aside."

Multon's face darkened but he stood back and held the door ajar for Sophie to exit. "Again, apologies. Your belongings are at the desk."

"You should get your blood pressure checked, Detective. Stress can be hard on your heart." Sophie breezed past him and down the hall, leaving ongoing bickering behind.

At the holding desk she collected her phone, external drive, tablet backpack, and various pocket tools, checking each item for tampering. Feirn hovered protectively nearby while Marcella continued her controlled demolition of Multon's career, ending with, "And we'll need copies of everything from that computer. And I mean everything. If a single file is missing . . ."

"You'll have it all," Multon muttered.

They walked out in formation—Marcella leading, Sophie in the middle, Feirn bringing up the rear. No one spoke until they reached the parking lot where the FBI helicopter waited, rotors already warming up.

As they strapped into their seats, Marcella made eye contact with Sophie. "You okay? Multon didn't—"

"I'm fine," Sophie assured her. "Meditation and yoga helped me get a good night's sleep, calmer than home has been lately with Sean having nightmares. A cup of coffee would be great, though. That stuff in the computer lab was terrible—and a long time ago."

Marcella handed her a thermal mug. "You can have mine. You earned it." She scowled. "That station's captain had everything shut up tight and had gone home by the time Feirn got ahold of me with the news of Multon's antics. We had to wait until morning for the facility to open up. I'm sorry."

Sophie shrugged, taking a restorative sip of Marcella's strong coffee. "Like I said. I was alone in there, thankfully. Better night's sleep than I expected." The blades whined louder, and the pilot instructed them to don their headphones. Once the comms were on, Sophie checked her phone; many messages waited for her to sort through, but as she hit the first one, the screen blanked out; it hadn't been charged overnight. "So, what did I miss, Marcella?"

Marcella's elegant brows drew down and her mouth made a shape as if sucking a penny. "I sent HPD to pick up Yoshimura at her house in Manoa once I got your message. She was gone. Neighbors say they saw her loading suitcases into her car before leaving."

"Right after she reported the 'cyber intrusion,' I'm guessing," Sophie said. "She must have realized her cover was blown."

"It gets worse," Marcella said. "The collectors who moved their artifacts to the Bishop Museum for safekeeping were robbed. The museum's vault was emptied last night. Professional job—no alarms, no evidence. Everything just gone."

Sophie shook her head. "Yoshimura gathered them all in one place. Made the job easy—if she didn't clean them out herself."

"She's stolen twenty-three pieces total," Marcella said. "Combined value in the millions. The museum's board has been calling SAC Waxman; they're in chaos. They're claiming Dr. Yoshimura must have been kidnapped, forced to give up the access codes."

"Do you believe that?" Sophie asked.

"We have to get her in custody to find out more."

"Or, I can hack all her personals and see what's going on behind the curtain," Sophie smiled. "Show her the real meaning of cyber intrusion."

"There's a Be On Lookout posted for her, and I'm working on a federal warrant for her house, office, computer, etcetera as we speak." Marcella smiled back; it was more of a baring of teeth. "Let's get you back to our computer lab where you can really do some damage."

The helicopter banked, heading inland. Below them, the Big Island's varied landscape spread out—black lava fields giving way to deep valleys, merging into rainforest as they left the dry areas behind. Soon they were streaking across the Pacific toward Oahu.

Sophie was grateful the wind was calm this early in the morning; she pressed her forehead against the window and watched for the telltale spume of whales, but none ever showed this time.

THE HELICOPTER TOUCHED down at the FBI's rooftop on Oahu as the morning sun bathed Diamond Head fully in golden light.

Sophie headed straight downstairs for the FBI's computer lab, familiar territory from her years there, Feirn trailing behind. Marcella peeled off to her office to brief Special Agent in Charge Waxman.

Sophie's mind was already racing through the digital infiltration she'd need to execute. Upon entering the cool, sound baffled space with its dimly lit work bays, the familiar hum of servers and clicking of keyboards was a form of greeting.

She dropped into an ergonomic chair in an empty workstation and immediately dialed Armita. The line connected on the second ring.

"Armita, it's Sophie. Calling from the FBI office. My phone is dead."

"Sophie! Marcella reached me yesterday, said you were detained. Are you alright?"

"I'm fine, really. How were the children last night?"

"They're good. Sean had a rough night again, but he settled around three a.m. I gave him some warm milk with honey, and it did the trick."

Sophie's chest tightened with regret that she wasn't there, but relief too. Motherhood was full of ambivalence. "And Momi?"

"Drawing pictures of dolphins this morning before preschool. She wants to show them to you when you get home." Armita took a breath, blew it out. "Sophie, are you safe? This case is worrying me."

"It's worrying me, too. I'm being careful, and Feirn is at my side. I'll try to be home for dinner."

After ending the call, Sophie cracked her knuckles and got to work. The federal warrant for Yoshimura's digital assets had come through while she was in the air; it was time to show the curator what a real cyber intrusion looked like.

Feirn dropped to the floor. He sat cross-legged beside Sophie in her computer bay, his back against the wall, and appeared to go to sleep.

Meanwhile Sophie's fingers flew across the keyboard, exploiting a vulnerability in Yoshimura's home router that she'd identified during her initial reconnaissance. Within minutes, she was inside the home's network, tunneling to Yoshimura's personal computer.

The woman had decent security—for an academic. But Sophie had cut her teeth infiltrating Russian crime syndicates and Chinese state hackers. Getting into Yoshimura's cloud storage backup was child's play.

"Come to mama," she murmured as she accessed Yoshimura's encrypted backup drives on her desktop. This took longer, but Sophie's custom tools chewed steadily as she cloned the entire information cache.

The artifact database, when she got it open, was breathtaking in its scope. Hundreds of Native Hawaiian pieces had been catalogued with obsessive detail: provenance, current location, owner information, estimated value, and detailed security assessments of each owner's home or storage facility.

"This isn't just research," Sophie murmured aloud. "It's a shopping list."

She forwarded the entire database to Marcella via the FBI's cloud storage, then began cross-referencing the entries with the stolen items from the Bishop Museum.

Her phone buzzed with Marcella's text: *"Got it. Contacting all the owners on the database now to warn them. This is huge."* Then, a few minutes later, *"Come upstairs to Waxman's office at 3:00 p.m. for a briefing."*

Sophie continued digging, finding encrypted communications between Yoshimura and someone using the handle "Mainland Buyer." The messages discussed shipment schedules, payment structures, and—Sophie's blood chilled—"removing obstacles."

She archived everything, creating redundant backups on the FBI's secure server. This was evidence that could put Yoshimura, and any of the Ancient Ways members they could catch, away for a long time.

An hour later, Sophie's eyes burned from screen glare and her shoulders ached from tension. She stood, stretching until her spine popped, and spoke in Thai. "Feirn, I need to hit something before we go to this FBI meeting."

Her bodyguard looked up from his position on the floor. "What kind of something?"

"Let's go to the gym. Now. Before I start breaking office equipment."

Twenty minutes later, they pulled up to a converted warehouse that smelled of sweat, determination, and sterile cleaner. The familiar sound of gloves hitting bags echoed through the space.

Alika, her ex and Momi's father, looked up from wrapping a fighter's hands. He smiled when he saw Sophie. "Soph. Good to see you."

"Just need a little workout." She kept her tone upbeat, neutral. Their history was too complex for small talk, and co-parenting Momi had no place here. "Mind if we use the ring?"

"You never have to ask." He gestured to the equipment wall. "Gear's where it always is. Try not to hurt your new recruit."

Feirn bristled, but Sophie was already heading for the lockers; she pointed to the men's area for his benefit.

Once in the locker room, she changed into workout clothes she kept in her go bag, wrapping her hands with the methodical precision of muscle memory and slipping them into padded gloves.

When she emerged, Feirn had changed too, looking slightly uncomfortable in borrowed shorts and gloves. "You sure you want to fight me, Sophie? I've had extensive combat training with the Yām Khûmkạn..."

Sophie slipped through the ropes. "Let's just see how we go."

They put in mouth guards, bowed slightly, and began circling. Feirn moved with the kinetic grace of someone who had spent years training in martial arts. Sophie's heart rate went up. She was rusty, but she'd once been a Mixed Martial Arts women's champion.

"Just like riding a bike," she muttered, an American saying Marcella liked.

Feirn moved in with a choreographed series of kicks and jabs that telegraphed hesitancy; Sophie evaded all contact and countered with a hook that tapped his jaw.

The young man's eyes widened as Sophie backed away, bouncing on the balls of her feet. "Come on, Feirn. Give me what you've got," Sophie said around the rubber between her teeth.

He came at her harder, throwing combinations that would have dropped most opponents. But Sophie had learned MMA fighting under Alika's tutelage. Years ago, she had found an outlet in the ring for rage against her violent first husband.

She flowed around Feirn's attacks and landed pokes, jabs and kicks that could have been knockouts if she'd followed through.

Sophie worked out her frustration with each sweaty, whirlwind round: *last night in jail.*

Connor's abandonment.

Her son's nightmares.

Yoshimura's betrayal of Hawaiian culture.

She channeled all of it into the pure physicality of combat.

Finally, she caught Feirn's arm, pivoted, and executed a perfect hip throw. He hit the ground hard but clean, and she followed him down into an armbar position, stopping just short of hyperextension of his joint.

"I yield," he gasped against the rubber mat.

Sophie released him, sitting back on her heels. Sweat dripped down her spine, and her muscles sang with exertion.

She felt like herself again. Her *real* self, not just the roles of mother, investigator, and CEO that seemed to consume everything these days. "I don't get enough of this lately," she said, rising to her feet. "Maybe we can make this a regular thing."

Feirn accepted her hand up. "Where did you learn to fight like that?"

"Here." Sophie grabbed a water bottle from the cache on the side of the ring, catching Alika watching from across the gym. She pointed the bottle at her ex, once her coach. "From him. But enough playtime. We should go; time to get ready for that meeting with Waxman and Marcella." She punched Feirn lightly on the arm. "Had to see if you were good enough to be my bodyguard."

Feirn's brown eyes gleamed. "I hope I passed the test."

"You'll do." She smiled. They touched water bottles and drank. As they exited the ring, Alika approached. "Sophie. Momi told me you're helping with the stolen artifact case. Something about endangered birds and feather capes."

"Yes. But I'm sorry—I can't discuss an ongoing investigation."

"It's fine. I just wanted to say—these sacred items belong here in Hawaii, with the people. I hope you get them back." Alika rubbed the stump of his missing arm, gone just above the elbow. He'd lost that limb in one of her cases; a final wedge that drove them apart. "You look good. Fighting, I mean. Haven't lost a step."

"Nice to hear since it's been so long." Sophie shouldered her bag. "Talk soon."

Once they'd cleaned up and were outside, Feirn shook his head as they walked to the car. "That was . . . a surprise. Remind me never to do anything to make you angry."

Sophie smiled; the last of the tension drained away. "I have a history you know nothing about. Never underestimate an opponent."

The drive to FBI headquarters was quiet as Sophie's mind shifted back to the case. The physical release of sparring had cleared her head and sharpened her focus. She was ready for whatever came next.

16

CONNOR

THE ANCIENT STRONGHOLD of the Yām Khûmkạn clung to the earth, its weathered, lichen-covered walls blending seamlessly with the jungle that had tried to reclaim it for centuries. Connor stood on the highest balcony, watching mist rise from the canopy below. Humid air pressed against him like a living thing, heavy with the fecund scents of life—and decay. Insects droned their endless chorus while fruit bats shrieked, their leathery wings flitting through the velvet night.

The stone beneath Connor's bare feet still radiated the day's heat, but a cool mountain breeze raised goosebumps along his arms. He could taste a coming storm on that wind; metallic and electric, it promised violence. Lightning flickered in the distance, harshly illuminating the landscape for milliseconds before plunging it back into darkness.

It had only been a few years since he'd killed the previous Master, a man with purple eyes whose real name Connor never learned. A man he'd respected, but one who'd been under the poisonous influence of Sophie's mother, Pim Wat.

The memory of their final confrontation still haunted him; he'd been the Master's choice of successor, but he'd never wanted to be.

Hadn't imagined or aspired to be the Yām Khûmkạn's leader. In defending himself and killing his mentor, he'd become trapped here.

His attempt to escape to another life with Sophie and her children had only brought them trouble and danger.

Behind him, the stronghold seemed to squeak and groan, ancient timbers and stones adjusting to the barometric pressure changes of the oncoming storm as he gazed out into the falling, flickering darkness; a night filled with the sounds of jungle life—and death.

"You sent for me, Master?"

Connor turned. The Healer stood in the doorway, his stocky frame filling the space. His sandaled feet had made no sound on the worn stones. Despite his sixty-odd years and graying beard, the man moved with a warrior's grace. His hands, thick-fingered and strong from massaging tired muscles, hung loose at his sides.

Of all the elders, he had never shown resentment at Connor's accidental ascension, and he'd saved Connor's life more than once.

The old man's eyes caught the lamplight, reflecting it as Connor observed him—and his royal blue energy field. There was something unsettling in that gaze—a depth of knowledge that came from his decades of spiritual practice.

"Welcome, Healer," Connor said. "Thank you for coming."

The Healer joined him on the open terrace, bringing with him the scent of medicinal herbs and woodsmoke as his robes whispered over the stone floor. "You look troubled, Master."

"I am. I've asked you here because I trust you."

"I'm honored, Master." The Healer bowed slightly; the oil lamp's light gleamed over his shaved scalp.

"I need information from someone who won't talk about what I'm asking for. Can I count on you?"

"Of course."

"Sunan's group, the Brotherhood of Ancient Ways, is gathering ancient Hawaiian artifacts for some purpose." Connor tugged at the sash of his white *gi* in agitation. "They've stolen twenty-three pieces so far. What could they want with them?"

The Healer moved closer; the old man's weathered face was grave, and the deep lines on it seemed to grow darker. "You know what day approaches?"

Another flash. Thunder rumbled closer, vibrating through the stone beneath their feet. Connor's jaw tightened, a muscle jumping beneath skin stretched taut with tension. "The anniversary. Three years since I became Master."

"The day Sunan has chosen for his challenge of you." The older man moved to the parapet; his thick fingers curled around the balustrade and whitened as he gripped it. "They prepare for the Ceremony of Claiming."

The lamp flames on either side of the door guttered suddenly, as if responding to the name. Shadows leaped and danced on the wall, and for a moment Connor saw shapes in them—warriors in battle.

He gusted out a breath, mastering fear. "I do not know of this ritual."

"An ancient one. The Brotherhood believes that by gathering artifacts of power and focusing their combined will upon them, they can channel that energy." The Healer looked up at him, dark eyes serious. "They seek to give Sunan every advantage when he faces you in the courtyard."

Connor felt cold settle in his chest, spreading outward like ice crystals forming in his blood. "A week from now."

"Yes. The ceremony will reach its peak when Sunan issues his formal challenge. His followers will be performing the ceremony, releasing the artifacts' power to flow into him as the Brotherhood's focused intention strengthens his spirit." The Healer's voice dropped lower. "He means to kill you. Not just defeat you."

"I know. That is how it's done in the Yām Khûmkạn. I learned that the hard way." Connor narrowed his eyes. "The part you said about releasing the artifacts' power. How is that done?"

"The artifacts are burned on an altar as the participants focus their intentions by chanting."

A gecko called from somewhere in the rafters—a sharp, mocking sound that raised the hair on Connor's neck. "That would be a tragedy. We must stop the ceremony from going forward."

The Healer said nothing. The stronghold seemed to press in around them, centuries of tradition weighing like physical force.

Connor moved to the balustrade again. Lightning split the sky, revealing the jungle in a snapshot of silver and shadow.

Somewhere out there, Sophie was hunting the same enemies he was. A fragile thread between them, but a real one. "What can I do to prepare?"

"Clear your mind and heart," the Healer said. His voice carried the weight of absolute certainty. "Meditate on the tiger's-eye plinth before the men, where they can see you and surround you with power. Set your intentions solely on victory." He paused. "And surround yourself with trusted comrades—though I know they are fewer without young Feirn by your side."

"I had to send him. Sophie needs protection more than I."

The Healer made a noncommittal sound, stroking his beard. "Train diligently all week. Use the healing pools beneath the temple to restore your body each night. Most importantly . . ." He paused, as if choosing his words. The silence stretched taut between them. "You must commit completely to the Yām Khûmkạn. No divided heart. No dreams of another life."

Connor's hands gripped the stone balustrade hard. The rough surface bit into his palms, grounding him in the present even as his mind reached across oceans. "You're saying I need to let her go."

"I'm saying you cannot defeat Sunan with half your spirit elsewhere. He has spent years preparing for this moment, gathering followers, planning each detail. His commitment is absolute." The Healer laid a hand on Connor's shoulder. Heat radiated from the old man's body, coiled strength that age had not diminished. "What is *your* commitment?"

Connor closed his eyes and saw Sophie's face with painful clarity.

The way she'd looked at him that last morning before he left. Her hair tousled, gorgeous eyes sleepy, not knowing he was leaving to protect her from this world. Momi and Sean calling him 'Uncle Connor.' Their laughter and young voices, so light and bright, couldn't be more of a contrast to the measured discipline of these ancient halls.

Rain began to fall suddenly, fat drops splattering against the stone. The air temperature dropped, raising goosebumps along Connor's arms.

"The Brotherhood went after her," he said. "They're in Hawaii right now. If Sunan wins against me . . ."

"He will not stop with claiming the mastership," the Healer confirmed. His voice was matter-of-fact, which somehow made it worse. "The Brotherhood sees her as your weakness. They will eliminate her and her family to solidify Sunan's rule."

In order to save Sophie, he had to survive. To survive, he had to win. To win, he had to become what the Yām Khûmkạn needed— not a reluctant leader with one foot out the door, but the order's true Master.

A lightning flash—then thunder crashed directly overhead, the rumble rolling through the stronghold like the drums of war— followed by the roar of the rain.

Connor and the Healer stepped inside at last. Connor closed the door to the balcony, shutting out the storm.

"I understand what you're telling me," he said at last.

The Healer studied him for a long moment, then nodded. "Come."

He led Connor through the stronghold's maze of corridors. Their footsteps echoed off stone worn smooth by centuries of passage. They passed the Hall of Blades, where weapons from a thousand battles hung in silent testimony. Connor's reflection flickered across polished steel—distorted, multiplied, fragmented. Like his identity, torn between who he was and who he needed to become.

The Healer stopped before a wooden door Connor had never noticed, carved with symbols that seemed to shift in the lamplight. The old man pressed his palm against a worn indentation, and the door swung open on hinges that made no sound.

The chamber beyond was simple: polished stone floors, a counter with a basin and ceramic jug, a wooden chest beneath it. In the middle of the room, a single wooden chair. Ancient weapons lined the walls, and lamplight twinkled off their surfaces, a parody of coziness. The air smelled of lamp oil and soap.

"Sit," the Healer instructed.

Connor took the chair and its wood creaked beneath his weight. He watched as the older man gathered items from the wooden chest that looked old as the stronghold itself. A straight razor emerged first, its blade gleaming. Then soap and water in a bronze bowl that rang like a bell when the Healer set it down. Finally, a large white cloth in fine muslin that reminded Connor of a shroud.

"New recruits shave their heads when they commit to training," the Healer said. His voice had taken on a ceremonial cadence. "It shows dedication, removes vanity, marks them as students." His gaze met Connor's, and in them was compassion mixed with iron resolve. "You have been Master for three years, but never truly committed. Always holding part of yourself back for a life that cannot be."

Connor's hand went to his blond hair, styled like the cyber security consultant he'd been in another life. He still remembered the pride he'd felt when he graduated training and no longer had to shave his head.

He closed his eyes and a memory of Sophie beside him in bed, running her fingers through his hair, swamped him. The memory was so vivid he could smell her, cutting through the stone scent of this ancient place.

"You want me to do this to show I choose this path?" His voice sounded strange, hollow.

"To show yourself." The Healer said. "And to show the men. It will unite you with them."

Outside, the storm had reached its full fury. Rain hammered against the stronghold's walls like fists, but down here, it was far away, muffled, a mere vibration.

Sunan would stop at nothing. He was preparing his ceremony, focusing the Brotherhood's will on Connor's destruction. The warriors here who followed him despite his reluctance deserved a Master who was fully present.

The chair's arms were worn smooth by the grip of countless hands. How many had sat here before him, making this choice to choose this life above all others?

"Do it," he said.

The Healer moved behind him and wrapped him in the shroud cloth. Connor felt the man's presence, could smell the herbs on his clothes. The first touch of the blade was shockingly cold; then cutting began. The razor whispered across Connor's scalp with a sound like silk tearing. Hair fell past his eyes, gathering on the white cloth. Each stroke took with it another piece of a man who'd dreamed of a normal life.

The storm sounds faded. There was only the whisper of steel on skin, the Healer's measured breathing, Connor's own heartbeat loud in his ears as the Healer wet his head and smeared soap over his scalp. He drew the blade over Connor's head in long, slow sweeps, swishing the razor in the bowl with each pass.

The lamp's flame bent and swayed, casting moving shadows that made it seem as if the weapons on the walls were stirring, eager for use.

The Healer handed him a bronze hand mirror when it was done.

Without hair, Connor's features were sharper, more dangerous; his cheekbones were blades, his jaw iron, his sea blue eyes flashed.

The scar on his temple from the previous Master's blade stood out white against tanned skin, a permanent reminder of how he'd come to be here.

He looked like what he was—a warrior preparing for battle. A killer shedding his humanity.

Connor's newly bare scalp tingled. He felt exposed, vulnerable, yet somehow lighter. As if the weight of his old life had been cut away along with his hair.

"Now," the Healer said, wiping the last traces of soap from Connor's scalp with surprising gentleness, "we begin."

They left the shaving room. The Healer took a lamp and led Connor deeper into the stronghold, down stairs carved from living rock. The temperature rose. The walls wept moisture that glittered in the torchlight like tears.

The stairs ended at a rough stone wall with a familiar door. The Healer opened it and they stepped inside into a natural cavern, expanded by human hands over centuries. Steam rose from cracks in the floor. The Healer led him through a maze of passages, past pools that bubbled and hissed, their waters colored impossible shades by dissolved minerals.

The healing pools were a secret known only to Masters and their most trusted retainers and Elders. Fed by hot springs that bubbled up from the earth's core, they'd been used for centuries to restore warriors between battles. Their existence still felt like something out of legend to Connor, though he'd been restored by them numerous times.

The largest pool lay in a chamber whose ceiling disappeared into darkness. Steam rose from its surface like the breath of a sleeping dragon. The water was dark as old blood, its depths unknowable. Around the edges, minerals had built up over centuries into formations that looked like melted bones.

The Healer reached into a pouch at his waist and withdrew packets of herbs. The smell hit Connor immediately; sharp, medicinal, with undertones of renewal. The old man scattered them across the water's surface while murmuring Thai words of an old dialect. The herbs dissolved, turning the steam acrid.

"Each night after training, come here," he instructed. "The waters will heal your body faster than nature allows. By the time the day comes, you'll be at your peak."

Connor stripped, his clothes falling away like another layer of his old self. His body told its story—scars from training, from the night he'd killed his predecessor. Each mark was a reminder of how far he'd traveled from the man who lived alone in Honolulu with his dog, and hunted criminals through cyberspace.

He entered the pool slowly, sighing as heat enveloped him. The water was almost too hot to bear, sending needles of pain through his skin before numbness set in. He sat on a built-in bench, closing his eyes, the water level with his chin. Deeper sensations moved through him: muscles unknotting, toxins being drawn out, old injuries twinging briefly before quieting as his tissues rejuvenated.

The Healer's herbs added layers to the experience. Connor's eyes watered from the fumes, his sinuses reacting. But beneath the discomfort was something else—a sense of something transforming at the cellular level.

"I'll gather those loyal to you," the Healer said, settling above Connor on a stone bench worn smooth by generations. "If you win the men's hearts in the coming week, their numbers will swell."

"How many do you think Sunan has?" Connor's words came slowly as if passing through syrup.

"Fifty? Sixty? The Brotherhood recruited well among the ambitious and discontent. Those who've left our stronghold since you ascended." The stocky man shrugged, his shadow huge on the cavern wall. "The challenge itself will be single combat. The rest is just . . . atmosphere."

Connor sank deeper into the healing waters until they covered him to his ears. The heat was pleasant, now. "Tell me about the Ceremony of Claiming. Everything you know."

The Healer's eyes grew distant as he stared across the pool. His voice took on the cadence of oral tradition, of stories passed down through darkness and blood. "Long ago, before the Yām Khûmkạn found its purpose as protectors, some members sought power through objects. They believed certain artifacts could store the spirits of great warriors, that gathering them together could call those spirits back."

Steam swirled between them, taking shapes that might have been faces, might have been Connor's imagination.

"And can they?"

"Does it matter? If Sunan's followers believe it, their faith alone makes him dangerous. Add their focused meditation, their absolute conviction of victory . . ." He spread his thick hands. "Faith can move mountains. Or kill Masters."

Connor thought of the Hawaiian artifacts, each one sacred to its culture—a stolen heritage being twisted to serve violence. "Twenty-three pieces. Why that number?"

"Seven times three, plus two for binding. It's an old formula." The Healer stood, his joints creaking. "Tomorrow, you train with the men. You set an example for them, all day long. You train in earnest. Take all the time you want. I will meet you in the massage room with restorative oils."

The old man's footsteps faded up the stone stairs, leaving Connor alone with the dancing shadows. He floated in the mineral-rich darkness, letting the waters work their slow transformation. His shaved head felt strange against the water. Every nerve seemed exposed, hypersensitive.

He'd spent three years trying to be two people—the Master of the Yām Khûmkạn and Connor Standish, who loved Sophie Smithson and her children. Living in the spaces between identities, never fully committing to either of his roles.

Connor submerged completely, letting the healing waters claim him. The heat pressed in from all sides, a liquid furnace remaking him from the inside out. His lungs burned for air, but he held himself under, embracing the pain. When he finally surfaced, gasping, his decision was made.

For the next week, he would be nothing but the Master. No name, no past, no future beyond the challenge. He would train with absolute focus, prepare with total commitment. He would use every advantage, every trick, every hard-learned skill from his years as both cyber vigilante and accidental inheritor of ancient traditions.

And when Sunan came, surrounded by his fanatics and empowered by stolen artifacts, Connor would be ready.

Not because he wanted to be Master. Not because he believed in the Yām Khûmkạn's traditions.

But because somewhere in Hawaii, Sophie was fighting the same enemies, and the only way to keep her safe was to survive what was coming.

Connor rose from the pool, water streaming off his newly shorn head and down his body. He wrapped in the muslin towel. Cooler air hit him, raising every hair on his body as he ascended the stairs. When he reached the massage chamber, the full length mirror against the wall showed a changed man: any softness was replaced by sharp angles, hard planes.

Good. The reluctant Master with a divided heart that Sunan expected to face was dead.

Connor Standish was gone. In his place stood only the Master, preparing for war.

17

SOPHIE

THE FBI CONFERENCE room's recycled air tasted like the burnt-coffee smell that seemed to have chased them from the Kona PD computer lab. The fluorescent lights set Sophie's teeth on edge—or maybe that was just the residual adrenaline from her sparring session with Feirn. She drank another bottle of water down as she entered, rolling her shoulders, feeling the satisfying ache of well-used muscles beneath a fresh button-down shirt.

Special Agent in Charge Ben Waxman was already seated and commanded the head of the table. His silver hair caught the harsh overhead lighting, and penetrating blue eyes, so like Anderson Cooper's that agents joked about his resemblance to the newscaster behind his back—swept the room. The years had left a few lines around those eyes since he'd been Sophie's boss, but his presence still filled the space with a tension that made everyone attentive.

"Sophie." Waxman's voice carried warmth beneath the professional tone. "Good to have you back as a consultant." He gestured to an empty chair next to him.

"Thank you, Ben." The padded plastic creaked as she sat. Feirn stood against the wall, ostentatiously absenting himself from the group.

The conference table's polished surface reflected their faces as Marcella sat straight on Waxman's left, her manicured nails drumming a staccato rhythm beside her case file.

A new face had joined them—an Asian woman. She took the chair beside Marcella and across from Sophie. Her precisely applied red lipstick and razor-edged, angled bob sent a message of professional sharpness.

"This is Special Agent Janet Chen," Waxman told Sophie. "Our art crimes specialist, on loan from the San Francisco office."

Chen nodded to the group. "I've been briefed on the basics. Twenty-three Hawaiian artifacts have been stolen, Dr. Yoshimura is a person of interest and missing, and there might be a connection to terrorists through this Ancient Ways group." Her even voice carried a slight rasp, as if she'd been up all night reviewing files.

"That's just the surface," Marcella picked up her tablet, fingers flying across its shiny surface. The conference room's wall-size smart screen flickered to life, casting artificial illumination across their faces. "Sophie's digital investigation has uncovered more. Sophie, care to bring us up to date?"

"I will, of course." Sophie stood. She picked up a presenter's remote. The small controller was cool in her palm, a lodestone. She activated her case file and paired it with the smart screen on one wall. "But first, I have a question. What happened with the raid on the private plane I identified as a possible transport?"

"A dead end. We raided the plane's hangar. Empty," Marcella said. "Just a charter with a clean interior and a shell company renting it."

"It was a long shot, but that's disappointing." Sophie opened the first of a series of spreadsheets on the wall display. "Dr. Yoshimura lured collectors into participating in a comprehensive database of Hawaiian artifacts. In it are thousands of items, not just those in the Bishop collection. As a part of the database, she documented provenance, item details, photographs, information on the owners' security systems and their contact data, and even noting which owners travel frequently." Each click of the remote punctuated her words as she clicked through the pages of the database, revealing a treasure trove of relics and information.

"A Hawaiiana catalog," Waxman said, his jaw tightening. "For the thieves to choose from."

"Exactly. Yoshimura had encrypted communications with someone called 'Mainland Buyer.' I believe that's the handle the Ancient Ways faction has been using. They discussed shipping schedules and—" Sophie paused, the words bitter on her tongue as she brought up a specific message, "—'removing obstacles.' Given the recent murder, we can guess what that means."

Chen leaned forward, her chair's wheels squeaking against the plastic floor mat. "These artifacts—feather capes, carved wood items, weapons made of organic materials—are extremely delicate. The feathers alone can disintegrate if the humidity's wrong. They need climate control, specific humidity levels, UV protection."

"That's what we've been thinking," Marcella said. "The thieves can't be storing these in some random warehouse. They need a proper facility in which to store the collection."

Waxman's fingers steepled, the light catching his gleaming, neatly barbered hair. "So where? Hawaii's not that big, but there are plenty of possibilities. Private estates, commercial buildings . . ."

"I have another idea. I cross-referenced Yoshimura's database with collectors' property records, searching for likely storage." Sophie pulled up a new screen, the data cascading and then stabilizing. "Several of the collectors have extensive personal storage facilities. But here's one that caught my attention—" She highlighted an entry, the name pulsing red. "William Thornfield. Owns a climate-controlled vault on his Wailea, Maui estate. State-of-the-art security system."

"What made you focus on him?" Waxman said.

"He spends six months a year in Switzerland. According to his social media—yes, this seventy-year-old billionaire has Instagram

—he left for Zurich two weeks ago," Sophie said. "Perfect timing for the thieves."

"An empty estate with a nice storage facility," Chen said. "But wouldn't the security go off with as much traffic as these burglars are creating?"

"Yoshimura had his codes," Sophie said. "Every alarm, every camera angle. It's all in her files."

Marcella's tablet screen reflected in reading glasses as she slid them on to focus on what she was studying. Her fingers danced across the sleek surface. "I'm checking flight manifests for the past forty-eight hours. If Yoshimura fled with the artifacts . . ." Her frown deepened, creating a crease between elegant brows. "No Catherine Yoshimura on any flights out of Hawaii."

"She could be using an alias," Chen said. "Or she could still be on-island, waiting for things to cool down."

Waxman pushed back from the table, his chair rolling smoothly. He paced to the window, his reflection ghostlike against the reflective bulletproof glass. Outside, Honolulu sprawled below, bright and oblivious. "We need to check every storage facility belonging to these collectors. They might not be aware of the thieves' incursion, or they might be a part of it. Start with the ones who are off-island."

"I can generate a prioritized list," Sophie said, already mentally crafting a way to sort through the data. "Based on facility specifications, owner absence. Other factors."

"Do it." Waxman turned back, his movement sharp enough to make Feirn tense. "Agent Scott, coordinate with HPD for the searches. We'll need warrants."

"Already drafting them," Marcella said without looking up, her fingers never stopping their rapid-fire typing.

"What about the 'Mainland Buyer contact?'" Chen asked, leaning back in her chair. "Any leads on their identity?"

Sophie shook her head in frustration. "The communications were routed through multiple VPNs, TOR nodes, etcetera."

"We need to find Yoshimura." Waxman's palm slapped the table, making everyone jump. "She's our most concrete lead. Every hour these artifacts are missing increases the chance they'll be shipped overseas and disappear forever." He glanced up at Sophie. "I want to check Thornfield's estate, since that's low-hanging fruit. Sophie, can you access his security system remotely?"

"I can try," Sophie said, her mind already racing through infiltration protocols. "I need to get back to the lab to work on it."

"And let's cast a wider net, too, in case the group's gone outside of Yoshimura's database. Agent Chen, compile a list of climate-controlled storage facilities in Hawaii, both commercial and private. Someone might have rented space recently. Sophie, help her with that if you have time."

"On it." Chen's voice was all business, and Sophie met the other woman's gaze with a nod of assent.

Waxman's phone buzzed against the table, the vibration seeming unnaturally loud. He sat, read the screen, and scowled. "The Bishop Museum board wants a press conference. They want to offer a reward for information."

"That'll cause chaos," Marcella's knuckles shone as she gripped her tablet. "Every conspiracy theorist and activist will come out of the woodwork and pile on pressure."

"I'll handle the museum board," Waxman said. "Buy us another 24 hours at least. But people," his gaze swept the room like a searchlight, lingering on each face, "we need results. These aren't just artifacts—they're Hawaiian cultural heritage that a man has died for already." He typed rapidly on his laptop and stood, dismissing them. "All right, team. Let's move. Check in every two hours."

18

SOPHIE

BACK IN THE COMPUTER LAB, the familiar hum of machines wrapped around Sophie like a cocoon as she sat down in her borrowed workstation. Her belly rumbled with a reminder that she needed food, and she frowned, remembering she'd promised Armita to be home for dinner. She couldn't take long on this if she was going to make it home on time; helping the new agent would have to wait.

She cracked her knuckles and dove into researching Thornfield's security system. Feirn dropped to the floor and did push-ups near the door.

The billionaire's digital setup was impressive—and it should be, because it was designed by Security Solutions, her own company. Sophie smiled at the sight of the familiar login screen.

"Well, this isn't even fun," she murmured. "But I can be efficient, at least." She used a universal admin code to open a back door, and moments later, "I'm in," she announced, triumph sharp in her voice as multiple camera feeds bloomed across her monitors. "Main house, guest house, pool house, and—hello."

"What?" Feirn came to her shoulder.

"The storage building. Temperature logs show it's been accessed three times in the past twenty-four hours." She enhanced one of the images, pixels sharpening into clarity. "And look at the power usage. It's spiked. Like someone's running additional climate control."

She contacted Waxman and Marcella quickly with the confirmation. A moment later, her screen lit up with Marcella's response to her urgent text: *Surveillance team en route. Good work.*

Maybe she had time to help Agent Chen with her storage facility searches after all, but the truth was, she was hungry and tired. She'd been away from home too long. "Not to mention, spending a night in jail," she muttered.

Sophie leaned back, the chair's springs groaning. They were close to these perps—she could feel it. But something scratched at her, fingernails on glass.

This felt too easy. Would they really use such an obvious location? She rubbed her eyes with the heels of her hands.

"What's wrong?" Feirn asked.

"I don't know. Maybe nothing." She pulled up Yoshimura's database again, the entries scrolling past. "Or maybe we're seeing what they want us to see."

The computer lab's ventilation system kicked on with a wheeze, stirring papers on a nearby desk. Sophie shivered as cold air hit her. She texted Chen, telling the agent she had to go home; maybe after the children were in bed she could help with the search for other storage facilities.

The woman texted back that she had it in hand and would reach out if she needed any further help.

"Okay, Feirn. We're out of here," she said in English.

The young man cocked his head and replied in Thai. "What is going out of where?"

She chuckled, remembering all the years American idioms had been a puzzle. "We're done for the day and going home."

"That I can say yes to," he replied with dignity.

Evening sun painted Honolulu's glass towers in shades of amber and gold as Sophie got into her SUV. Feirn folded himself into the passenger seat beside her with the fluid grace of someone used to cramped spaces, his eyes scanning the shadows between parked vehicles.

"Seat belt," Sophie reminded him in Thai, hearing a maternal note in her voice. The click of the buckle was reassuring in its normalcy as she navigated her SUV through the FBI building's parking garage. The concrete walls amplified every sound—the squeal of tires on the smooth surface, the echo of a distant car alarm.

They emerged into the beginning of Honolulu's heavy commute traffic, a river of red taillights stretching toward the Pali Highway. Sophie merged, the familiar route to Kailua unfolding before them.

"This traffic," Feirn said, his tone carrying a note of wonder. "Bangkok is worse, but here the cars actually stay in their lanes."

Sophie smiled. "Give it time. You haven't seen what happens when there's a surf competition on the North Shore."

They crawled past the gleaming shops of Ward Village, where tourists clutched shopping bags and locals hurried home from work. The mountains rose to their right, their peaks shrouded in clouds that promised evening rain. Sophie's stomach growled again, loud enough that Feirn raised an eyebrow.

"When did you last eat?" he asked.

"There hasn't been time today." She changed lanes to avoid a city bus belching exhaust. "I texted Armita we're on our way. She's making her famous pad krapow tonight. You'll like it. She does it spicy for us adults."

Feirn's expression softened. "I look forward to eating food from home."

They entered the Pali Highway, the road beginning its winding climb through the Ko'olau Mountains. The temperature dropped a few degrees as they gained elevation, and Sophie cracked her window to let in the rain-scented air. Bamboo and wild ginger crowded the roadside, their leaves rustling with the wind, flowers a bright contrast.

"This reminds me of the mountains outside Chiang Mai," Feirn said, his face turned toward the jungle-covered slopes. "But the trees are different. Everything here is so . . ." he searched for the word, ". . . soft. Even the mountains seem gentle."

"Don't let them fool you. The trails around here have claimed plenty of hikers who underestimated them." Sophie downshifted as they approached the first of the highway's notorious curves. "Connor and I used to—"

Her phone rang through the car's Bluetooth system, the display showing Connor's name as if she'd conjured up the man once known as the Ghost. Her heart did a familiar skip-and-ache.

"Speak of the devil," she muttered in English, then answered in Thai. "Connor. You're on speaker with me and Feirn."

"Good." Connor's familiar baritone filled the car. She heard strain beneath his calm. "I have new information."

Sophie's hands tightened on the steering wheel as they entered the first tunnel, the sudden darkness making her headlights flare to life. The tunnel's orange sodium lights turned everything sepia toned as an old photograph.

"Sunan will challenge me in seven days," Connor said, his words echoing slightly. "On the anniversary of my ascension as Master."

They burst from the tunnel into filtered green light, the road now cutting through dense rainforest. Sophie had to force herself to focus on driving. "Seven days? Connor, that's soon."

"I know. Not much time to prepare. Meanwhile I've found out what they want the Hawaiian artifacts for—they're for something called the Ceremony of Claiming."

"Ceremony of Claiming?" Feirn said. "I've never heard of such a thing."

"Neither had I," Connor said. "The Healer says it's one of the old ways that were discontinued under the last three Masters. The worst part is that the artifacts will be burned to release their *mana*

—their spiritual power—during Sunan's challenge. It's supposed to make the one who orchestrated the ceremony stronger."

Sophie swerved to avoid a tourist vehicle that had stopped to photograph the view and hadn't pulled far enough out of the road. Her horn blast scattered a flock of mynah birds. "Burned? We can't let that happen! Those artifacts are priceless. They're irreplaceable pieces of Hawaiian history!"

"I know what they are." Connor's voice carried an edge. "That's why the Brotherhood of Ancient Ways chose them. They want every advantage. At least, that's what they believe the relics will give them."

"Is that the group's official name? Brotherhood of Ancient Ways?" Sophie flexed her hands on the wheel.

"Yes. So I've heard from a reliable source."

They passed the Pali Lookout where King Kamehameha had once driven his enemies over the cliffs. Sophie spotted the ocean in the distance, Kailua Bay a perfect crescent of turquoise against the green shore. The Technicolor beauty of it mocked the darkness of their conversation.

"Where would they perform this ceremony?" she asked. "Here in Hawaii?"

"As close to our fortress here in Thailand as they can get, to amplify the effect of the ceremony. The Healer thinks they'll try to create a sacred space near us. I have contacts in the Yām Khûmkạn watching for any Brotherhood movement in our area," Connor said, referring to his network of informants in Thailand's martial arts underworld. "But nothing so far. Sophie, those artifacts can't leave your country. If they make it to Thailand—"

"They'll be destroyed." She finished his thought, anger tightening her chest. "Priceless antiquities of Hawaiian culture burned for some twisted fanatic's magic ritual. What a waste."

Feirn shifted in his seat. "There is power in belief," he said.

"Yes, and it's called the placebo effect," Sophie snapped. "Perhaps that's why Dr. Yoshimura hasn't left the island yet. She is safe-guarding the items for transport."

"That's what I'm thinking," Connor agreed. "The Brotherhood would want everything in place before moving the pieces."

"But since they're planning to burn them, they might not care about their storage and preservation like we assumed they did," Sophie said. "I have to get back to the FBI with this."

They descended toward Kailua, the town spreading before them like a postcard with red-tiled roofs among swaying palms, the ocean beyond shifting from turquoise to deep blue as clouds raced across the sun. Sophie took the Kailua Road exit, muscle memory guiding her through the familiar turns. "I tracked unusual activity at a collector's storage facility. William Thornfield's estate in Wailea, Maui. The FBI is checking it now."

"Good. But Sophie. . ." Connor's voice dropped. "The Brotherhood has been planning this for years. They'll have contingencies. Don't assume anything."

"I know." She turned onto her street, the familiar sight of her neighbor's rainbow shower tree making her throat tighten. "We're almost home. I need to see my children."

"But I will not see them again," Connor said, his voice flat and unemotional.

"Don't say that." She pulled into the driveway. The facial recognition software on the plinth by the gate read her face, and the heavy metal portal rolled slowly open. "You'll win against this challenger. You always do."

"Even so. My life is here now. My death, too. Goodbye, Sophie." The call ended with a soft click.

Sophie frowned. What did he mean by that? Apparently she wasn't the only one who'd made a permanent choice about their relationship.

She pulled through the turnaround past the guesthouse where the security team operated, and parked in front of her home's entrance.

"Seven days," Feirn said quietly. "That's not much time."

"No." Sophie grabbed her backpack, exhaustion and hunger hitting her gut like a physical punch. "It's not."

They entered the house to a chaos of children, dogs, and cooking smells. Sean launched himself at her knees while Momi chattered about her day at school, something about a gecko in the classroom and how she'd been the only one brave enough to catch it.

Normal life flowed around Sophie like water around a stone. But as Sophie hugged her children, breathing in their scent, tousling heads, she couldn't stop thinking about those missing artifacts.

Fanatics were preparing to destroy pieces of Hawaiian history for imagined power.

They had a week to stop them. Less, if you considered that the Brotherhood would want to be set up in Thailand for their ceremony before the anniversary that marked Sunan's challenge to Connor.

She kissed Momi's forehead and made herself smile. "Who wants to help Mama set the table?"

It was time to be a mother. Anything else could wait until after bedtime.

19

SOPHIE

Sophie jolted awake to the buzzing of her phone on the nightstand. The digital clock glowed, showing 5:47 AM. Outside, the first birds were just beginning their dawn chorus, and pale light made a line beneath the heavy blackout bedroom curtains.

She grabbed the phone before it could wake Feirn in the guest room beside hers; the young man's circadian rhythm was still adjusting to Hawaii time. "Sophie Smithson," she answered, her voice rough with sleep.

"It's Marcella." The FBI agent's tone was terse. "We hit Thornfield's storage facility. It was empty, but . . ."

"But what?" Sophie sat up, instantly alert. The sheets pooled around her waist as she swung her legs over the side of the bed. "Empty as in cleaned out, or empty as in never used?"

"Oh, it was used alright. We found packing material left behind. Specialty foam for delicate objects, climate-control gel packs, bubble wrap, etcetera. But whatever was there is gone now." Marcella's frustration crackled through the connection. "Security footage at the estate shows a commercial moving truck leaving yesterday afternoon, about two hours before you flagged the location."

"Foul breath of an inbred goat." Sophie padded to her bathroom, closing the door softly. She splashed cold water on her face with one hand, holding the phone with the other. "We were so close."

"Gets worse. The truck had fake plates. We lost it on traffic cams heading toward Kahului."

Sophie's stomach tightened. "Marcella, I have new intel from my source. The artifacts are intended for a ceremony in Thailand. The splinter group is planning to burn them."

"Burn them?" Marcella's voice rose. "Those artifacts are priceless!"

"I know. My source says it's some kind of power ritual tied to a challenge to leadership in the Yām Khûmkạn, which is happening in six days. They will be trying to take the stolen items to Thailand for the ceremony. We need to check every flight—commercial and private. They are on a clock."

She heard Marcella's keyboard clicking. "Do you have any idea how many flights leave Hawaii daily? And that's just the direct routes. They could fly to Japan, Singapore, anywhere in Asia and connect to Thailand from there."

Sophie grabbed her robe from the hook, her mind already racing through possibilities. "Private jets are the biggest risk. Easier to hide cargo, less scrutiny."

"Already thinking that. But private aviation is a nightmare to track. They file flight plans, sure, but those can be amended in-flight. Say you're going to Los Angeles, then 'divert' to Bangkok for 'weather' or 'mechanical issues.'"

"What about cargo manifests?"

"Required for commercial flights, optional for private unless they're carrying restricted items. And let's be honest—anyone smart enough to steal these artifacts isn't going to list 'priceless Hawaiian cultural relics' on their customs forms."

Sophie opened her bathroom door quietly and peered out. The house was still silent, her children still sleeping. She moved to her walk-in closet and reached for clothing.

"We need to think like the group, which is called the Brother-hood of Ancient Ways," she said, switching the phone to speaker as she dressed. "They've had this planned for years. They won't risk commercial flights with X-rays and customs inspections. It's got to be private."

"Agreed. I'm pulling records of every private jet departure scheduled for the next seventy-two hours. But Sophie, Hawaii's a hub. We're talking dozens of aircraft, maybe hundreds if we include island hoppers that could transfer cargo to larger planes."

Sophie tugged on a pair of black yoga pants, her movements sharp with frustration. "Focus on jets with range to reach Asia. Gulfstreams, Bombardiers, the big ones. And check recent arrivals too—they might have flown in specifically for this."

"That narrows it some." More keyboard clicking. "What about boats? Harder to track than planes."

"Possible, but slow. The event is in six days. Would they risk an ocean crossing with that timeline?"

"Good point. Unless . . ." Marcella paused. "What if they're not taking them directly to Thailand? What if they have a staging point? Somewhere to perform preliminary rituals or wait for the optimal moment?"

Sophie tugged down a snug-fitting tee. "That's exactly what they'd do. The Brotherhood of Ancient Ways are fanatics about tradition. They'd want everything perfect."

"So we're not just looking for flights to Bangkok. We're looking for flights to anywhere they might have allies. Japan has ancient martial arts connections to Thailand. So do the Philippines, Indonesia . . ."

"Yes, we need to cast a wider net," Sophie agreed. "But we're running out of time."

She heard voices in the background on Marcella's end. "Hold on —Chen just ran in. What? You're sure?" A pause. "Sophie, we might have caught a break. Chen found a climate-controlled shipping container booked on a private cargo flight this afternoon. Destination listed as Singapore."

"Singapore's a major hub. They could go anywhere from there."

"The booking was made through a shell company registered in Delaware. Chen's tracking the ownership now, but these things are designed to be opaque."

Sophie finished dressing and moved quietly through the house to the kitchen. The coffee maker, already set up, gurgled to life at her touch, a small comfort in the predawn darkness. "What about the plane itself?"

"Registered to a leasing company. These jets change hands like trading cards. But here's the interesting part—the flight plan shows a refueling stop in Guam."

"That's not the most direct route to Singapore."

"No, it's not. And Guam has much lighter security than Honolulu International. Maybe easier to adjust the cargo without anyone noticing. Take on more passengers or something."

Sophie poured coffee, the bitter scent sharpening her focus. Though she still preferred tea, coffee gave a faster caffeine hit and today, she needed it. Through the kitchen window, she could see the ocean lightening from black to deep purple.

"Can we intercept at the airport?"

"Already mobilizing a team. But Sophie, if we're wrong—if this is a decoy or just coincidence—the real artifacts could be halfway to Asia while we're chasing shadows."

"It's a risk we have to take." Sophie took a sip of coffee, letting the heat warm her. "Send me everything you have. I'll start analyzing, looking for more information."

"Sending now. And we need to consider another possibility. What if they're not shipping the items together? What if Yoshimura and the Ancient Ways members are planning to fly with the artifacts personally, as luggage? It would be harder to track individuals than cargo."

Sophie headed to her office. As she hit the lights, her tablet, plugged in on her desk, chimed with incoming files. She hurried over and opened the first one, her eyes scanning the data. "Then we need to check the passenger manifests too and alert Homeland Security and use facial recognition to look for anyone connected to Yoshimura, or the Brotherhood. Maybe target Thai passengers, since we don't know what to look for."

Marcella blew out a breath; Sophie could almost see the lock of hair that usually rested on her forehead lifting in the breeze of it. "That's a lot of ground to cover with limited time."

"I know. But what's the alternative?"

"I think it's time to get more agents on this, and loop in the CIA in case we can't intercept the artifacts before they leave the islands," Marcella said.

Sophie swallowed a hot gulp of coffee, remembering her call to Agent McDonald, a call that hadn't been returned. "I already reached out. My contact there hasn't gotten back to me."

"We'll have to do this through official channels. I'll wake up Waxman next; he's going to love hearing from me." Marcella's tone softened slightly. "We'll find the artifacts. Chen's got half the cyber division working on this, and I'll have Marcus help and call in favors with TSA, private aviation security, anyone we can think of."

"I'll work from here for now, but I'll come in if you need me." Sophie sat in her chair and activated her rigs with a key fob. "I want these unsubs more than you know."

"Sophie . . ." Marcella hesitated. "Is this about a challenge to Connor's leadership in the Yām Khûmkạn? This ceremony—it sounds like something out of a movie."

As her rigs booted up, Sophie stared into her coffee, seeing Connor's face in the dark liquid. She had to protect him however she could and the details of the Brotherhood's challenge weren't relevant to the FBI's investigation. "I did not name my source and I won't. I can't. Just trust that he's not lying about what the Brotherhood are planning for the artifacts. These fanatics are capable of anything."

"All right. We'll proceed on the assumption that this timeline is real and removal of the artifacts from the USA is imminent. I'll let you know when I have more." Marcella ended the call.

Sophie pulled up the files Marcella had sent over. Somewhere, in all the ways a treasure trove of precious artifacts could leave this island, was the answer to where they could be recovered. She just had to find it before they left American soil.

Once they did, it was a CIA matter—and that was a whole other animal to deal with.

The soft creak of her office door closing made her turn. Feirn stood in the entry holding a mug of coffee, fully dressed in his usual ninja black despite the early hour. "I heard you talking," he said in Thai. "You have news?"

"The artifacts are gone from Thornfield's estate. Possibly heading for a plane off this island today."

His eyes narrowed. "Then we hunt. How can I help?"

Sophie frowned. "I can give you my tablet to work on. I'm going to engage some software that looks for keywords and have it sift all this departure info and variables. But I could use someone to help with facial recognition. So far, we only have a name for Sunan. Did you ever see him?"

"I was very new at the Yām Khûmkạn when he left, but yes, I've seen him."

"Good. I've got a program on my laptop that you can use to reconstruct Sunan's face, so we can put the airports on alert and circulate a general Be On Look Out." She paused, touching the scar on her cheekbone. "Have you personally seen any of the other warriors he recruited for the Brotherhood?"

"I don't know who they are." Feirn cast his eyes down, troubled. "I wish I did." The mug he held featured a grumpy-looking cat curled asleep with the caption, "DO NOT SPEAK TO ME UNTIL THIS MUG IS EMPTY." The incongruity of the young ninja holding that mug brought a smile to Sophie's face.

"Well, Sunan's the most important unsub anyway. I'll get the program going for you and show you how to use it. Wish we'd thought of this before, I'm sure Marcella will put anything you come up with right to work."

"Unsub?" Feirn's dark brows lifted.

"Unknown Subject. It's how the FBI refers to suspects." She was already opening her tablet to the facial reconstruction drawing program. "See here? First you choose the shape of the face . . ."

Moments later they were both hard at work; Sophie texted Armita that she wouldn't be able to help with breakfast but she'd join the children briefly when they were eating. When Armita replied cheerfully in the affirmative, once more Sophie thanked all that was good in the world for her nanny; Armita had truly earned the title "Auntie" that the children called her.

As Sophie scanned her screens, a new email notification popped up—from an address she didn't recognize, with a subject line that made her stomach drop: "Regarding your message to Agent McDonald." The sender's domain was **cia.gov**, but it wasn't from McDonald.

Sophie's belly tightened; she had a bad feeling about this.

20

SOPHIE

Sophie stared at the **cia.gov** email for a long moment before clicking it open.

The message was brief: *"Ms. Smithson, regarding your recent attempt to contact Agent McDonald, please call 703-482-1100 extension 4421 at your earliest convenience. Time sensitive. ~CIA Liaison Office"*

Her fingers hesitated as she held her phone. McDonald had given her his direct line years ago, and she'd never had to go through official channels to reach him before. What had changed?

Morning light streaming through her office window had grown stronger, painting golden rectangles across her desk. The office door was cracked, and Armita's voice drifted from the kitchen mixed with the children's high tones. A clink of dishes added context—breakfast was almost ready, and she'd promised to be there.

"Feirn," she said, closing her email. "Let's take a break. Come have breakfast with us."

The young man looked up from the facial reconstruction program, rubbing his eyes. "I'm close to finishing—"

"It can wait twenty minutes. You need to eat." She managed a smile in spite of the tension in her gut. "Besides, the children haven't got to know you hardly at all. I want them to spend more time with you."

The kitchen was chaos in the best way. Momi was wondering aloud if dragons could swim and deciding they could, while Sean ran a dump truck back and forth making rumbling noises. Armita was just dishing up a mass of scrambled eggs.

"Everyone, this is Feirn," Sophie announced. "He ate dinner with the security team yesterday, but he's staying with us for a while."

"Are you a ninja?" Momi asked. "You look like a ninja."

Feirn glanced at Sophie, who smiled. "Yes, a little," he said in heavily accented English, sliding into the empty chair beside her. "You make picture well."

"I like art," Momi said. "This is my pet dragon, Rupert. Can you draw?"

Feirn shook his head. "Not good."

She promptly pushed her tablet and box of crayons over. "You make a dragon, now. I'll help you."

The familiar breakfast sounds were comforting, but Sophie found herself hyperaware of every detail as she seated Sean in his highchair and served up his eggs and her own—the way the morning sun caught the steam rising from the dish. The faint scent of plumeria drifting through the open window from the tree outside. The sound of mynah birds squawking in the yard. Even Armita humming as she buttered toast, and the scrape of the knife over crisp bread.

Everything felt too sharp, too present, as if her senses were trying to memorize this moment of normalcy before it shattered.

"Mom, you're not eating," Momi observed, pointing her fork at Sophie's untouched plate.

"Just thinking, Little Bean." Sophie forced herself to take a bite of eggs, then another. Fuel for the body. Who knew what the day would bring?

After breakfast, as Armita herded the children upstairs to dress,

Sophie loaded the dishwasher while Feirn cleaned the table and highchair. Done with chores, Sophie touched Feirn's shoulder and spoke to him in Thai. "I need to make a private call. Would you mind going back to your room for a bit? You can take my laptop and keep working on the reconstruction there."

His dark eyes studied her face intently. "Is everything all right?"

"Not sure. I'll let you know after the call." She followed him down the hall and went into the office, waiting until he closed the door to his room before picking up her phone. The house felt too quiet now, the walls pressing in. She could hear her own heartbeat as she dialed the number the CIA had sent.

The phone rang twice before a crisp male voice answered. "Extension 4421."

"This is Sophie Smithson. I received an email about Agent McDonald—"

"One moment, Ms. Smithson. I'm transferring you to a secure video line."

Her phone screen flickered, prompting her to accept a video call. She did, and found herself looking at a young black man in a navy suit, his CIA badge visible, clipped to his jacket pocket. Behind him, the sterile white walls of what was clearly a government office glowed in fluorescent lighting that made his richly toned skin look ashy.

"Ms. Smithson, I'm Agent Clive Davis." His tone was professional but cool, his expression neutral. "I understand you've been trying to reach Agent McDonald."

"Yes, I left a message yesterday about an urgent matter."

"Agent McDonald retired six weeks ago," Davis said. "I've taken over his caseload. How can I assist you?"

Sophie hadn't realized she was holding her coffee mug. She set it down carefully, noting the faint tremor in her fingers. "Retired? But he never mentioned . . ." She shook her head. "Do you know who I am? I've been a witness and confidential informant for the CIA for years."

"Yes, I know who you are. I have verified your identity using your IP and voice recognition." Davis's voice had not warmed.

"Well, that's something at least. I'm working with the FBI on a case involving Hawaiian artifacts being smuggled to Thailand. It connects to the Yām Khûmkạn and—"

"I'm aware of the organization." Davis's eyes glanced away at a monitor; his fingers moved over his keyboard with mechanical precision. "I'll need the FBI case file and your liaison agent's name and identification number." He paused. "Also, is this a sanctioned or unsanctioned report?"

"What do you mean?" Something about his haughty demeanor set her teeth on edge. The air-conditioning in her office kicked on, raising goosebumps on her arms. "Before we proceed with the case information, can you tell me how my mother is doing? Pim Wat Smithson. Agent McDonald was . . . monitoring her situation."

Davis's fingers paused. He looked directly at the camera, his expression unreadable. The pause stretched too long into silence. "Give me a minute," he said at last. "I'm searching my database now." A few more rattling keystrokes, each one seeming to echo in the quiet room. "I show no one by that name in my caseload. I have all of McDonald's cases and files."

"Are you telling me you lost her?" The blood drained from Sophie's face, leaving her lightheaded; her mouth tasted metallic.

"I'm telling you there's no such person in our database."

Sophie had to swallow twice to get enough saliva to speak. "That's impossible. I handed her over to McDonald myself." She focused on the man's face with an effort. "Check again. Pim Wat Smithson. She's also gone by other names. She's a USA and Thai national."

"Ms. Smithson, I've checked twice. There's no record of that name or any variants or associations in any of my inherited cases, or elsewhere in our database." His tone had shifted from cool to arctic. Outside, a cloud passed over the sun, throwing her office into shadow. "Let's get back to the artifact case—"

"I want to speak to your supervisor," Sophie interrupted, her voice steady. "Get him or her for me. Now."

Davis's jaw tightened; he clearly didn't like her attempt to go over his head. "That won't be possible. If you have information relevant to national security, I suggest you share it through proper FBI channels. I assume we will be hearing about your artifact case that way. Good day, Ms. Smithson."

The connection went black.

Sophie sat frozen, staring at her reflection in the phone screen.

House sounds filtered back into her awareness—Armita's voice upstairs, a door closing, water running, the patter of Sean's little footsteps. Normal sounds that felt surreal after what she'd just heard.

Her mother's file couldn't just disappear. True, she'd been so relieved to have Pim Wat taken into custody that she hadn't followed up until now, and it had almost been a year since their showdown that led to Pim Wat's capture.

Maybe her mother was hidden in some offshore black site, and McDonald had made sure her case wasn't part of his documented work. That had to be it.

She had to find McDonald. Speak to him directly, and find out what he'd done with her.

Her phone buzzed against the desk, making her jump. A text from Marcella: "*Come into office now. Found the truck from Thornfield's. It seems contents were loaded into a Matson shipping container. It's on a cargo ship but destination unknown. Waxman wants strategy meeting ASAP.*"

Sophie could use this opportunity to talk with Marcella and Waxman about what she'd discovered. Use their access to the CIA to probe for Pim Wat's location. It was past time the CIA was involved with the artifacts case, anyway, now that chances were good the group was moving the artifacts outside the USA.

Sophie's hands shook as she grabbed her keys. The metal ring felt cold, real, grounding her back to the immediate crisis. She hurried to Feirn's room and knocked. "I have to go to the FBI office. Keep working on that facial reconstruction."

He opened the door, laptop in hand, reading something in her expression. "What's wrong?"

"There's a problem at the CIA," she said, the words tasting bitter. Feirn had been with Connor last year when everything went down with her mother's attack; she could tell him anything. "McDonald's gone, supposedly retired. My mother's file has vanished, and Marcella wants me to come in right away. They have a lead on the artifacts. You can stay here and work."

"No. The Master said I was to stay at your side at all times." He tucked the laptop under his arm. "I'll keep working when we reach the FBI. Let's go."

As Sophie drove toward town in the morning traffic, white cattle egrets flying overhead, locals in trucks heading to work—all of it felt like a thin veneer over something dark and shifting.

The Matson shipping container could be heading anywhere in the Pacific. And with McDonald gone and his replacement clearly hostile, she'd lost her only window into what the CIA was doing with her mother—and what they might be planning regarding Connor and the Yām Khûmkạn.

She pressed harder on the accelerator, and the response of the SUV's engine was immediate and reassuring. Whatever game was being played, it was time to involve the CIA—even though she had lost the only contact in the agency that she knew.

21

SOPHIE

Sophie had texted, and Marcella was waiting in the foyer when the elevator doors of the Federal Building opened. "Finally. Waxman's been asking for you." Her eyes flicked to Feirn with professional assessment. "I see he's got a laptop. What gives?"

"Feirn's assisting with facial reconstruction on one of our unsubs," Sophie said. "Is there somewhere he can work while we meet?"

"Interview Room 3 is empty." Marcella signed them in at the intake desk, and handed Feirn a visitor's badge without taking her eyes off Sophie. "You look—upset. What happened?"

"I'll tell you when we get a private moment."

After settling Feirn in the interview room with his laptop and a bottle of water, Sophie followed Marcella to her office. Her friend shut the door. "Spill. We only have a minute."

"I called to check on Pim Wat a few days ago because—I was uneasy. This situation with the Yām Khûmkạn is just her kind of toxic mess to get involved with. I wanted reassurance she was still safely locked up." Sophie shut her eyes, her gut churning. "Turns out Agent McDonald's gone. Retired, apparently. His replacement is . . ." Sophie searched for the right word. "Unhelpful."

Marcella's eyebrows rose. "That's going to complicate things. What did Agent Replacement say about your Satan-mom?"

"Claimed not to know of her. Can't find any trace of her in the system. Says he inherited all McDonald's cases. Hung up on me when I asked for his supervisor."

Marcella's eyes widened. "Think she's in an off-the-books black site?"

"That's my hope."

"Well, damn. Getting answers out of those guys is like getting blood from a stone. But maybe we can get a dialogue going through channels via the boss; it's time to alert the CIA anyway. Come on, let's get this meeting over with. I'll warn you, Waxman's pissy today." Marcella opened the door with a swish and strode down the hall ahead of Sophie, her fashionable slingback heels clicking.

In the SAC's corner office, Ben Waxman stood before a wall-mounted screen displaying shipping manifests and satellite imagery. His silvery white hair caught the light as he turned abruptly. Chen was already seated and helping herself to coffee from the tabletop carafe.

"Sophie. At last." He gestured to the screen. "Marcella, bring her up to speed."

Marcella clicked a remote, zooming in on grainy security footage. "The truck leaving Thornfield's estate was tracked to Pier 3 in Kahului. The container was loaded onto a carrier vessel registered in Guam called the *Moku Pahu* at 0300 this morning." Another click showed a massive cargo ship. "The ship's manifest lists the container as agricultural equipment bound for Los Angeles, but that's false."

"How do we know it's false?" Sophie studied the screen.

"Because thirty minutes after leaving port, the *Moku Pahu* changed course." Waxman pointed to a red line veering southwest on the maritime tracking display. "They're not heading to California. Current trajectory suggests either Tahiti or American Samoa as first port of call."

Chen frowned. "Those are both transshipment points for cargo heading to Southeast Asia."

"Exactly." Waxman's jaw was a corded line. "The artifacts could go anywhere from there—Singapore, Bangkok, Hong Kong, via air or ship. Once they leave U.S. territorial waters, our options become limited."

"What about the Coast Guard?" Sophie asked. "Can't they intercept?"

"On what grounds?" Marcella pulled up maritime law regulations on her tablet and cast the dense page of text over to the screen. "The ship hasn't violated any laws we can prove. The manifest says agricultural equipment. Without probable cause to board and search that specific container . . ."

"But we do have probable cause, and this case will become international trafficking with ties to terrorism if we can't stop the relics from leaving the USA," Sophie said forcefully. "We need the CIA to get involved. I was wondering what your plans for that were, SAC Waxman."

Marcella shot her a glance from under her lashes, but Sophie kept her gaze on the chief and her expression, one of respectful attentiveness. Waxman had never been privy to the drama with Pim Wat's capture the previous year, and she didn't want to pull him in on her situation unless it was unavoidable.

The SAC sat down heavily at the head of the table. "I've reached out to our CIA liaison and alerted him to the case, but I don't want to pull that agency in any further unless we have to. They're notoriously bad at sharing—on any level." He took a sip of water and then set the glass down deliberately. "Let's focus on the immediate problem. We need a court order to stop and search the ship, and we have maybe eighteen hours before the vessel reaches international waters. After that, even with CIA help, intercept becomes complicated, if not impossible."

"Okay, I'll focus on the justification for stopping and searching the ship," Sophie said. "The artifacts came from specific sites that

have been documented extensively. If we can prove their provenance, show they're stolen native Hawaiian cultural patrimony, that
gives you probable cause under the Native American Graves Protection and Repatriation Act."

"Yes! Good angle. But NAGPRA only applies to interstate
commerce," Chen pointed out. "Once the relics are in international
waters—"

"They're not there yet," Sophie interrupted. "And if I can document that these specific pieces were illegally removed from
protected sites, you have the grounds you need to stop the ship
before it leaves U.S. jurisdiction."

Waxman leaned back in his chair. "How fast can you put that
documentation together?"

Sophie glanced at her watch. "Give me two hours. I'll need
access to my files and the State Historic Preservation database. And
. . ." she hesitated, ". . . I'll need to make some calls to the Hawaiian
cultural practitioners who oversee those sites. They can provide
sworn statements about the artifacts' significance."

"I'll help. This is my area, too," Chen said. "Let's use my office,
okay?"

"I was planning to go to the computer lab," Sophie said. "Feirn
is using my laptop."

"We've got extras," Chen said. "And we're going to be doing a lot
of phone calling, so I think my office is more appropriate."

Waxman nodded. "Let Chen host you this time," he directed.

"Too bad Yoshimura's in the wind," Marcella said with a touch
of bitterness. "She'd have been our best go-to resource. Anyway,
while you two address the relics angle, I'll get the court order
roughed out and reach out to a federal judge to let them know that
the order will be coming through soon. Sophie, when you have
your document prepared, punt it to me

"Do it," Waxman said. "Also, Agent Scott, coordinate with the
Coast Guard. Have them track the *Moku Pahu* and develop an

approach plan, but don't execute yet. We'll have one shot at this and we need it to be legally airtight."

A gentle knock came from the door. "Come in," Waxman said.

Feirn slid the door open, holding Sophie's laptop open. "Sorry to interrupt," he said in halting English. "I done with face."

He turned the laptop screen to reveal Sunan's likeness. The man looked younger than Sophie had expected; there was a belligerence to his direct stare.

"This could be a game changer," Waxman said. "Thank you."

Feirn inclined his head with dignity. "I happy to help."

"Move out, team, and get this picture out and about everywhere. Let's wrap up this case and bring home the goods," Waxman said.

Sophie hoped to hell it was that easy.

22

PIERRE

PIERRE RAVEAUX WAS REVIEWING security footage from the Ala Moana Center for one of this Security Solutions cases. The Security Solutions office hummed with its usual activity—analysts at their screens, the soft murmur of phone conversations, the coffee maker gurgling in the break room.

His phone buzzed. The familiar Hawaii number made his heart jump—Sophie rarely called during work hours unless something important was happening. "*Bonjour*, Sophie. To what do I owe the pleasure?"

"Pierre, I need you at the Federal Building. Now." Sophie's voice was tight with an underlying urgency that made him sit up straighter. "Can you bring the artifact database you compiled? The one with all the provenance research?"

He minimized the security footage and pulled up the file in question. "Of course. What's happened?"

"The shipment of artifacts is on a cargo ship heading for international waters. We need to document that the artifacts are protected cultural patrimony to get a court order to stop the vessel. I'm working with Special Agent Chen, but we need your expertise and that work you did on the stolen items."

Pierre was already saving the file to an encrypted thumb drive. "I'll be there in twenty minutes. Anything else I should bring?"

"Just yourself and that brilliant mind of yours." His neck flushed at her praise. "And Pierre? There's something else I need to discuss with you. Privately. It's about my mother." The call ended.

Pierre stared at the phone for a moment before pocketing it along with the thumb drive containing the records.

Sophie rarely mentioned Pim Wat, the woman who had nearly destroyed all their lives the previous year. He'd been injured in an attempt to capture her in Greece, and two young Yām Khûmkạn operatives he'd been working with had lost their lives.

If that devil woman had come up, something was very wrong.

He locked his workstation and grabbed his jacket. Kendall Bix, the chief of operations, looked up from his desk as Pierre passed. "Heading out?"

"FBI needs assistance with the artifacts case. Sophie called me in." He adjusted his leather satchel, a nervous habit from his Interpol days. "I may be gone the rest of the day."

"Good hunting," Bix said, already turning back to his screens.

The drive to the Federal Building was mercifully quick since traffic was flowing smoothly through downtown Honolulu. Pierre ran through the implications of Sophie's call. If the artifacts were already on a ship, they were running out of time. Maritime law was complex, and once that vessel reached international waters, boarding it was going to be difficult to justify.

He parked in the visitor section and made his way through security, the thumb drive metaphorically heavy in his pocket. The elevator ride seemed interminable. When the doors finally opened on the FBI floor, Sophie stood in the foyer area, waiting.

"Pierre, thank you for coming so quickly." Stress had tightened the skin beneath her eyes and left the scar on her cheekbone a stark line. "Special Agent Chen's in her office pulling together the NAGPRA documentation. Let's take her your data."

They made their way inside and down to Special Agent Chen's

office. The agent's space was organized chaos—law books piled on every surface, multiple computer monitors displaying databases and documents. An Asian woman who must be Agent Chen looked up as they entered; her glossy bob was frazzled and she had pen marks on her blouse.

Sophie introduced them. Chen came around with a hand extended and they shook. "Monsieur Raveaux, excellent. Sophie said you have comprehensive provenance documentation on the artifacts?"

"Everything that was stolen has a backstory." He handed over the thumb drive. "Cross-referenced with museum records, archaeological surveys, and cultural practitioner statements."

"That last part is what we really don't have time for." Chen hurried around her desk and plugged in the drive, her eyes widening as she scrolled through the files. "This is incredible. How long did this take you?"

"I had help from a number of sources at the Bishop Museum and elsewhere, including Dr. Yoshimura," Pierre said. "Each piece tells a story.'"

"Special Agent Chen, can you pull up the photos of the twenty-three stolen pieces?" Sophie asked.

The FBI agent opened another file, displaying high-resolution images of the artifacts and casting the image to a wall-mounted monitor. Pierre leaned in, cataloging details. "I recognize these."

"Now we need to match the documentation you brought to each of the pieces." Chen's fingers flew over her keyboard. "I'm building the legal argument with each identified piece. And thank you, this background is exactly what we need. I'll pull this together and then you can check the matches, Monsieur Raveaux."

"Pierre, please," he said.

She glanced up through her lashes with a brilliant smile. "And you can call me Janet."

Sophie leaned in, ignoring the byplay. "Janet, now that you've got what you need, can I borrow Pierre for a minute?"

"Of course."

Pierre followed Sophie's confident departure from the office—clearly, she was no stranger to the layout. A few minutes later, they got off the elevator at the top floor. Storage and mechanical items took up the open space, but a hallway led to a plainly marked exit.

Sophie led him through the service door, out onto the roof.

A running track had been installed along the perimeter of the building, offering spectacular views of Honolulu, the ocean, and the mountains behind them. Several covered picnic tables in the middle of the space provided a place for meals. Trade winds whipped across the open space, carrying the scent of the sea and faint sounds of traffic below.

"We can talk here," Sophie said, beginning to walk briskly along the track; she was clearly anxious about something. "No cameras, and the wind makes audio surveillance impossible."

Pierre fell into step beside her. "Very cloak-and-dagger," he said lightly. "What's happened with your mother? I take it there's bad news?"

Sophie's jaw tightened. "She's disappeared. Completely erased from CIA databases. Agent McDonald, my contact there, has supposedly retired. His replacement claims to have no knowledge of her."

Pierre stopped walking. "That's impossible. There must be documentation—"

"No." Sophie resumed walking with her long-legged stride, and he hurried to catch up. "I've tried every CIA contact I had—disconnected. I even tried hacking their database, but they've changed all the protocols and I wasn't able to get in."

Implications hit Pierre like a blow to the solar plexus. Pim Wat Smithson was one of the most dangerous individuals he'd ever encountered in all his years of international law enforcement. "Do you think she's escaped?"

"I don't know what to think." Sophie's voice was controlled, flat. "Maybe she's in some black site McDonald never documented.

Maybe someone higher up decided she was too valuable to waste in a cell."

"Or too dangerous to leave alive," Pierre said quietly.

Sophie flinched but nodded, speeding up her pace. Pierre almost had to jog to keep up. "I need you to reach out to your Interpol contacts. Quietly. See if there's been any trace of her. New identities, unusual activity in her old networks, anything."

"I'll make some calls." He touched her shoulder gently. "We'll find out what happened. But right now, we need to focus on stopping those artifacts from getting out of our waters."

"Yes. You're right. One problem at a time." Sophie took a deep breath, visibly pulling herself together. She stopped and faced him; the wind blew her hair around and sun struck her light brown eyes, turning them almost amber. She seemed to be observing him with the same intensity, then spoke. "Chen's waiting for us. She's reached out to a federal judge who's sympathetic to cultural patrimony cases, but we need rock-solid documentation before we have the Coast Guard serve the documents and send a team to the vessel."

"I'm glad I could help."

"You did. Thanks for coming. It helps to have someone I can confide in." Sophie's phone vibrated. She glanced down at it. "Feirn has been helping with facial reconstruction of Sunan and other possible members of his group. He has some more results for us to see."

They hurried back downstairs. Pierre entered Chen's office while Sophie went to a nearby conference room, emerging minutes later with a young Asian man that Pierre recognized as Connor's second in command. He carried a laptop.

"This is Feirn," Sophie said. "My bodyguard. Show them, please."

Feirn set the laptop on Chen's desk, opened it, and turned the screen toward them. "This a face who may be Brotherhood," he said in careful, heavily accented English. "He left Yām Khûmkạn same time as Sunan."

The screen displayed a 3D facial reconstruction featuring a hard-looking Asian in his mid-forties, with a distinctive scar through the left eyebrow.

Pierre started. "*Merde*. That's Khun Sakchai."

"You know him?" Chen asked sharply.

"Only by reputation. He's wanted by Interpol. A thief of high-end art and valuables. Former Thai special forces, suspected in a dozen assassinations across Southeast Asia." Pierre met Sophie's eyes. "He's a white whale for Interpol; they've been hunting him for years."

"He's likely the one masterminding the artifact thefts," Sophie said. "And we're running out of time to stop him."

"Show Pierre Sunan's picture," Chen urged. "We didn't have any hits on him in the criminal databases, but maybe you recognize him too."

Feirn hit a button, and another visage filled the tablet's surface. This man was younger, with high cheekbones, heavy black brows and a shaved head. "Don't recognize him," Pierre said.

"We've got two faces to circulate everywhere around the world through law enforcement," Sophie said. "Good work, Feirn."

The young man ducked his head in embarrassed acknowledgement.

"I'll make sure these images get out," Sophie said. She and Feirn left.

Chen's phone rang. She listened for a moment, then hung up. "The judge will see us in two hours. We need everything ready by then."

Pierre took a seat at a chair by the window. He opened his laptop.

"I'll add you to the document I'm creating. You can access the matches I've made, pairing your material to the missing pieces as I'm assembling them," Chen said. "We can check them together in real time."

"*Oui*. Yes," Pierre said. A moment later his computer pinged with the access to the file.

This document was a critical step to getting the artifacts back and possibly stopping Sunan's bid for power; but a darker worry gnawed at him.

If Pim Wat was truly missing, and assassins like Khun Sakchai were part of Sunan's group, then Sophie was in more danger than she realized. He was glad she had a bodyguard. Hopefully Feirn would be enough.

23

SOPHIE

A DAY AND A HALF LATER, Sophie and Waxman, with Feirn seated cross-legged on the floor, tuned in via remote camera to watch the raid on the *Moku Pahu*. Button cams mounted on Janet Chen's and Marcella Scott's ballistic vests provided a grainy live action feed.

The FBI conference room smelled of burnt coffee and the alcohol cleaner someone had used on the whiteboards. Sophie sat forward in her chair, eyes fixed on the wall of monitors showing live feeds from button cameras. Her reflection ghosted across the screens—a pale shadow against the bright displays.

They'd timed the rendezvous in the conference room for when the coast guard cutter was nearing the huge cargo ship, and it happened to be past sunset.

"Thank you for inviting us to follow the action," Sophie told Waxman.

"You deserve to be here, and I know you'd rather be on board with Chen and Scott than sitting in this conference room," Waxman said, his eyes on the screen as he typed.

Sophie stayed silent; that wasn't strictly true. She didn't have a strong stomach for boats, and it had been nice to be able to spend a day at home while the raid got organized; even now her hands smelled like the baby shampoo she'd used on Sean's hair just before she left for the FBI building.

A crackle of static.

"Coast Guard Cutter *Kimball* to FBI One, we have visual on target vessel," the speakers spat. "*Moku Pahu* bearing two-seven-zero, range three thousand meters."

SAC Waxman stood up and paced back and forth at the head of the table, arms crossed, jaw tight. The room's fluorescent lights cast harsh shadows across his silver hair and the planes of his face. "Chen, Scott, status report."

On the center screen, Chen's camera showed the view from the Kimball's deck—black ocean stretching and heaving, broken only by the cargo ship's lights piercing the darkness like a small city. The image lurched and swayed with the cutter's movement. Sophie's stomach rolled in sympathy.

"In position," Chen's voice came through the speakers, breathless. "Boarding team ready."

Marcella's feed appeared on the adjacent monitor. Her camera angle showed Coast Guardsmen in tactical gear checking weapons, their faces green-tinged from night vision. The wind whipped past her microphone, creating bursts of static.

"Signaling now," the Coast Guard commander announced.

Sophie watched as spotlights blazed to life, illuminating the *Moku Pahu*'s rust-streaked hull. The cargo ship seemed to freeze for a moment, but maybe that was the connection, as the plunging movement resumed.

Sophie dug her fingers into the conference table's edge, grounding herself.

"They're responding," Chen reported. "Reducing speed, turning on deck lights."

On screen, the two vessels drew closer. Sophie could hear the engines' throb through the agents' microphones, feel the vibration in her chest. The Kimball's crew shot lines across the gap, securing the ships together with practiced efficiency.

"Boarding ladder secure," someone called out.

Chen's camera tilted up, showing the ladder stretching up the *Moku Pahu's* side; twenty feet of swaying metal over black water.

Sophie's palms grew damp.

"FBI! We're coming aboard!" Marcella shouted over the wind into a bullhorn. "Put your hands up and visible!"

"Copy that," came through an amplifier. "We are unarmed and prepared for boarding."

The camera lurched as Chen began climbing after fastening a sliding safety harness to one side of the ladder. Sophie caught glimpses of gloved hands gripping rungs, boots finding purchase on metal. Below, the ocean churned white between the ships' hulls. One slip, one missed grip . . . yes, Chen would be safe, but the fall sure wouldn't be pleasant.

"Halfway up," Chen panted.

Marcella's feed showed her following, the ladder bowing under the women's combined weight. Sophie could almost taste the salt spray, feel the wind trying to peel them off the ship's side.

"Contact on deck," a new voice reported. "Crew members visible, hands raised."

Chen hauled herself over the rail, camera swinging wildly before stabilizing on a group of casually dressed multiethnic sailors, their hands high, eyes wide in the spotlights' glare. The deck beneath her feet shone with spray and the rainbow glare of grease.

Moments later, Marcella joined Chen, followed by the cadre of armed Coast Guardsmen. Marcella stepped forward, holding an official document in a plastic cover. "This is a joint venture by the FBI and Coast Guard. We have a warrant to search this vessel."

The captain, a weathered man in stained khakis and a yellow slicker, stepped forward. "We cooperate, yes? All legal here. Agricultural equipment for American Samoa." His speech was accented.

Sophie leaned closer to the monitors. The captain's body

language seemed genuine—confused, worried about his job, but not guilty. He took the warrant, turned on a flashlight, and scanned it.

"Where are the containers?" Marcella's voice cut through the wind and static.

"This way, please." The captain gestured toward a massive hatch. "Everything is on the manifest and it's in the hold."

The Coast Guard men preceded the FBI agents, following the captain down steep steel stairs. The cameras, moving up and down with the women's strides, descended into the ship's belly as the agents followed.

Sophie's nose filled with phantom smells—rust, diesel, stale air recycling through inadequate ventilation. The LED work lights mounted in the ceiling carved harsh circles in the darkness, revealing container after container stacked like giant building blocks.

"Looking for container MSKU-7892341," Chen read from her phone. "Should be third tier, port side, according to the manifest."

They moved deeper into the maze. Sophie's chest tightened with each turn. So many hiding places. So many ways to lose something or someone in this metal labyrinth.

"There," Marcella's camera focused on a blue container, partially hidden behind legitimate cargo. "That's our target."

"Crane operator!" Chen called. "We need this container on deck, now!"

Sophie got up and fetched a fresh cup of coffee for Waxman, and hot water for tea as they waited. She handed water and a teabag to Feirn, then dunked her teabag up and down.

The crane's mechanical groan filled the conference room speakers as the crew got it activated. Waxman hadn't moved, his attention laser-focused on the screens—though he sipped the black coffee Sophie had brought as if on autopilot.

Eventually, the container settled on deck with a resonant clang.

Chen and Marcella approached as one of the sailors produced bolt cutters.

"A heavy lock," Chen observed. "Not standard shipping security."

The lock snapped as the sailor applied brute force to the long handles. Sophie held her breath as the Coast Guard men swung the doors open, and moveable work lights flooded the interior.

"Holy sh—" Marcella caught herself. "Sir, we have visual confirmation. The artifacts are here."

Sophie's heart leaped with excitement as the cameras revealed the interior—custom foam cradles, archival packing, each piece carefully stacked, pristine and accounted for. The feather cape's red and yellow plumage seemed to glow even through the grainy feed.

"Every piece from Thornfield's compound," Chen confirmed, checking her inventory as the men moved the items to be counted.

Marcella turned back to the captain. "Do you have any passengers?"

"No."

She nodded to the Coast Guardsmen who'd accompanied them. "Verify this, please."

The search of the ship for hidden passengers or guardians of the artifacts took another hour. Finally Chen confirmed. "No extra personnel or passengers. Container's empty except for the artifacts."

"Check again," Waxman ordered. "Look for hidden compartments, false walls."

They searched for another hour, obtaining blueprints of the ship layout and comparing them to what they faced. The Coast Guardsmen took the lead; they did this work often, using fiber optic scopes to probe for potential voids.

"Sir," Chen's voice carried disappointment. "No suspects. The crew checks out—all legitimate employees. No one matching our suspect photos."

Sophie slumped back. They'd recovered the artifacts but missed the real prize—actual Brotherhood members.

"Begin transfer of the relics to the Kimball," Waxman ordered. "Carefully."

The next hour passed in tense concentration. Sophie watched as each artifact was photographed, catalogued, and placed in a transfer chute to the Coast Guard cutter. Chen's camera showed her cradling a boxed *lei niho palaoa* like a newborn. The whale tooth hook was ancient and irreplaceable.

"Seas are picking up," the Coast Guard commander warned. "We need to expedite."

A swell lifted the ships, the gap between them yawning wider before the lines snapped taut. Marcella's camera showed a crate teetering at the chute's edge.

"Hold it!" she shouted, lunging forward.

Sophie's fingernails bit into her palms as Marcella's camera went wild—sky, deck, ocean, then stability as she steadied the crate. "Secured. That was close."

Finally, the last piece was transferred. The cameras showed agents and Coast Guard personnel exhausted but victorious, the artifacts safe in the Kimball's hold.

"Outstanding work," Waxman said, the first emotion he'd shown all night. "Bring them home."

As the ships separated and the monitors went dark, Sophie fell back against her seat in the sudden quiet. Waxman's coffee had gone cold, her tea was forgotten.

"They sent the artifacts off without an escort," she said. "Put the container on an unguarded ship, probably paid the shipping company through shell corporations."

Waxman's jaw worked. "But we got the artifacts. That's what matters."

"We wanted the thieves, too."

"Of course. But sometimes you have to make the best of what you can get." Waxman stood up. "Let's call it a day." He headed for the door. Feirn followed, gesturing that he was going to the restroom.

Sophie continued to stare at the blank monitors. Her mother was still missing. Connor still faced death in four days.

This victory tasted like ash in her mouth. She sipped the weak, cold tea to wash the flavor away.

The conference room door opened again. She turned; Feirn was back. His gaze was direct. "Sophie," he said in Thai, closing the door behind him. "We need to talk."

"What's wrong?" she replied in the same language. "I can tell something is bothering you."

He moved closer, voice dropping to barely above a whisper in case they were overheard, though the language provided extra protection from eavesdroppers. "I received a message. From a contact in the Yām Khûmkạn. About the Master."

Her breath caught. "Is Connor all right?"

"Yes. For now." Feirn glanced at the door, then back to her. "The ascendancy anniversary is in four days. Then Sunan will challenge him for leadership of the Yām Khûmkạn."

"I know." Sophie's mouth went dry at the reminder of ritual combat and ancient rules, with death of one of the challengers the only acceptable outcome.

"Connor has been training with the men every day," Feirn continued. "Growing the bond he has with them. He meditates, sometimes all night. He's physically ready, but . . ."

"But?"

"My contact says he is still not as strong as he could be. Spiritually. Emotionally."

Sophie turned to the window, her reflection wavering in the glass against the dark outside. "Why are you telling me this?"

"Because you're the one who made him want to live for something more." Feirn moved to stand beside her. "When you were with him, he was stronger. Not just in body but in spirit."

"That was a long time ago."

"Not so long." Feirn pressed a folded paper into her hand. "This is the information for a contact in Bangkok, someone who can get you close to the compound, to a surveillance structure, before the challenge. So you could watch the contest and encourage him. If you choose to."

Sophie's heart thudded with hard, heavy beats as if it were squeezed in a fist. She hated the Yām Khûmkạn, its jungle fortress, and everything that pile of crumbling stone stood for. She'd sworn never to set foot in that place.

She glanced down at the paper—coordinates written in Feirn's careful hand, a phone number, a name: *Kamon.*

"The CIA is watching everything now," she said. "They'll know if I leave the country."

"There are ways. Your friend, the Frenchman—he has connections overseas, yes? Perhaps a private plane, a flight plan with unscheduled changes. You could be in Bangkok tomorrow night."

"And then what? I can't stop the challenge. Connor would never run from it. I'd only be a distraction."

"No, you can't stop the challenge." Feirn agreed. "But I would argue that with you nearby, he will want to win even more. To have something precious to fight for."

"He can't have me, in any case. We're over and done." Sophie's hand closed tightly around the paper, crushing it. "Yet I do owe him for saving my life from that volcano disaster on the Big Island."

"There's something else," Feirn said. "My contact shared that there are rumors in the compound about a woman who escaped CIA custody. A woman who knows the old ways, who might be heading home to the fortress. A powerful woman who supports Sunan."

It had to be Pim Wat. Sophie's pulse evened out into a rapid thundering. *"Foul daughter of Death,"* she cursed, her eyes closed. *"May your corpse rot forever."*

"Yes, I am talking about your mother." Feirn's brown eyes twinkled with a touch of humor. "And I can't promise you'll find her, but if Pim Wat is returning to Thailand, the Brotherhood of Ancient Ways would want her as an ally. It could be your chance to capture her."

"I can see her joining forces with them. The only person she hates more than me is Connor." Sophie looked up at Feirn. "If I do this—"

"I'll be on the same plane and never leave your side," he said.

Sophie gazed down at the crushed scrap in her hand again. *Four days.*

In four days, Connor would face Sunan in combat that could only end in death for one of them.

Whatever they'd been to each other, whatever they could never be again, the thought of him dying while she sat safe in her home in Hawaii and her mother prowled the world—*no*.

She couldn't let it stand.

"Thank you," she said quietly. "For telling me this. I'll talk to Pierre about chartering a plane to Bangkok."

Feirn bowed slightly, understanding in his eyes.

She pulled out her phone and scrolled to Pierre's number. He didn't pick up, but she left an urgent message for him to return her call.

She then texted Connor that she was coming to support him— and was startled to see *Message undeliverable* come back.

Something must have happened to his phone. Hopefully he'd reach out soon. She'd try contacting him in the protected chat room they used online.

She had four days to save a man who'd once saved her. Four days to find her mother and close a chapter she'd thought was already written and ended.

As she turned away from the window, the harbor sparkled in the morning sun, peaceful and deceptive as the calm before a storm.

24

SOPHIE

SOPHIE STOOD in her kitchen with a cup of coffee, watching her children eat breakfast the next morning. Momi carefully arranged her Cheerios into patterns on the table, while Sean wore more yogurt than he'd eaten, babbling happily to himself in a mixture of English and Thai that only Armita fully understood.

Feirn sat beside the toddler's highchair, eating a bowl of oatmeal and chopped fruit mixed with protein powder with swift economy. Sophie wished she could make herself do the same; she needed fuel for the day ahead—but her stomach revolted at the thought.

"Mama, where you going?" Momi asked, her voice accusing. She had that perception some children seemed to possess. "You just got back from a trip."

Sophie's throat tightened. She'd rehearsed this moment during the sleepless night before, but the words were still hard to find. "Mama has to go help a friend. Just for a few days."

Ginger, Sophie's yellow lab, whined softly from her bed in the corner, sensing the tension. Anubis, Connor's graceful and well-trained Doberman, hopped up from his dog bed to nose her thigh, as if sensing her distress. Then he paced, moving between the kitchen and the hallway leading to the front door as if already guarding the family in her absence.

Armita joined them, dressed in her usual plain black clothing and braiding her long hair. She'd been with them since Momi was born, had seen Sophie through Jake's death, through the dark months that ended brighter with Sean's birth. Her wise eyes took in the travel duffel in the hall, the way Sophie gazed at her children's faces. "Don't worry. I'll take care of them," Armita said in Thai. "You do what you must do."

Sophie came over and hugged her, murmuring thanks into Armita's ear. "I will count the hours until I'm back."

Her phone buzzed with a signal that Pierre had arrived; he'd insisted on driving them to the airport where an unregistered private jet awaited.

It was time. Sophie hugged the children fiercely, breathing in Sean's baby shampoo scent, feeling Momi's small arms tight around her neck as she kissed her goodbye. "Mama loves you more than all the stars in the sky," she whispered, as she said in their nightly bedtime ritual.

"And all the fish in the sea," Momi whispered back, completing their call and response.

Sophie's heart squeezed painfully as she touched her daughter's nose and gave a watery smile. "See you very soon. Be good for Armita."

Both dogs walked Sophie and Feirn out to the car. In the driveway, Pierre waited beside a black SUV, its engine running.

"This is a mistake," Pierre said without preamble as she approached. "Whatever debt you think you owe Connor—"

"You already said all you had to say last night. Do not strain our friendship with a repeat," Sophie said. "And, for the record, it's not about debt. At least, not entirely." Sophie placed her bag in the trunk; Feirn did the same. "He would come for me. Has come for me. If the situation were reversed."

"That was before. You have children, responsibilities . . ."

"My mother is out there, Pierre." She met his serious brown eyes; her own gaze was fierce. "And Connor could die. I won't go into the compound, but I have to give him what support I can while trying to find Pim Wat."

Pierre's expression changed, softened; he pulled her into a quick embrace, surprising her.

Their bodies pressed close; she smelled sandalwood soap, and shut her eyes, feeling his breath on her neck, her ear. Sensing the longing coursing through him. She leaned into his arms, shocked by the answering desire he'd sparked, until he set her back and away abruptly.

"The plane is fueled and ready. I worked with a contact in Interpol to make sure your flight plan shows a charter to Los Angeles, then mechanical problems requiring an emergency landing in Bangkok." He pressed a satellite phone into her hand. "For emergencies only. Your most important numbers are already programmed in, including mine. Be careful when you use it—the CIA has ears everywhere."

"Thank you." Her body buzzed; her lips tingled as if they'd kissed.

The ride to the airport passed in silence with Pierre at the wheel. At the private terminal, a Gulfstream G650 waited on the tarmac, its white hull gleaming, sleek wings tilted up at the ends like a bird in flight. Feirn exited the back passenger seat as Pierre unlocked the trunk remotely.

They were alone for a moment—and once again Pierre surprised her, this time with a kiss. Quick and soft, just a promise, the light but intimate touch made Sophie want more—as his hug had.

"Come back to us," he said. "Be safe."

"I will." She got out and slammed the door, her cheeks hot.

Feirn emerged from behind the car, holding their duffel bags. Both were the type that converted into backpacks. "Ready?" he asked.

Sophie nodded, not trusting her voice. As she climbed the jet's stairs, she glanced back at Honolulu spreading up the mountains. On the other side of them, her children played, trusting she'd come home.

THE JET'S interior was all cream leather and polished wood, but Sophie barely noticed the luxury as she and Feirn took seats across from each other. The weight of what they were doing settled between them like a third passenger.

As the plane lifted off, banking over Pearl Harbor, Feirn finally spoke. "You should rest. It's fourteen hours to Bangkok, then another eight on horseback to the stronghold."

"I can't sleep right now." Sophie watched the Pacific disappear beneath clouds. "Tell me about the ascendancy rules. What exactly will happen?"

Feirn was quiet for so long she thought he wouldn't answer. When he spoke, his voice was heavy, rough. "The Yām Khûmkạn way is old. Older than the kingdoms that rose and fell around us. When an anniversary or ascendance day comes around, any warrior can challenge for leadership. It is how the Master is always the strongest among his followers."

"Do you have any sense how much support Connor has among the men?" Sophie leaned forward, propping her chin on her hand. "I tried to reach him at his private number, but it's no longer in service or he's blocked me."

"I let my contact, Kamon, know that we're on our way. Word will get to him. And to answer your question, there were many who were doubtful of Connor when he first ascended, though his gifts and strength were obvious."

"He could do remarkable things for which there was no explanation."

Feirn smiled. "Such things are not uncommon among the Masters. They are taught to manipulate energy, time and space."

Sophie shook her head. "He told me he saw energy fields around everyone."

"That is basic to the disciplines. I was honored he chose me as his personal . . .squire, I guess it would be in Western culture. He was beginning to teach me the deeper Ways when he sent me to you."

"And I'm glad he did," Sophie said, smiling at the earnest young man before her. "I see why he trusted you."

Outside the window, dawn was breaking over the Pacific, painting the clouds in shades of rose and gold as they rose above them. "He never stopped loving you," Feirn said, pulling her back to the present. "But I think that has to end for him to win."

"I agree," Sophie said. "It's a gamble, me coming to support him. I hope I won't be—in the way. Make him lose focus."

"You will not," Feirn said. "I will make sure of it."

She smiled again, this time at his youth and simple faith.

FOURTEEN HOURS LATER, they landed in Bangkok as the sun set. The city sprawled beneath them in a maze of lights and shadows. No immigration, no customs—Pierre's connections had ensured they ghosted through the airport like smoke. A car waited, driven by a Yām Khûmkạn contact. Within an hour they were beyond the city limits, heading north into the darkness.

At a river village that had no name on any map, they transferred to a long-tail boat. The pilot, an ancient woman with teeth stained red from betel nut, guided them up tributaries that grew narrower with each turn. Sophie gripped the wooden sides as the handmade vessel skimmed over rapids. The jungle pressed in on both sides, and the air was thick with moisture and the scent of decay.

"Nearly there," Feirn shouted over the engine noise.

The boat scraped against a muddy bank where horses waited—small mountain ponies, sure-footed and patient. Sophie's mount, a bay mare with intelligent eyes, picked her way through the jungle trails with confidence, as if she knew the route by heart.

They moved through the night, heading into foothills and navigating paths that switchbacked through dense forest. Somewhere in the canopy, monkeys called to each other, their cries echoing like shrieking birds.

The air grew cooler as they gained altitude. Sophie pulled her jacket closer, glad of its protection in the dank humidity.

Feirn had been on his satellite phone periodically; Sophie had only used hers twice, both times to briefly check in with Armita and the children, keeping the time under what it would take to trace the call.

"Have you heard anything about my mother?" she asked, as they paused to eat and rest the horses near a gurgling stream.

Feirn tilted his head, eyes going up and to the left as he considered his words. "They say a woman matching her description came through Bangkok a week ago; she was traveling with the Brotherhood."

"So they are all here in Thailand."

"Yes. Your mother had supporters among those loyal to the former Master. She seeks revenge on Connor. That is the rumor."

"Nothing new there," Sophie said. "The former Master was her lover. She was displaced when he died. She has been on the run ever since, and not happy about it."

"But she always lands on her feet." Feirn remounted his horse. "Like a bad cat."

"A bad cat." Sophie had to smile a little. "An evil one, actually. That is exactly what she is."

They crested a final ridge. Feirn led them on a side path to a clearing large enough to see past the trees surrounding them. Below them, a valley opened up, mist clinging to its depths like pale, filmy scarves. Along one side, the Yām Khûmkạn stronghold rose from the jungle. Its ancient stone walls were topped with modern steel watchtowers; traditional wooden buildings mixed with barracks. It was a fortress between worlds, between times.

"There," Feirn pointed to a cleared area near the center. "The challenge ground is in the middle of the complex."

A man with a shaved head dressed all in black approached Feirn from the jungle. Four others, heavily armed, accompanied him. Feirn slid off his horse to greet the man. They briefly embraced and exchanged an update in rapid Thai.

Sophie paid no attention. She had a pair of binoculars to her eyes, and from atop her horse, she could just make out figures moving, forming a circle in the courtyard. Drums began to beat, their rhythm carrying across the valley and up the slope, primal and demanding.

"We're too late to stop it," she said. She'd known that; still, the reality was terrifying. "When does it begin?"

"We could never have stopped it, and the challenge begins at dark." Feirn returned to Sophie and mounted his horse. "We will watch from the surveillance tower. This is Kamon, my contact and liaison to the Yām Khûmkạn."

Sophie nodded to the man as he bowed. "We are honored you chose to support the Master," he said in halting English.

"No, it is my honor," Sophie returned in Thai. "Thank you for your help and invitation."

"The Master knows you are here. He told me to tell you he is thankful you came. You can call briefly before the contest. I will give you the number," Kamon said. "But keep it short. We do not want to alert any enemies to your location."

Sophie nodded in acknowledgement. She and Feirn nudged their horses to follow Kamon and his men as he led them into the trees.

Sophie reflected on the passage of the past five years as the mare moved through deeper shadows under the jungle canopy; the closest she'd been to this place was that many years ago, when she came to Thailand following Pim Wat, who had stolen Momi as an infant.

She'd done her best to walk away from this world and build a safe, normal life for her children—but some part of her knew she might have to return and face the ghosts and demons of her past. "And now that time has come," she whispered. "Please, God, may Connor win quickly."

25

CONNOR

Connor felt Sophie's presence before he saw her.

Six months since he'd left her, and suddenly the air felt different—charged, life-giving. He didn't turn toward the surveillance tower hidden in the jungle canopy. Didn't acknowledge what his every instinct screamed.

Sophie was here. Sophie was watching.

But the knowledge settled over his bones like armor.

His satellite phone vibrated—the encrypted one only three people had the number for. He stepped away from his men, into the shadows of the teak pillars.

"Sophie." Not a question.

"How did you know?" Her voice moved through him like an energizing elixir.

"I always know when you're near." He closed his eyes, memorizing the sound of her breathing. "You're in the north tower. I'm glad you're here." The words came out raw. "Whatever happens tonight, I'm glad you'll witness it."

"Connor—" Her voice broke. "I came to support you. Nothing more."

"I know we won't be together again. I understand." He watched the sun sink toward the horizon, painting the compound in shades of blood and gold. "Your children, your life in Hawaii—that's where you belong. And I belong here."

"Please be careful. We captured the artifacts, so hopefully that weakens him, but . . ."

"I am ready." Sunan's preparations, his chemical enhancements, his growing army didn't matter. Connor would prevail with her at his back. "Sophie, I will say this one last time. I love you. I'll always love you."

A long pause, then she whispered. "Win this. Please. Just . . . win." The line went dead.

Connor stared at the phone for a moment, then powered it off completely.

No more distractions. It strengthened him that she'd come at all.

"Master." Niran, his new second since Feirn left, touched his shoulder. "The sun sets. It's time."

Connor nodded, rolling his shoulders beneath the raw silk white *gi* he wore. Night challenges were more difficult—low visibility made the combat harder to navigate. But Sunan had insisted, and Connor had accepted. When he was in the zone he used all of his senses, not just his eyes.

The courtyard below his balcony blazed with torchlight, shadows dancing across stones worn smooth by centuries of bare feet. His soles knew every bump and crevice of that courtyard.

He descended the steps from his quarters, each movement deliberate, meditative. His closest men flanked him—Niran on his right, steady as granite; Yai on his left, young and fierce; others falling into formation behind. Twenty-three men out of hundreds who'd chosen him during the ascension, who'd stayed loyal through three years of reforms that had angered the old guard. Twenty-three who'd chosen exile if he lost tonight. The rest would accept a new Master.

The crowd of silent onlookers parted as he entered the courtyard. Three hundred of the Yām Khûmkạn had gathered, travelers from every camp between Bangkok and the Golden Triangle. He recognized most faces: men who'd trained beside him, women who'd stitched his wounds, elders.

Some met his gaze with respect and a bow. Others looked away.

At the courtyard's center, a circle had been drawn with blessed chalk, ten meters across. That circle was ringed with torches that made the chalk glow like phosphorus. The drums shifted rhythm, and the eastern gate opened.

Sunan swaggered in like a conquering king wearing gold satin. Where Connor came with a modest escort, Sunan brought fifty Brotherhood warriors in black, moving in perfect synchronization, gleaming swords at their sides. The faction's philosophy showed in modern tactical clothing marked with traditional symbols.

Sunan himself had transformed in the three years since Connor's ascension. He wore a cloth of gold robe over fighting shorts, an outfit that cost more than most Thai families saw in a year. His body was oiled and gleaming, pumped-up muscles enhanced by whatever chemicals his pet doctors had prescribed.

Connor saw past the pompous display to the truth beneath. Sunan's energy field was red and pulsing with aggression and pride. His hands were wrapped in hemp rope, the old way, his knuckles covered with resin and ground glass. He was ready to tear flesh, shatter bone.

"Brother," Sunan said, his voice carrying across the courtyard. "For three years you've led us away from the old ways and the days of greatness. Tonight, when I defeat you, we'll be great again."

Connor didn't respond. Words were wind. Only action mattered now.

Elder Prasong stepped forward. Ninety years old, he was still straight as a spear. He'd overseen challenges since before either of them were born and had watched the Yām Khûmkạn rise and fall and rise again.

"We gather as our ancestors did," Prasong intoned. "To witness a leader revealed in blood. Who challenges this Master's right?"

"I do." Sunan had slipped his arms out of the sleeves of his robe and as he stepped forward, he rolled his shoulders back and raised his fists, tossing off the golden robe to be caught by an acolyte. "By right of blood spilled, by right of strength proven, by right of the old ways over the new, I challenge you."

"And I accept." Connor's voice carried across the throng. "By right of honor maintained, by right of loyalty earned, by right of combat, I stand ready."

Prasong raised his staff. "Then let all who would interfere be cursed. Let all who would flee be shamed. Let the circle be sealed until the truth is shown."

The crowd pressed closer, forming an unbreakable wall of flesh. Somewhere above, out in the darkness, Sophie watched. Connor felt her hope and support as clearly as if she stood beside him.

She came. Even knowing it's over, she came to witness. I'm not alone. I will prevail.

Both men entered the circle, moving to opposite edges. The drums stopped.

In the silence, Connor heard his own heartbeat, steady and sure. Heard the crowd's collective breathing. Heard the torches crackling, casting wild shadows that made the fighters seem like giants, like gods.

Prasong's staff came down and struck stone.

Sunan attacked instantly, crossing the distance in a blur. No feeling out, no testing—just pure violence aimed at ending the contest quickly. His right foot whipped toward Connor's head with enough force to shatter his skull.

As Sunan's kick moved through space, Connor slipped inside the arc. His elbow found Sunan's ribs, drawing a grunt, but Sunan was already spinning away, a glass-encrusted fist whistling past Connor's ear.

They separated, circling. First blood to Sunan—a cut had

opened above Connor's eye where his wrapped knuckle had grazed. He shook his head as blood ran into his eye, and the drops spattered on the courtyard's rough surface. The crowd murmured.

In the darkness beyond the torchlight, Connor imagined Sophie leaning forward in the tower, intent on the battle.

Watch, and remember why you loved me, even if we can't be together.

They clashed again, and this time Connor met violence with violence, shin checking shin with impacts that echoed like gunshots. Sunan's fist found his ribs; Connor's knee found Sunan's kidney. They broke apart gasping.

"You insist on dragging out the inevitable," Sunan said, spitting blood that looked black in the torchlight. "I represent all those who want to return to greatness."

"Your greatness is lies." Connor swiped blood from his eye with a forearm. "Drug trafficking, gun dealing—you would make us into a cartel, nothing more."

"A rich cartel that runs the world." Sunan bared his reddened teeth. "Ask your woman, cowering from her perch in the jungle. She chose comfort in Hawaii over you, but I'll make sure she meets the new Master of the Yām Khûmkạn."

Connor didn't react to confirmation that Sunan knew Sophie was here; he could not be distracted.

They engaged again, and this time Sunan's Israeli training showed. He mixed Krav Maga brutality with Muay Thai traditions, creating combinations Connor had never seen. An eye gouge flowed into an elbow strike. A groin attack set up a head kick.

Connor absorbed the punishment, waiting for the man to tire, waiting for those pumped-up muscles to run out of juice. His style had always been different—the mountain that endures the storm, finding the perfect moment to send an avalanche.

Each time Connor positioned for a finishing strike, Sunan was gone, leaving only air and adding another slashing cut to Connor's collection.

Five minutes became ten. Ten became fifteen. The torches burned lower, making the shadows dance faster, turning the fight into something mythic. Both men bled from dozens of wounds, their movement slowing but never stopping. The crowd had gone silent, recognizing they were witnessing not a challenge, but a war of philosophies made flesh.

Connor's left eye was swelling shut. At least two ribs had cracked. His lead leg was slick with blood from Sunan's kicks. But he kept moving, kept pushing back.

"She's not yours anymore," Sunan taunted during a clinch, as their bodies heaved and strained against each other. "After I kill you, I'll thank her properly for returning to witness your end."

Connor let the words wash over him. Connor had already accepted that Sophie wasn't his—but she'd come to watch him fight, knowing it might be his last effort. That gift of her presence, even at a distance, was more than he'd dared hope for.

He could not fail or he'd be failing her too.

Sunan loaded up for another leg kick but as he did, he dropped his right fist, protecting ribs that were more damaged than he wanted to show. Connor didn't think. He simply moved, flowing under the kick.

His fist found Sunan's liver with precision. Sunan's eyes went wide and his body folded involuntarily. Connor's elbow followed, crashing into the man's temple, sending Sunan spinning. Before he could recover, Connor's knee drove into his spine, knocking him to the ground in a strike that might have paralyzed a normal man.

But Sunan was not normal. He rolled with the impact and came up swinging, desperation replacing calculation.

They traded blows, then grappled, gladiatorlike, in the center of the circle. No more dancing, no more technique. Just two men trying to break each other before they themselves shattered.

Connor's nose broke under Sunan's palm in a white-hot eruption of pain. He didn't stop, though, and Sunan's knee buckled under his kick.

They were destroying each other piece by piece, inch by inch. The largely male crowd roared with excitement as two of the Yām Khûmkạn's greatest warriors fought like cornered tigers.

The torches guttered in a gust of night wind as Connor and Sunan pummeled on, too stubborn to fall, too proud to yield, better matched than either could have believed.

Through the blood and pain, Connor felt Sophie's presence at the periphery, a heartbeat of hope and support.

Still watching. Still there. A witness to his triumph or his end.

I will prevail. For the future of the Yām Khûmkạn. For the memory of what we were, what we could be again.

I will win.

THE TORCHLIGHT TURNED the ancient stones of the combat circle into pools of gold and shadow. Connor tasted copper in his mouth, felt the warm trickle of blood from his split lip mixing with sweat. His ribs screamed with each breath—at least two cracked, maybe three. But he was still standing.

Sunan wasn't.

The younger man knelt in the dirt, one hand pressed to his side where Connor's knee had found its mark. The arrogance that had carried him through the first rounds of combat had evaporated like morning mist. Now there was only pain and the dawning realization of defeat.

Connor's bare feet found their stance in the packed earth, feeling every grain of sand, every small stone. The night air was thick with torch smoke and the metallic tang of spilled blood. Around them, the brotherhood watched in silence—some his men, some Sunan's, all bound by the ancient laws that governed this moment.

His body catalogued its damage: the gash above his left eye that kept trying to blind him, the fire in his ribs, the deep bruise spreading across his right thigh. Sunan had been fast, trained in modern brutality. But Connor had survived worse. Had endured when others would have fallen.

"Master," his second called from outside the circle, his voice carefully neutral. "I will bring the sword." Connor inclined his head, keeping Sunan in his peripheral vision. His man approached with the blade—not the ceremonial *katana*, but the practical *dao* that had served the brotherhood for generations. Its weight was familiar in his palm, the leather grip worn smooth by countless hands.

The steel sang softly as he raised it, catching the torchlight. Around him, the assembled warriors shifted, recognizing the moment. This was the way. Challenge issued, combat joined, victory claimed. And now, a final duty.

Sunan's eyes met his. The younger man's jaw worked, but no words came. Perhaps searching for some final insult, some last defiance. But there was nothing left. They both knew how this ended.

Connor adjusted his grip, the blade's balance perfect. One clean strike. Honor satisfied, order restored. The brotherhood would survive another generation.

"Make it quick," Sunan said, his voice conversational.

Connor took the couple of steps needed to reach his adversary, the sword raised overhead.

Sunan bent his head, baring his neck—and Connor swung, putting weight and power into it. A clean stroke.

The head rolled free. Blood pumped.

A flicker of movement caught his eye—not in the circle, but beyond. High near the trees where the observation towers pierced the canopy.

His instincts, honed by years of survival, prickled.

Someone, or something, was coming their way. Someone who didn't belong.

He knew it with the same certainty he knew his own heartbeat.

Connor turned toward the darkness where he felt Sophie's presence, the heavy sword's tip dropping to hit the earth. He searched the shadows for her, this woman who'd taught him there was so much more to life than loneliness and the pursuit of justice. She'd shown him what it meant to love, to laugh and play, to look forward to tomorrow.

But it was too dark to see Sophie; the tower was unlit so it wouldn't be a target. He couldn't see her.

The sound came from nowhere and everywhere at once. A high whine that didn't belong in the jungle night. Not insects, not night birds. Mechanical. Modern.

Drones.

"Run!" Connor roared, but his voice was swallowed by the scream of the first missile.

The eastern wall exploded in a flower of orange flame. The shock wave hit him like a giant's fist, lifting him off his feet. He had a moment of weightlessness, almost peaceful, before the world turned to chaos.

Stone shrapnel whistled past his head. Heat seared his skin. He hit the ground hard, the sword spinning from his grip. Through the ringing in his ears, he heard screams, shouts, the crash of ancient masonry surrendering to modern warfare.

He tried to rise, but his body wouldn't obey. Blood ran into his eyes from the gash on his scalp. Men were trying to crawl away, the faction's black uniforms scattering like roaches from light.

The second missile shrieked down.

Connor saw it coming toward him, a bright star falling from the heavens. Time dilated, stretched like taffy.

He thought of Sophie in the vantage point of the tower outside the fortress walls. Watching this. Watching him die.

In that instant, suspended between life and death, Connor saw it all with perfect clarity: the CIA was making a big move. Taking out all the players at once.

There was no time for rage. No time for anything but the

strange peace that came with understanding. He'd lived by the sword and expected to die by it.

That the sword turned out to be a Hellfire missile changed nothing.

He shut his eyes. Saw her face.

I'm sorry. For everything we couldn't be. I love you.

The missile struck the center of the combat circle.

The world went white, then—nothing.

26

SOPHIE

SOPHIE'S KNUCKLES were white as she leaned against the bamboo railing of the observation tower, her whole body coiled tight. She watched Connor's battle through military grade binoculars.

The torches in the courtyard created pools of shifting light and shadow, turning the ancient combat ring into something mythic, primordial. Even bloodied and staggering, he was magnificent. So was Sunan. They were a force of nature pitted against a natural disaster.

A nightjar called from the canopy above, its liquid notes floating incongruous through the darkness. Sophie barely heard it. Her world had narrowed to the ten-meter circle where the man she'd once loved, and still cared for, despite everything—fought for his life.

Through the painful closeup of the high-powered binoculars, she saw Connor's elbow crash into Sunan's jaw. The impact looked brutal. Sunan stumbled back, his stance cracking. Connor pressed forward with a flurry of blows and kicks.

The tide was turning. Where Sunan had been flash and modern brutality, Connor was endurance and grit.

"He's winning," Feirn murmured beside her, lowering his own binoculars, voice tight with something between hope and disbelief.

Sophie couldn't speak. Her throat had closed around prayers in three languages. The air was cool at this elevation, but sweat soaked her shirt. They were too far away to hear the impact of flesh on flesh, but she could see it—every strike, every stumble, every drop of blood that splattered, black in the torchlight.

She adjusted the focus as Connor landed a devastating knee to Sunan's ribs. She read the body language—Sunan's bravado shattering as he gasped, stumbling, falling to his hands and knees.

"The crowd's reacting," Kamon observed from her left, his night vision scope tracking the action. "Look at Sunan's men. They're getting nervous."

Sophie tore her gaze from the combat long enough to see the black-clad fighters shifting uneasily.

She refocused on the two men in the circle.

Both fighters were streaked with blood in the torchlight. Sunan had raised his torso but he was still on his knees, swaying now, making no effort to rise. Connor turned his head and extended a hand; his second ran to put a sword into it. He raised the blade for the strike that would take Sunan's head.

A sound came that didn't belong. Distant, easily mistaken for thunder if not for the clear stars above.

No one in the courtyard noticed. Connor swung the sword and ended Sunan's bid for power.

Sophie had heard that sound before, in classified locations where American interests superseded human lives: *high speed drones approaching.*

"No," she breathed, the binoculars trembling as she lowered them, searching the sky. "No, no, no—"

The sound of engines cut through the velvety black night. High-pitched, mechanical. Precision death on its way.

"Radio the fortress!" Sophie yelled at Kamon. "All frequencies! Incoming strike! Everybody needs to run!"

Kamon reached for the tower's communications gear, but it was too late.

Even as Sophie screamed Connor's name, she knew no one would hear—but somehow, he turned toward her. Searching the dark for her, the sword dripping at his side.

The first missile hit the eastern wall. Even from two kilometers away, the explosion was incandescent. Sophie's night-adjusted eyes were blinded as the detonation turned ancient stone to powder. A shock wave rippled out, visible in the smoke and debris, and bodies were flung like dolls.

The second missile struck the courtyard, obliterating the combat circle and all those in and around it.

When Sophie's vision cleared, where the ancient fighting ground had been was an expanding ball of fire.

The circle where warriors had tested themselves for centuries, where Connor had just won his greatest battle, was gone—and so was he.

"No!" The binoculars fell from her nerveless fingers as Sophie gripped the railing. "NO!"

The third missile obliterated the main hall. Then came a fourth, a fifth. One after another, the ancient towers and buildings fell—flurries of flame, smoke and debris rising in a hellish glow.

"They're gone," Feirn said, his scope tracking the devastation. "Sophie, they're all gone!"

This was not an attack; it was an erasure.

Sophie sank to her knees on the platform, unable to look away as the entire complex below was annihilated. Secondary explosions tossed debris into the air as ammunition stores and fuel depots exploded from beneath, turning the stronghold into a scene from one of Dante's rings of inferno.

"They knew," she whispered. "The CIA knew about the challenge. They waited until everyone was gathered to send in the drones and strike. Take out all the terrorists at once."

"Of course." Feirn's voice was bitter. "They were probably tracking us this whole time."

"I led them here," she said, voice hollow. "I killed him."

"The CIA killed him. And everyone else." Kamon was already packing their equipment, his movements efficient despite the horror. "Now we move, or the Master's death means nothing."

But Sophie couldn't move.

Couldn't think beyond the last image of Connor through the binoculars—turning, searching for her, even in that final moment.

The drones screamed overhead, circling to return for another pass. The valley that had hidden the Yām Khûmkạn for centuries was lit up like the cauldron of a volcano, smoke rising in a column that would be visible all the way to the coast.

By dawn, there would be nothing left but rubble, ash, and the scattered bones of warriors who'd believed in honor and died in a world ruled by drone strikes and plausible deniability.

"Your mother might still be alive," Feirn said, tugging Sophie to her feet. "We never saw her down there. Connor would want—"

"Connor's dead." Sophie's dry mouth tasted foul. "They're all dead. The CIA must have used me as a targeting beacon."

She'd come to strengthen Connor. To honor their history and the complicated love they'd had by giving him the gift of witnessing him defeat his enemies.

Instead, she'd brought a worse enemy to his door.

As the group abandoned the tower, moving quickly through the dark jungle and away from the systematic extermination of the Yām Khûmkạn and its fortress, Sophie felt something fundamental crumble inside her.

Not her heart—that had been torn apart and knit together too many times.

Something deeper died this time: the part that had believed, despite everything, that good would always prevail in the end.

27

SOPHIE

SOPHIE'S AUNT Malee had a house on a street lined with orchid trees, across from the Ping River on the outskirts of Bangkok. Her home was a place where Sophie had always felt safe; Sophie told her companions that's where she wanted to go as they fled the site of the drone attack.

Even so, she barely registered their arrival in the neighborhood through the fog of shock. The last eighteen hours were blurred together in a haze of dark jungle paths, wet hidden boats, and Feirn and Kamon's grim and creative efficiency at avoiding checkpoints.

Now that they'd arrived, Bangkok's humidity pressed against her like wet wool. Moving robotlike through the motions of travel, Sophie felt nothing. Could feel nothing.

When she closed her eyes, all she saw was Connor, turning toward her, searching—and then that blinding first explosion.

So she didn't close her eyes—but exhaustion threatened to win and take her to a hell of flaming destruction.

Once the group reached the city Kamon and his men scattered, but Feirn stayed with her.

He paid for an hourly-rate room where they were able to clean up and change their appearance by dressing in clothing bought at a bazaar. He hired a motorcycle taxi to take them close to Sophie's aunt's address, then paid the driver extra to forget their faces.

He guided Sophie through a narrow alley that smelled of fish sauce toward her aunt's house. Invisible from the main road, the narrow two-story wooden house stood like a dignified folded fan, its teak facade dark with age and monsoon stains. The entrance was hidden, a small gate inset in the tall wooden fence behind a tangle of bougainvillea.

"Are you okay?" Feirn asked as they approached, his first words to her in hours.

Sophie nodded, dimly aware that she was deep in shock. Unable to do anything about the muffled quality of everything around her except to keep moving.

The door was carved with lotus patterns; she placed her palms on the smooth, warm wood, resting her forehead on the carving. Anchoring herself with something familiar.

From somewhere inside came the soft chime of wind-bells, and a whiff of jasmine rice steaming. The fragile petals of bougainvillea blossoms brushed her cheek as Sophie reached into a hidden alcove and pulled a string that rang a bell inside.

A few minutes later, the door opened a crack, then wider as she was spotted. "Sophie Malee!" Her namesake aunt Malee sat in a wheelchair, backlit by afternoon sun filtering through latticework over a walkway to the house.

"Auntie," Sophie said. "This is my bodyguard, Feirn. I'm sorry I didn't call . . ."

"Ah, my favorite niece. No need, you are always welcome."

"I'm your *only* niece."

"And you'd still be my favorite." Malee's dimples showed in a wide smile. Sophie came inside; Feirn followed, locking the gate behind them. Sophie leaned down to hug her aunt. She hadn't seen her mother's sister in five years. Malee's fine-boned face was still beautiful despite lines of pain etched around her eyes and a streak of white in her dark hair. Her legs, visible beneath a simple blue sarong, were withered—the price of crossing Pim Wat when she helped Sophie get Momi back.

"I am so delighted to see you." Malee's voice was water over stones, soothing and full of affection; it brought quick tears to Sophie's eyes. "Come. You look like you need food and a bed, both of you. And for that, you've come to the right place."

Sophie pushed her aunt's chair up a ramp into the elevated first floor of the house. The interior of the old place was a sanctuary of polished teak and aged silk. No air-conditioning, just ceiling fans turning lazily, stirring air perfumed with incense and the earthy sweetness of dried flowers.

The smell of rice cooking grew stronger when they reached the kitchen and eating area. A plump young woman, wiping her hands on a sacking apron, joined them.

"This is Ema. My helper," Malee said. "Ema, my niece Sophie and her friend Feirn. Can you put on more food for us? And they will be staying here, so freshen up the guest rooms upstairs when you have a chance."

"Of course. My pleasure," Ema said, and bustled off.

Feirn leaned on a wall, monitoring the outside world with his ears and phone. Through the windows, from a distance, came the sounds of the neighborhood—vendors calling their wares, the sputter of motorcycles navigating narrow lanes, someone's radio playing music, the distant clang of temple bells.

The Sig Sauer strapped to Feirn's hip on one side and the sheathed blade on the other were discordant but currently welcome notes in the peaceful home.

Sophie collapsed more than sat on the woven floor mat cushions Malee indicated. Her hands wouldn't stop shaking. "I'm so tired, Auntie, but I can't go to sleep."

"Tea first," Malee said, wheeling herself to a low table where a ceramic pot waited. "Ema just made it for me when you rang. Talk and food next. Then, you rest." The cup Malee pressed into

Sophie's hands was thin porcelain, painted with tiny blue flowers. "You can tell me what brings you here when you're ready."

Sophie paused to sniff the fragrant chrysanthemum tea, then sipped. Light and faintly sweet, the herbal brew was counterpoint to the sticky ball of grief lodged in Sophie's throat.

Through the windows she glimpsed the Ping River; brown water moved slowly in the afternoon heat, long-tail boats stitching white wakes across its surface.

"I need to get it out." Sophie told her aunt why she was in Thailand, and what had happened at the fortress. She didn't know she was crying until dripping tears hit her hands holding the teacup.

Malee's voice was gentle. "The Americans and their solutions. So final, so . . ."

"Destructive. Three hundred people died. At least." Sophie's voice cracked. "Maybe more. The whole stronghold, gone. And Connor—" She couldn't finish.

"The man you loved." Malee had been Sophie's pen pal; they'd kept up via periodically exchanged old-fashioned letters. "Your mother spoke of Connor. She hated him. Because he killed her lover."

"She told you about him?" This bit of information pierced through Sophie's numbness.

"Once. Here, actually." Malee gestured to the room around them. "The last time I saw her. When Pim Wat—cut me."

"What?" Feirn roused from his place on the wall. "Pim Wat, your sister—she hurt you?"

"Pim Wat crippled me." Malee tugged aside the blue silk sarong draped over her lap. She extended her shriveled legs, turned them at the ankle so vicious, knotted scars above her heels were revealed. "Cut my Achilles tendons and left me to die. A punishment for helping Sophie get her child back."

Feirn's eyes went wide; he shook his head, seemingly unable to speak.

Sophie had known of Malee's injury at her mother's hands, but seeing it was another story. "Oh, Auntie. If there were any justice in the world . . ."

Malee shrugged. "She did not kill me. I was rescued in time to live, though not for my mobility to be saved. I am grateful to be alive. And that her attack did not make me bitter; I refused to let it do so. The greatest freedom we have is to choose how to respond to the blows life deals out."

From the kitchen came the homely sounds and smells of Ema cooking—garlic and onions hitting hot oil, filling the air with comfort. Sophie realized she hadn't eaten in an endless long time; her stomach growled.

"You need sustenance," Malee said, hearing the sound. "The meal will be ready soon. Then, sleep. We must plan how to keep you safe in case the Americans want to tie up loose ends."

"My father will protect me." Sophie finished her tea and set down the cup. "They've done enough. Blowing away the entire Yām Khûmkạn. Speaking of—I have to let him know I'm okay." Sophie took out her satellite phone. She made quick calls to both Ambassador Frank Smithson and Armita, letting them know she was safe and making her way home.

Soon Ema brought out a tray loaded with savory stir-fry and a big bowl of rice. Feirn joined them; they ate companionably around the low table, Malee with the tray across her knees.

Sophie wanted to stay awake, but now that her stomach was full, exhaustion was pulling her under like river current. The room had taken on a dreamlike quality—dust motes dancing in shafts of light, the wooden walls expanding and contracting with each gust of wind, the distant bells marking a sort of minute-by-minute eternity.

"There are clothes in the guest room," Malee said. "Your mother's, from when she stayed here. You're taller, but otherwise close to the same size."

"Thank you, Auntie, I'll—"

The front door opened without warning, flying back to hit the wall with a bang.

Sophie's body reacted before her mind did. She rolled sideways, her hand reaching for a weapon she wasn't wearing. She took cover behind a large ornamental vase, peering out to assess the threat as Feirn reached for the gun at his hip. Before he could get it free, the silenced shot of a weapon rang out with a muffled spit. The young man dropped his weapon, falling backward to the floor. Ema screamed, throwing her apron over her head as if it would protect her.

Pim Wat Smithson stood in the doorway, dramatic as a figure from a shadow play. Her mother wore tight black leather and tall shiny boots that probably cost more than a new car. Her hair was a short, spiky platinum, and its cut emphasized the architectural perfection of her face. She wore no jewelry but a single jade bangle on her left wrist—the one that concealed a garrote wire, if the CIA's reports were true.

"Sister." Malee's voice was flat. "You always did like to make an entrance. At least we finished our meal before you ruined it."

Sophie was frozen, unable to react or respond. Her mother had come to kill her at last. She'd probably kill everyone here—and what about Armita and the children? She had to do something!

Feirn groaned. Blood bloomed on the shoulder of his weapon arm.

Pim Wat lifted her weapon and shot him again, this time in the leg.

He screamed in agony. Ema screamed too. Sophie bit her lips to keep from crying out as well, thus giving away her location.

"Quiet, or I'll put you out of your misery," Pim Wat said to Ema. The only apparent change in her mother was that Pim Wat's voice was hoarse, unfamiliar. Maybe the torture Agent McDonald had promised to put her through had left a mark after all.

Sophie scanned for something, anything, to use to defend them; but couldn't see anything nearby effective enough. Her mother wasn't just deadly with a gun, and right now Sophie was too far away to intervene without a weapon.

Pim Wat moved into the room with an assassin's grace, inclining her head to Malee seated in her wheelchair. "Malee. Sister. You're looking crippled, as usual." Pim Wat then turned her beautiful brown eyes—Sophie's eyes—to her daughter, hiding in her fragile, cowardly spot behind the urn. "Hello, Sophie. I heard you were in the country. Thought I'd drop in for a visit with family."

Sophie found her voice. "I was looking for you, too."

"You came to support Connor, you mean." Pim Wat settled onto a chaise with fluid dignity, her weapon now pointed at Sophie. "Foolish girl. Always leading with the heart." Her expression didn't change, but something flickered in her eyes. "It was fun watching him die. Worth everything to see that whole place burn."

The cruelty of it—so casual, so precise—took Sophie's breath away.

But before she could respond, Malee spoke. "Pim, please. The child just watched hundreds die. Including the man she—"

"Why are you here?" Sophie interrupted. "To hurt your family more?" Rage rose in her chest like lava, extinguishing the shock and exhaustion that had muffled her responses. Her gaze found Feirn's fallen pistol on the floor. One good lunge and maybe she could get it in time ...

"I'm here to take over. There's a hole in the ground and in the markets where the Yām Khûmkạn used to be. Room for a new organization to rise; one with me as its Master." Pim Wat picked up Feirn's abandoned teacup and sipped. "The CIA wiped the fortress and everyone in it off the face of the earth. They announced they're done with subtlety. And they work for me now." She set down the cup with a soft click. She smiled. "They've given me *carte blanche* to rebuild the organization as I see fit."

"What?" Sophie stuttered.

"I made a deal, you see. Intelligence so they could do their worst in a targeted strike. In return, they gave me my freedom—and more." Pim Wat leaned forward, and through some trick of the air, Sophie smelled gunpowder and her mother's expensive perfume. "The question is: are you your father's daughter, content to pine and die for love? Or are you mine, ready to make the CIA pay for every drop of blood spilled?"

Outside, a street vendor's bell announced the evening food carts making their rounds. Through the windows, the Ping River gleamed like hammered bronze in the dying light. A mynah bird squawked.

Sophie stared at her mother—the woman who shaped her worst nightmares.

She had to find a way to get closer to the weapon. Any weapon. Move Pim Wat somewhere further away from the vulnerable hostages in the room.

"What did you have in mind?" Sophie felt something cold and patient wake where her heart used to be. She stood slowly, and stepped out from cover to stand tall, her hands loose at her sides. "I'm all ears, as the Americans say."

Pim Wat's smile widened; for the first time Sophie could remember, she saw approval in her mother's eyes. "You're finally asking the right questions, daughter."

28

SOPHIE

THE APPROVAL in Pim Wat's eyes wasn't maternal pride—it was the satisfaction of a spider watching prey step onto her web. Sophie recognized that particular gleam; it was also in the eyes of snakes before they struck.

"You're finally asking the right questions," Pim Wat repeated, propping her silenced weapon on her thigh and swinging her boot gently. "Though I think you already know I don't need you. But I do want to see you crawl and beg to save the lives of these people you care about. So do it, Sophie. Crawl. Beg. Maybe I'll spare them; you never know."

"It wouldn't do any good." Sophie's numbness had evaporated, replaced by energizing fury as Pim Wat's words sank in. "So it was you, after all, who gave the CIA coordinates and schedules. You knew about the gathering. The exact time of the fight."

"Of course." Pim Wat couldn't resist preening. "Ever since I slit that pig McDonald's throat and escaped the black site in Macau, I've been feeding the CIA information. They think their assets in Bangkok have been so clever, 'developing local intelligence.' Once I found out about Sunan's plan to unseat Connor, I aligned with him." Her chuckle was brittle. "And the Americans. So eager to believe what confirms their assumptions about us. They didn't know it was me they were dealing with."

Malee's hands tightened on her wheelchair arms as she interrupted. "Pim, please . . . let Ema go, at least. She's nobody to you."

"Quiet, sister. I might still need to hurt your little housekeeper because she matters to you." Pim Wat narrowed her eyes. "You lost your chance to speak when you helped steal my granddaughter from me." Her tone remained conversational. "Sophie was guaranteed to come here too, once we salted the path with plumerias and stolen artifacts. She made the perfect cover for my double cross of both Sunan and the CIA."

Pim Wat's deception overwhelmed Sophie like a black wave. "You set me up. That whole case. You lured me in and used me as bait."

"Bait. Distraction. Justification." Pim Wat shrugged. "The Americans needed a reason to move against the Yām Khûmkạn. A former FBI agent rushing to support her cyber vigilante lover and all the terrorists in one place? Perfect excuse to erase everyone."

"Connor wasn't a terrorist." Sophie's words came out raw.

"No, worse. He was an idealist." Genuine disgust colored Pim Wat's cheekbones with a rosy flush. "Do you know what he did when he came to power after killing my beloved, the *real* Master? He tried to reform the Yām Khûmkạn. Tried to return it to its 'noble roots.' Started interfering with business arrangements, like the opium trade, that had worked well for centuries. He was the reformer—not Sunan."

Sophie thought of Connor in the circle, magnificent even in brutality, fighting for something he wanted to believe in. "So you had him killed."

"I had them all killed. Connor, that usurper who believed honor mattered more than profit. Sunan, who was getting too ambitious, starting to question why his operations kept facing mysterious setbacks. The elders, who resisted power and influence. The young, stupid trainees, waiting to be told what to do." Pim Wat nibbled at a sesame cookie on the tray. "One night's work took care of it all. By next month, I'll control every major smuggling route from Myanmar to Malaysia. I'm building a legacy that will last for generations."

"Pim," Malee said quietly. "That is where I draw the line. You can't take Sophie's children."

Sophie's eyes widened. "*What* about my children?"

"*Your* children?" Pim Wat's lip curled into something that might have been pity—or contempt. "You mean *my* children. The ones you've hidden away in your little Hawaii paradise." She stepped closer. "Like I said. I'm building a legacy. They will be my heirs."

"Over my dead body!" Sophie started forward, but froze as Pim Wat raised her sleek weapon, its barrel lengthened by the silencer.

"Yes. That was always the plan. Don't worry. I'll tell the children you died heroically. They'll grow up hating the Americans who killed their mother. Perfect motivation for the tools of my empire they'll become."

The unmuffled booming report of a decades-old Colt .45 was impossibly loud in the wooden house.

Pim Wat's eyes widened as her body jolted; her weapon fell from her hand. She looked down in genuine surprise at the glossy, spreading stain on the breast of her black leather outfit, then at her sister. She choked suddenly, and blood bubbled from her mouth and down her chin.

Malee held the old six-shot pistol steady in both hands. A tendril of smoke rose from the barrel like incense. Her face held a resoluteness that Sophie had never seen before.

"I should have done this years ago," Malee said. "Good riddance to bad rubbish."

Pim Wat tried to reach for her fallen weapon, but Sophie darted in and kicked it out of the way, then backed up out of reach.

Pim Wat opened her mouth, a ghastly rictus filled with red. More blood pumped out of her chest, bubbling with each beat of her dying heart and drowning breath. She sat abruptly on the chaise. "You," Pim Wat coughed through the fluid filling her mouth, frothing from her lips. "You were always weak. Gentle."

"Gentle isn't the same as weak," Malee said. "Die, please. I've had enough of your theatrics."

Pim Wat's panicked gaze found Sophie's.

Sophie saw something almost human in her mother's face in that moment—fear, regret, sorrow perhaps. Then Pim Wat's perfect features contorted as she heaved up a final gout of blood and fell forward off the chaise.

Even dying, her mother managed to position herself to fall gracefully. The liquid spreading beneath her body, creeping across the shiny teak floor, looked like red satin in the evening light.

Sophie hurried to check on Feirn.

The young man was unconscious, breathing shallowly, and bleeding from two wounds that looked nonfatal if she could get blood loss stopped and some first aid on its way. She grabbed a couple of cloth napkins, wadded them up, and pressed down on Feirn's shoulder wound.

"Ema! Come here. Put pressure on this," she yelled at the shell-shocked housekeeper. The woman, white and trembling, came and leaned down on the wad of napkins. "Auntie, call for an ambulance. Now!" Sophie found a silken table runner and wrapped it around the welling hole in Feirn's leg. She tightened it mercilessly, glad for Feirn's unconsciousness as she manhandled his wound to stop the bleeding.

In the background her aunt's voice was raised and urgent as she phoned for the police and emergency assistance on a landline.

Outside, the *som tam* vendor's bell continued its rhythm. A boat chugged by on the distant river. Bangkok was teeming with life, unaware that one of its shadow queens had fallen dead in a modest wooden house that smelled of rice and stir-fry.

"Are you all right?" Malee asked, setting her gun on the table with a clunk.

Sophie gazed at her mother's body, then at the aunt who'd

saved her. She thought of her children, finally safe from their grandmother. "No," she said honestly. "But I am uninjured. Thank you, Auntie."

Malee nodded. "Now might be a good time to call those friends of yours in the FBI. Pim Wat was wanted in a dozen countries, but you never know who among the police here in Bangkok was on her payroll."

"You're right about that. And I need to let my father know she's gone, anyway. Sadly, she matters to him."

But as Sophie reached for her phone, she paused. Her mother's jade bangle had rolled free of the body. After a moment's hesitation, Sophie picked it up and slid it into her pocket. Not to use—never to use—but to remember who her mother had been.

She took out the sat phone and called her father. "Dad? She's gone. Pim Wat is gone. Auntie Malee shot her to save me. I need you to make sure we don't run into any legal problems."

Sirens sounded. The bell rang at the gate. Sophie hurried to let the first responders in, filling Frank in on the current situation as she did so.

Soon she would be going home to Hawaii, where her children slept safely, dreaming ordinary dreams. She couldn't wait to join them.

29

SOPHIE

AFTER A BRIEF and unremarkable police investigation, Pim Wat's death was chalked up to a family dispute and ruled self-defense in favor of Malee. Money changed hands, forms were signed, and one of the world's deadliest assassins became smoke and ash with the same efficiency she'd brought to killing others.

Sophie had overseen every stage of her mother's body's handling and disposal, superstitious that somehow Pim Wat would find a way to cheat death yet again.

Now she stood alone in the viewing room, watching as flames in an incinerator consumed the woman who'd given her life—and very nearly taken it. She held up her phone on video mode so Frank Smithson could watch too.

No monks chanting. No mourners weeping. No flowers, except a plastic bag of marigold heads the crematorium provided as part of their basic package.

"Some people just need killing," Sophie murmured to herself, echoing something her mother had once said.

"What was that?" Frank asked from the video chat on the phone.

"Nothing." Sophie turned the camera back, frowning at the

sight of her father's face. His color was ashy and pouches hung beneath his eyes. Frank had survived being shot and treated for cancer in the same year, but he'd appeared healthier than this the last time she saw him. "You're not looking well, Dad. Are you sure you're okay?"

He shook his head; gray was edging out the black of his short-cropped hair. "Sadder than I expected to be," he said at last. "I had a good cry about her last night. The world is better off without Pim Wat, but she wasn't always . . . like she became."

"Corrupt? Evil? A psychopath, you mean?" Sophie sighed, gazing at the wall of white-hot flames, strangely silent behind the heavy glass of the crematorium. "I know, Dad. I was there. She could be loving when I was small."

"I'm glad it wasn't you that had to pull the trigger. At the end of the day, she was still your mother."

"Honestly? Me too. Auntie Malee was stone-cold about taking the shot. Took Mother—and me—completely by surprise."

"I guess your aunt decided she was done being abused by her sister."

"That's it exactly."

"You sure you don't want to do some kind of . . . memorial in Hawaii?"

"Who would come? Thieves, gangsters, killers for hire? The CIA who were her handlers? Auntie, who shot her?" Sophie shook her head. "I'll figure out something to do with her ashes, but I won't grieve her. I have others to mourn."

Like Connor.

She wouldn't have so much as a pinch of his ashes, though; the bombing site was inaccessible to her. Sophie's heart gave a painful squeeze, but she rallied. "I'm bringing Auntie Malee back with me to Hawaii for her first visit to the Islands. It's past time she spends some time getting to know the children."

"Great idea. I will look forward to seeing her again; it's been too long."

"I have to go, Dad. Thanks for witnessing this with me. It was good we could share this."

"We both wanted to make sure Pim Wat was really dead and totally gone," he said.

"Macabre, but true," Sophie said.

When the crematorium delivered the urn the next day—plain ceramic, unmarked—Sophie gave the ashes to her aunt's temple to scatter in their garden of unmarked remains.

In death, Pim Wat would share space with strangers, commoners, and the poor. She would've hated that, and thus Sophie smiled.

THREE DAYS LATER, Sophie pushed Malee's wheelchair through Honolulu International Airport toward the baggage claim, where Armita and Bill were picking them up. Feirn limped on crutches behind them; she'd invited him to Hawaii to become part of her permanent security team.

Trade winds carried the scent of plumeria through the open-air terminal. Her aunt hadn't stopped smiling since they'd cleared customs, marveling at everything from the multilingual signs to the casual mixing of cultures that defined Hawaii.

"There," Malee said softly, pointing. "There they are."

Sophie glanced up, and her heart cracked open.

"Mama! Mama!" Momi broke free from Armita's grasp, her five-year-old legs pumping as she ran across the baggage claim area, silky curls streaming behind her. Sean toddled after his sister, chubby arms outstretched, his loud cries of "Mama!" echoing off the high ceiling.

Sophie dropped to her knees to catch them both, pulling their small bodies against her so tightly they squeaked and wriggled. She breathed them in: Johnson's Baby Shampoo, Goldfish crackers, and the indefinable sweetness of family.

Tears she couldn't shed for Connor, for her mother, for all the death and waste, welled and overflowed in a hot, silent gush.

"Mommy crying," Sean observed with concern, patting her cheek with a sticky hand.

"Happy tears, baby," Sophie managed. "Mama's glad to see you."

"We made you pictures!" Momi announced, pulling back to study her mother's face with serious eyes. "And Sean only broke two crayons this time."

"Me draw!" Sean laughed, the big belly chuckle that always reminded Sophie of his father, Jake.

Sophie smiled through her tears, gathering them close in a hug once more. Armita stood back, hands clasped, her stern face soft with a smile. When Sophie finally looked up, the rest of her group had convened.

Frank Smithson looked older, his ambassador's bearing intact but his face showing the strain of recent days. When Sophie stood, still clutching her children in her arms, he came forward and embraced them without words. She closed her eyes, breathing in his scent—the same aftershave he'd worn since she was small, a touchstone of stability.

"I'm sorry about Connor," he said quietly against her hair. "I meant to tell you before."

Sophie nodded against his shoulder.

Pierre hung back beside Bill, hands in his pockets, waiting.

When Sophie saw him, she set the kids down and walked over. She reached for him, pulling him into an embrace that marked, for everyone who witnessed it, a change in relationship status.

Pierre wrapped her close in his steady warmth; those easy tears came to her eyes again at the relief, the safety, the companionship and support of his hug.

"I've been terrified," he murmured in her ear.

"It's over now," she whispered back. "All of it."

Frank cleared his throat after a moment, drawing their attention as he stepped away from greeting Malee. "I was hoping you all might be hungry. I made a reservation for all of us at the club. They have good hamburgers."

"Pizza!" Sean yelled, getting a laugh as Armita took him by the hand.

Not to be outdone, Momi grasped her grandfather's hand in both of hers. "I like burgers, Grandpa."

Her father was still strong enough to swing her up into his arms. "I knew I could count on you, Little Bean."

Standing there in the terminal, watching her patchwork collection of friends and family knit itself together, something shifted in Sophie's chest.

This was what she'd been searching for. *This.* These people right here—and yes, a few ghosts too.

30

SOPHIE

THE BISHOP MUSEUM'S Great Hall thrummed with subdued celebration as afternoon light filtered through the Victorian era windows to cast geometric patterns across the polished koa wood floors. The air carried the subtle scent of *pikake lei* mixed with the museum's distinctive aroma—old paper, lemon polish, and the faint mustiness of centuries-old artifacts.

Sophie stood near the climate-controlled display cases, their lighting making the recovered treasures glow against black velvet backdrops as white-gloved curators arranged each piece with reverent precision—the *lei niho palaoa* with its polished hook of sperm whale ivory catching the light like aged bone, the feathered cape's red *ʻiʻiwi* and yellow *ʻōʻō* feathers still vibrant after generations, the *leiomano* war clubs with their embedded tiger shark teeth gleaming.

Twenty-three pieces in all, each now bore a small brass placard noting its provenance and the donor family's name. The newly christened *Aliʻi Collection* commanded the hall's central display area, surrounded outside by potted bird of paradise plants and stands of bamboo that rustled softly in the air-conditioning.

"Ladies and gentlemen," the museum director's voice echoed

slightly in the vaulted space, amplified by speakers hidden among the carved ceiling beams, "today we celebrate not just the return of these priceless pieces of history, but the dedication of those in law enforcement who made their recovery possible." The director called them forward: Sophie, Pierre, Agent Marcella Scott, SAC Waxman, and Agent Janet Chen.

Sophie's heels clicked against the floor as she came to stand with her colleagues, and the sound seemed to echo in her skull with the persistent ringing that had plagued her since the explosions in Thailand. Applause washed over her like distant surf, muffled and unreal: the sunlight too bright, the trade winds too fickle.

Life kept moving hectically forward as if a fortress in Thailand hadn't been blitzed to rubble, ash, and bone.

" . . . and we give particular recognition to private investigators Sophie Smithson and Pierre Raveaux." Camera flashes burst like small explosions. Pierre's palm touched the small of Sophie's back through her sheath dress, his scent of cedar and sandalwood cutting through the numbness. She let herself lean into his gentle touch, using it to anchor herself in the present moment.

Sophie accepted the cool wood of a koa plaque etched with Security Solutions' logo, along with the weight of multiple lei: *maile* leaves with their spicy green scent, *mokihana* pods smelling of anise, and a simple string of *kukui* nuts that clicked softly when she moved.

Afterward, SAC Waxman asked for a private word.

The trio of Sophie, Pierre, and Marcella followed SAC Waxman's silver head through the quieter galleries, their footsteps muffled by runners protecting the floors. They passed cases of ancient *poi* pounders and displays of tapa cloth, entering the Hawaiian Hall where afternoon light filtered through frosted glass to illuminate feather standards and carved tikis.

The door clicked shut, sealing them in climate-controlled quiet.

The room smelled of lemon wood polish as Waxman stood beneath a portrait of King Kalākaua, his hands folded.

"First, I wanted you both to know that Dr. Yoshimura has been taken into custody and is cooperating fully. She's agreed to a plea deal—turns out the Brotherhood was threatening her daughter, a freshman at UH. They had people watching the girl, made it clear what would happen if Yoshimura didn't use her position to help identify and collect the artifacts."

"That explains why she called in the cyber intrusion and the obviousness of the relics' storage at the end," Sophie said. "She was leaving breadcrumbs."

"She wanted to be caught," Pierre concurred.

"Yes. She's provided names, locations, everything she knew about the splinter group and its operations here in Hawaii. Most of the operatives went to Thailand with Sunan, but we've been able to round up the few that remained." Waxman paused, frowning. "Speaking of Thailand. I wanted to address the illegal drone strike that occurred there." His steel blue eyes met Sophie's with sincerity. "The CIA never informed my office. The Thai government hasn't even acknowledged the incident."

"Of course they wouldn't," Sophie said. "They don't want to appear weak. And the CIA doesn't generally share their plans with anyone."

"Indeed." Waxman said. "I'm glad you got out safe, and I want you both to know how much the Bureau appreciates your unique skills and connections. We'd like to work with you again in the future."

"Of course. We're available anytime you need us to support a case," Sophie said.

Waxman shook their hands and left.

Pierre stepped out to take a call that came in on his cell, and Marcella approached Sophie. "I'm sorry about Connor," Marcella said quietly. "I know you loved him."

"At one time I did." Sophie stared at a feather cape's colorful design, seeing instead a sword raised in victory moments before obliteration. "We weren't together anymore."

"That doesn't make it easier. What happened."

"No," Sophie said. "But it's over now."

"And your mother." Marcella reached out, pulling Sophie's stiff body into a hug. "That's a lot all at once. I'm so sorry."

Pierre appeared in the doorway, phone still in hand, frowning in concern as he took in Sophie's rigid posture, Marcella's attempt at comfort. Sophie met his warm brown eyes over Marcella's shoulder.

"I'll be okay," Sophie said. For the first time since the missiles fell, it might even be true. "But I need time."

Marcella let go and patted her shoulder. "Take those kids to that private island you love so much. Get some vitamin sea."

"A great idea." Sophie smiled at her friend.

As they walked out of the museum, Pierre's hand found hers. Sophie squeezed it, welcoming the touch.

Together they walked forward into whatever came next, as yellow and white plumeria blossoms, knocked loose by the wind, cartwheeled across the walkway ahead of them.

31

EPILOGUE

THE TURQUOISE WATERS of Phi Ni Island stretched away into the distance, each wave catching sunlight like scattered diamonds. Sophie lay on a beach lounger beneath a large umbrella, watching Pierre help Momi pat wet sand into turret shapes while Sean glee-fully smacked his sand shovel on the watery "moat" surrounding their drip castle construction.

Anubis sat alert beside the children, his pointed ears swiveling, while Ginger dozed in the shade beside Sophie's lounger, her belly full of bits of the family's lunch.

They were on their third week of vacationing on Connor's island—*her* island, now, she had to remember.

Everything Connor hadn't left to charity had come to Sophie in his will: Phi Ni Island and everything on it, including the house and boats, several Swiss bank accounts, the jet, and controlling interest in Security Solutions' stock. Even in death, Connor had taken care of her; it had been a humbling revelation she'd always be grateful for.

"He's going to get sunburned," Armita observed in Thai from the adjacent lounger, nodding toward Pierre's lean, muscled shoulders.

234   TOBY NEAL

"At least he's wearing a hat," Sophie said in the same language. "And he put sunscreen on with the rest of us."

Armita snorted. "Men. Like another child to care for," she said. She'd never made a secret of her opinion of Sophie's various relationships.

Sophie rolled her eyes, then slanted a teasing glance at Armita. "You're just annoyed because he's as good a cook as you are."

"Pierre's all right." This was high praise from Armita. "I want you to be happy."

"And I am happy," Sophie said, surprised to find it was true. Though grief for Connor and her mother could still ambush her, the sea and sun of Phi Ni were working their restorative magic.

"Mama, look!" Momi called out in her piping voice. "Uncle Perro helped me make a mermaid!"

Sophie shaded her eyes to admire the sand sculpture. "Beautiful, Little Bean!"

Sean toddled over with a bucket of seashells, presenting them to Sophie. He was all Jake with his high energy, unique brown-with-gray eyes and easy smile. "Thank you, son," she said, getting off the lounger to sort the shells with him.

"Hard to believe we leave tomorrow," Armita said. The weeks of rest and relaxation had restored color to her face and erased tension from both of their bodies.

"Back to reality." Sophie watched a fishing boat pass on the horizon. "School for Momi. Sean starting preschool. New investigations to work on and a company to run. Normal life."

"Normal," Armita said. "That's not a word that's ever applied to you."

"True." Sophie closed her eyes, feeling the weight of all that had brought them to this moment pressing down on her with the tropical heat.

"Go swim," Armita said, coming around to examine Sean's shells and take Sophie's place. "Some people need rest, but you need exercise."

"Don't mind if I do." Sophie reached into her beach bag for a pair of goggles.

Pierre looked over as she slipped on a Lycra swim shirt. "Going in?"

"I need to cool off and get my blood moving."

"Mind if I join you? I missed doing my laps today."

"Sure."

"Armita, okay to keep an eye on the kids for us?" Pierre asked.

"You never need to ask," Armita said with a huff. "Though you should put on a little more sunscreen. Your shoulders are getting red."

"Thanks." Pierre reached for a nearby tube of lotion. "I'll see you out there, Sophie."

She nodded, shedding her pareu on the lounger and walking toward the water. The sand was hot beneath her feet until she stepped into water only slightly below body temperature. She waded in slowly, stepping carefully on the sandy bottom in case of sea creatures. She let the water rise around her legs, her waist, her chest, and finally donned her goggles.

Then she dove.

The underwater world was silent except for the rush of bubbles past her ears. She swam hard, scanning the sandy bottom for fish and coral outcrops, pulling herself through the crystal clear water until her lungs burned. When she surfaced, she was many meters from shore, treading water in the deep blue.

From here, she could see her family as tiny figures on the white sand, framed by the backdrop of colorful umbrellas. Behind them rose a high golden bluff, highest point on the island, crowned by Connor's beautifully designed house; now her home.

The children were bright splashes against the beach, the dogs, loyal companions—with Armita watching over them all with the fierce protectiveness of someone who'd learned how precious life was.

Pierre was wading in and putting on his goggles—coming to join her.

This was what remained, and it was good.

Sophie floated on her back, letting the sun warm her face as the gentle swells rocked her.

One by one, she said goodbye to the ghosts she'd loved: Jake, his gray eyes intense as he asked her to marry him from his hospital bed. Connor, searching for her in the dark in that last dramatic moment of his life. Pim Wat's beautiful face caught in astonishment as the knowledge that her meek little sister had killed her sank in.

Salt tears flowed from Sophie's eyes to join the salty sea around her as she grieved. Said goodbye.

When Pierre swam to her side, Sophie moved upright and smiled at him, a gust of energy moving through her body with the release of letting go.

"Ready to race? Bet you cooking duties tonight that I can beat you to that rock outcrop." She pointed to one of the spectacular limestone karsts rising from the sea floor that was unique to the area.

"You're on," Pierre said, and was churning away before she could pull in a breath. Laughing, Sophie hurled herself into his wake.

When they eventually reached the outcrop, they climbed out of the water onto the narrow skirt of stones around the limestone tower's base. "I guess we have to suffer while I cook," Sophie said. "Since you beat me so handily."

"Don't forget, I swim every day. But you don't see me challenging you to a foot race." Pierre tugged one of her curls so it stretched, a long coiled spring. "Or a round in the ring."

"You're a wise man, Pierre Raveaux." Her voice softened. "One of the things I like about you."

"So you like me." His deep brown eyes sparkled; that almost-smile tugged up one side of his mouth. "Or is it my cooking?"

"The cooking doesn't hurt." She leaned forward; they kissed, a gentle exploration. So far, that's all they'd done—but she was looking forward to more when they had time and privacy.

It felt good to look forward to something.

She finally turned and dove off the rocks, swimming vigorously back—and this time she narrowly beat Pierre to the shallows, turning to splash him with a laugh. "I just needed a head start!"

Momi spotted them. "Mama's coming in!"

Sophie opened her arms as both children splashed toward her, shrieking with delight.

Later, they all walked toward the long, zigzagging flight of stairs that led up the bluff's face to the house. The dogs leaped ahead, hurrying up to the clifftop mansion where faithful staff would have their bowls filled with water and food.

The tired children were much slower to begin the long ascent. Momi whined, and Sean cried to be carried. All three of the adults were already burdened with picnic detritus, towels, umbrellas and toys, but Sophie found a way to get Sean on her shoulders so she could still carry a beach bag. He folded his arms on her head, using it as a pillow.

Sophie paused with one foot on the stair, looking back at the vast ocean. Somewhere beyond that vivid horizon lay the ruins of the Yām Khûmkạn fortress, and her aunt's house, with its blood-stained living room floor. She was glad that Auntie Malee was here with her and her family, waiting in the house with Feirn for the rest of them to return.

Somewhere in the opposite direction lay a return to "normal" life on Oahu.

Wherever she was, Sophie had all she needed: an eclectic family blended together with love. Resilient as a palm tree that bent with the winds but was strong enough to weather whatever might come.

She turned away and began to climb, carrying her precious burden, leaving nothing but footprints behind.

ACKNOWLEDGMENTS

Aloha dear readers!

We've come to the end of another wild ride with Sophie—and wow, what a journey this one was! My heart is still racing from writing some of those scenes.

Thank you for sticking with Sophie through all the twists and turns and ups and downs of her romantic life. I know this book took her to some dark places—losing Connor that way still makes my chest tight—but she keeps going, keeps fighting for what's right, even when the cost is almost too much to bear.

And Pim Wat! It seemed like perfect justice that Malee, finally done being bullied, was the one who did what needed to be done.

And to you, wonderful reader—you're the reason I keep writing. Your emails, messages, and reviews brighten my days and inspire me to dig deeper with each book. The Paradise Crime World exists because you care about Lei, Sophie, Kat, and their ever-growing supporting cast of characters.

Which brings me to a small request: if you enjoyed this book, would you consider leaving a review? It doesn't have to be long or fancy—just a few words about what you liked (or didn't like!) helps other readers discover the Paradise Crime World. Reviews are like gold to authors. They truly make a difference in keeping this series alive.

Sophie's not done yet. She's got more mysteries to solve, more battles to fight—and yes, more of her complicated heart to sort out.

Until next time, keep reading—and I'll be writing!

With warm aloha,
Toby Neal

P.S. Want to know when Sophie's next adventure releases? Join my newsletter at **TobyNeal.net**, get a free full-length mystery, *Torch Ginger*, along with insider updates, exclusive content, and the occasional photo of a Hawaiian sunset to brighten your inbox.

If serial reading is your thing, join my Substack and follow the books as they're written. We have a fun community there with lots of commenting and interactions. Annual subscribers get free ARC copies of my books when completed!

P.P.S. If you're curious about my other series, you can find them all on my website and begin with free, full-length *Blood Orchids*. Sophie began as a character that you'll meet in Book 4 of the *Paradise Crime Mysteries* with Lei! Eagle-eyed readers will spot familiar faces crossing over between all the series.

ALSO BY TOBY NEAL

Paradise Crime Thrillers Books 1-15 (with Sophie)

Paradise Crime Mysteries Books 1-17 (with Lei)

Paradise Crime Cozy Mysteries 1-6 (with Kat)

Paradise Crime Standalone (Marcella)

Memoirs (TW Neal)

Romances (Toby Jane)

ABOUT THE AUTHOR

Kirkus Reviews calls Neal's writing, *"persistently riveting. Masterly."*

Award-winning, USA Today bestselling social worker turned author Toby Neal grew up on the island of Kaua`i in Hawaii. Neal is a mental health therapist, a career that has informed the depth and complexity of the characters in her stories. Neal's mysteries and thrillers explore the crimes and issues of Hawaii from the bottom of the ocean to the top of volcanoes. Fans call her stories, *"Immersive, addicting, and the next best thing to being there."*

Neal also pens romance and romantic thrillers as Toby Jane and writes memoir/nonfiction under TW Neal.Visit tobyneal.net for more ways to stay in touch! Or... Join her Facebook readers group, *Friends Who Like Toby Neal Books,* for special giveaways and perks.

www.ingramcontent.com/pod-product-compliance
Lightning Source LLC
Chambersburg PA
CBHW022109240626
47153CB00007B/2293